THE LEGACY OF ZIG

A RETURN TO MARBLEHEAD

S. SCOTT

Author's Tranquility Press
MARIETTA, GEORGIA

S. SCOTT/Author's Tranquility Press
3800 Camp Creek Pkwy SW Bldg. 1400-116 #1255
Atlanta, GA 30331
www.authorstranquilitypress.com

Ordering Information:
Quantity sales. Special discounts are available on quantity purchases by corporations, associations, and others. For details, contact the "Special Sales Department" at the address above.

THE LEGACY OF ZIG: A RETURN TO MARBLEHEAD/S. SCOTT
Hardback: 978-1-959930-10-5
Paperback: 978-1-959930-11-2
eBook: 978-1-959930-12-9

Contents

DEDICATION

For all those who search for identity, personality and true worth.
For all those who believe magic and mystery are the vibrancy of romance and
For all those who struggle to make their dreams realistic myths to live by.

I dedicate this book to you.

CHAPTER ONE

The gulls hovered low over the beach in Marblehead, skimming the low tide for fish; a pathway of rocks and mussel shells jutted out from the boatyard to Brown's Island. The old house stood disheveled, yet not hollow for the imagination, and a dreamer dreamed of secret booty buried somewhere in the house by pirates of long ago.

Marguerite Scott Paine, ten years old, sat in a crevice of a massive rock overlooking the beach, the island, and the noble sea. She searched the ocean with her young blue eyes, serious mouth and tilted head. Chestnut hair, chin length and whimsical, slapped her face. The gull's songs, boat bells, and distant fog horns never ceased to mystify her from this perch of God.

"Scotty!" Someone was calling her. She stopped to listen. The call became louder until she saw Barbara Miles popping her head into the opening in the rock.

"I thought I'd find you here," said Barbara, her lanky friend. "Your mother's looking for you."

Scotty looked up with a cheerful expression. "I wonder why. It's not supper. Usually, she's still in school now."

"Well, she said something about a meeting and wanted you to come home and help with dinner." Barbara gingerly reached down to pull Scotty out of her cave. "How come we didn't fish today?" she pouted while tugging; her marble black hair shone in the sun and waved with the wind. Scotty popped to her feet.

"Sorry, my dear buddy, I felt like being alone today. I'll be gone in three months, my heart here, my body in California. Oh, why is my father making us move! Fishing is swell. We can do it tomorrow, but right now I'm too sad for fishing."

"We gotta do things before you go, our haunted house and all."

The Mystery House stood on Brown's Island, a legend of wonder dating back to the 18th century. Folktale had it that English pirates, after capturing booty from merchant ships, headed for the colonies to bury a treasure and reclaim it later. One haunting tale of the house renders an account of beautiful Victoria Snow, a captain's daughter, taken as chattel with the treasure of her father's ship. The legend goes that Victoria and jewels were buried in revenge by Boot Black Charlie on Brown's Island. Unrequited love and a lust for gold turned Sir Charles Westgate, first mate of the Ship Princess into a mutinous rogue, a chameleon pirate. Questfully, kids dreamed of the house during winter snows and March muds. At least three kids did, Scotty, Barbara, and Neil.

Neil Montague lived on the cliff, just one sumac and two rocks away from Scotty's hangout. A banker's son, a prep schoolboy, he was remarkably free of his pompous background. Neil had a crush on Scotty, if one could call it a crush, for it was more of a love for the sea in her. Both of them were by birth and nature bonded to the sea, cliffs, and woods that surrounded this romantic town of the pre-Revolution era.

"Marblehead forever, God bless that dear old town." The girls sang the town song as they climbed through the fence leading down Fountain Park and up to Old Burial Hill. Redd's Pond lay on the other side of the cemetery. The pilgrims had bathed in the pond, so they say. It was a fishing pond now for the kids and sailors launching their small vessels and racing them on windy days.

Barbara's house was to the left of the pond and Scotty's to the right. The ducks perched mostly on the mound encasing the Paine house. Two stately ceramic lions reclined on the hill and pathway to the house. Rows and rows of lobster traps lay near the house adjacent to the pathway. There were landings on both sides where the girls could fish for crawfish and minnows, all thrown back after the angler's adventure. Neil joined them at times; he especially liked to sit with Scotty on her rock, near his house, rather than fishing. Mysterious affinity seemed to connect them.

"We'd best wait for summer for our treasure pillage of the house."

It was April and still bitterly cold. Billowy clouds reflected in the pond. Scotty winced with painful thoughts of moving away.

"See ya tomorrow after school, on your landing, Barb."

"Bye, Scotty."

The girls parted at the bottom of the hill each taking her own path home.

Lois Paine's patient face masked a personality, a woman responsible to others, a woman of her time.

"What else, what else," she spoke to herself bobbing out of the refrigerator to throw a warm glance at Scotty. Rarely out of sorts, Lois Paine controlled her daughter's world with dutiful serenity.

"Scotty, how about tossing a salad for the two of us, everything else is ready. I have to hurry off to the PTA."

"What about Eric?" asked Scotty.

"He's at Jerry Brown's," said Lois.

"Good, I'm sick to death of that stupid song he plays on the record player."

"Which one?"

"You've got to be kidding, Mum. 'Cross Over the Bridge.' I don't know who sings it, some sick female."

"Patti Page has a beautiful voice," Lois laughed.

"Not if you heard her morning, noon and night! I am going to break it; I'm just waiting for the right moment."

Lois seemed preoccupied. Ed Paine was in California, preparing a new home. One month has passed, and he would be gone for three more months. It would be hard to leave the pond. Her mother, dad and sisters were all she knew. Was she still stunned by her husband's near death from Hodgkin's disease? Was she glad to adhere to his last wish, a hope to go West? Somehow, she translated it as pained stoicism. How could Scotty be other than good, her mother was so docile and dutiful, and her father almost died. She wanted to be happy; after all, she was just a kid. Her friends were happy that Scotty was like them. They were cared for by their families, but they were nurtured by the land, sky and sea. They obeyed their parents, but they revered nature.

"That was good," said Lois. They had consumed their meatloaf and salad in silence. "Now off to the Hill!" quipped Lois.

The Hill was the McFinch foundry. All the aunts, three of them, had been born there. At one time or another, one of the sisters had lived there with their families. Surrounded with cousins, Scotty was happily lost there, a "cock-a-button," her grandfather's nickname for her. Many fields around the home were filled with briars and weeds. Buried in the fields, Scotty would become enmeshed in her natural souvenirs of nature.

It was Aunt Marjorie's time on the Hill. Big bosomed nanny, Aunt Marge, spoke a child's lingo to impress the hardest of crybabies. Marjorie McFinch had married Francis Jeep O'Leary. Everybody called him Jeep from the war days when he maneuvered an army Jeep. Well, there were Kate, Penny, and Candy, too. Scotty's compadres and cousins of secret clubs, midnight walks on the bridge over the railroad tract, and wars on thugs who threw cats in the ponds.

On entering the clan home, Kitty McFinch could be found in the kitchen. Grammy McFinch, the cook, somewhat of a cross between Winston Churchill and W. C. Fields, was stout and portly, a drinker of ale. She sat at the kitchen table like a garrulous Hawaiian Queen attired with a crown of gray braids on her head, sucking on cloves, for she had a breath that smelled of libations. A loose-fitting gown and black Red Cross shoes completed the posture of the family matriarch.

In the afternoon, Grampy Roy McFinch sat, cigar in mouth, feet on hassock, in the deer mounted game room with a glass of squirt and whiskey in hand.

The renegade cousins could be found in the arbor or elsewhere outside the house hunting butterflies or plotting a new ritual for club membership.

Aunt Marge was hanging laundry and Uncle Jeep, by this time of night and year, was plowing the ground hoping for an early planting, dreaming of cucumbers and chard, their summer staples.

Lois gave Scotty a peck. "Back by nine or shortly after." Off she went in their 1949 Buick convertible, the only convertible in town. They reached the Hill, and Scotty jumped out in search of her leader. Kate hung upside down on the grape tree, named so because the grapevine entwined the tree and made it a September feat to climb the tree for a juicy Concord reward.

"Hey, Scotty, I'm up here!"

Kate, age 12, was the vulpine leader of the cousins. Fearing Scotty's magnetism with the kids, from time to time, Kate would challenge her to reinforce and secure her lead of their gang.

"Bet you can't do this!"

"I was hanging upside down in Seaside Park when I was four." She said, as alacrity won the better of her and she joined her cousin.

"Actually, Scotty, you look better upside down."

"Oh ya?"

"Oh, yeeah!"

Kate's glorious auburn hair hung like a red waterfall.

"Well, let's get down and talk about it," Scotty retorted.

Scotty was an ordinary cousin of the family; her chestnut hair and blue eyes not remarkable, she stood out for her honest, demure spirit, attractive to all.

"What we really have to talk about is our club," said Kate.

"Right" said Scotty, "I had forgotten about our club."

"Well, we were talking about what our members should do to get into the club. Last time, that is. I think." Kate continued. "Members should be blindfolded and made to touch and feel the most repulsive things, like chicken livers and skinless grapes. We will, of course, tell them that these items came from dismembered bodies."

Scotty grimaced as she thought back to her induction into Kate's club. How she was made to take coffee grounds from the sunken garbage can outside of Mrs. Boile's house. Scotty had lost sleep and peace over that incident, for anything that smacked of the unethical to Scotty was supremely upsetting to her. The grounds were to be thrown away but there seemed to be something of a sinister nature in creeping around Mrs. Boile's house and taking anything, even though it was only waste.

"Well, who will be in the club? Penny, Candy?"

"Too young and boring."

"Then who?"

"Geraldine Jones. Or how about Teddy Hutch? Two more would be enough," said Kate. "Too many kids make things tough for plans and stuff."

They were now walking back to the chicken coop, long house and designated club house.

"When do you suppose we're going to horrify our new club members?" Scotty said as she looked at a small stool which Kate had supplied with a kerchief for a blinder.

"Well, next Friday is an in-service day. Your mum will have to work but all the kids are out of school. Let's do it next Friday."

"That is if Mum brings me to the Hill."

"Where else is she going to bring you? Eric is never home."

"Even if he were," said Scotty, "he's too busy to be bothered about me. I might as well be in a loony bin if I have to listen to that confounded song, 'Cross Over the Bridge' again. I'm afraid to scratch it for fear he'll hit me, but I know I'll hide it one day, when I get up my nerve."

"Can I invite Barbara?"

"This is just a Hill Club, Scotty. I'll talk to Geraldine and Teddy tomorrow. Now, let's get going, I'm starved."

As they entered the house, Kate and Scotty were overwhelmed by the aroma of Grammy's fresh baking. It was like manna from heaven, pure ambrosia. Grammy McFinch now sat at the table slicing the warm bread and with a twinkle in her eye pointed to the pantry. The girls popped in to see a lavish display of jams and jellies. They chose a Concord jar and placing themselves next to their Grammy, spread mounds of butter and jam on the fresh bread. Oh, what heaven was that kitchen, full of scents to whet the appetites!

Grampy McFinch was puffing on his cigar. Red, his hunting beagle, was asleep beside him. McFinch was somewhat like Popeye with a stubby beard, cropped haircut, but with cigar replacing pipe. Squirt and whiskey replaced the spinach in his hand.

Penny and Candy sat next to him on the davenport, while Kate and Scotty stole Grammy's twinkling eyes as they stuffed munificent mounds of bread and jelly into their mouths, confident that the smaller tots did not understand their oblation. Beef stew simmered on the stove. The air steamed with hardy aroma, until giggles and rebukes came from the game room. Grampy McFinch had splattered his cigar all over the clean window next to him, thinking that it was open, because it was clean. The girls on the divan were reeling in laughter. Grampy was chastising Red; when things went wrong, he always chastised Red. Red looked like a sullen Norman Rockwell print, unwilling to bark for the moment. Red was a dog of character.

Kate and Scotty furtively looked in, wiping Concord jam off their mouths. These were ordinary times on the Hill, in value second to none.

CHAPTER TWO

These were happy times. Children were delighted with nothing more than broken shells and haunting tales. Sin was sin and beauty, beauty. Men were characters living by the rules of nature in the shadows of heroes and patriots. Out of the boredom and the repetitious sea came ideas and new dreams to be completed for mankind. Scotty was happy with broken pieces of that understanding in this landscape of life, in her effort to become fluent with the greater world.

There was something so real about her life with Barbara and Neil. She didn't know them as much as she knew the sea in them. With Kate, there was competition, family pride, excitement and anxiety, emotion to be dealt with, egos to be accounted to. She was drawn both to the mania of the Hill and the candor of nature with Barb and Neil. In their contrast was her light.

Today, she thought she'd fish with Barbara after school. She lay in her bunk bed, a single bed next to an ominous hole in the wall, a relic of a former tenant. She looked to the ceiling, avoiding the hole she imagined having all kinds of beetles and spiders. She would soon rise and bring coffee to her mother. While her father was in California, Scotty cared for her mother. She made English muffins and eggnog for her brother's breakfast, endured "Cross Over the Bridge" before grabbing her schoolbag and darting through the lion's lair on the dewy path, past the pond and around several brownstones to Lincoln Street.

Barbara went to Star of the Sea School. She would not see her until midday at their meeting place. Scotty tossed and turned in bed but it was the insidious hole in the wall that jarred her back to reality. She rose to meet the day. "Good morning, Mum," said Scotty, placing the instant coffee on the bedstand. Scotty knew only how to make instant coffee. But for Lois this simple gesture was appreciated, for Lois loathed mornings. Scotty loved her mother, and never thought much about her total service to family. She just did life; she didn't question it much.

Glad on the cracked path, to school again. It was the "again", the movement of life that carried her. Only Zig could stop her. Zig, the local beggar, was more munificent than niggardly. Disillusioned with his clerical bank position, twin daughters and proper wife, he donned the clothes of a vagabond, left a nest egg for his family, duly appropriated by the bank, and lived on a pittance: one dollar per day. For months he roamed the streets, a five o'clock shadow on his life.

As gossip subsided, Zigfried became a common sight to the town people but a celebrity to the children who seemed to value his eccentricity as special. Something in his patient smile overshadowed his tattered appearance. There was always a kind recognition when he met them. Not for the sniffling storekeeper at Shube's Market, nor for the milkman in his impeccable uniform with the milk bottles in impeccable order, nor for the mailman; even the garbage men brushed him aside and he in turn sent muffled oaths in their directions. The adults were lost in outward appearances, but children's feelings were genuine, still part of their beginnings and their feelings for life were as yet untainted and pristine.

Zig was walking backward, trying to find something he had not found the first time around. Remedial wonder now connected him to the children.

Scotty was standing on the landing side of the pond, after leaving her mother and brother to go to school. Zig came by the pond in his beggarly way. In his shabby clothes he looked quite the clown, with an empty look to the ground. When he passed the pond, he took note of Scotty and her pensive gaze toward the water. He stopped for a moment and observed her; Scotty was unaware of his stare. For a time, a cheerful composure enveloped Zig, as if they shared some bright cloud of thought. He shuffled quietly toward Scotty and placed his daily allotment, a one-dollar bill, in her hands, clasped behind her as she was observing the water pond.

Scotty gasped at his touch and then catching her breath said, "Oh, it's you, Zig! What are you doing creeping up on me like this? Hey, what did you give me?" She looked at the dollar bill.

The children knew Zig's name, but he did not know theirs. Scotty looked at him and understood that he did not know her, yet she felt some common bond as two human beings sharing a brilliant many-hued rainbow. For one moment, he felt this need to give because he recognized himself in her contemplation of the water, and so he gave a gift from his heart, his daily sustenance. It was a brief look they shared; he said nothing and then he was gone.

Scotty did not look at the dollar bill because she would be late for school. She quickened her gait now to make it to school on time. Putting aside something of significance, she realized the incident could not be forgotten. This episode with Zig would flash in her mind on many of her street walks to come.

Plodding on to school, not aware of the bare trees but intrigued with the brownstones and old houses of the Revolution, Scotty marveled at this spring that was still winter. The narrow streets, the forgotten hollyhocks, the cold stone and barren garden, these reminders of desolation only prodded Scotty to dream and find in her mind the lost treasure of Brown's Island.

Gerry School loomed ahead like a prison and strangely another Gary imprisoned the school, crude and overbearing, traumatizing the fifth-grade classroom, and more particularly, Scotty in the third row, third seat. Gary occupied the second.

"Miss Orne, Gary is looking down your bosom."

"Piss on you!" retorted Gary.

"What, dear?" scoffed Miss Orne, raising her eyes and pulling out her hanky which was lodged between her two pear sized breasts. Her eyes peeked up from her spectacles. "Is there a problem?"

"Gary is looking down your dress."

"Hark," she said, "I hear Abbot Hall. Let's count the chimes. Maybe we can guess the location of the fire."

Scotty thought for a moment about herself and Gary. She had never really developed an ego, so part of the sea was she. Nature had stamped her early in life. Gary, what an intrusion in her life! He had an ego that had to stamp her out, Scotty and her "prissy self." She really had nothing against him. She just didn't want to be around him. In a way he was like Kate, controlling her with fear as Kate did with her dictatorship of the club.

She would not be smeared with Gary's muck. But dealing with the muck and keeping the sea would always be her theme in life.

"Zip up your lip, Gary," Scotty mumbled as she circled the inkwell with her index finger not looking him in the eye.

"I'll get you, you little bitch, after school, just wait!" He looked at her. Her eyes were cast down, her fine chestnut hair masking one eye.

"Right, Gary," Scotty still circled the ink well as if in some hypnotic spell. The shells had given her the idea to withdraw inside, a defense system that would aid her for life. When in danger, would she fight or flee? She would go home to herself.

The bell rang and the kids leaped up, running for the playground for their kick ball game, no sweaters, young blood. Scotty was captain.

Gary had disappeared, probably to the brick gate encasing the school, to smoke. She wouldn't put it past him. The brisk April air reddened their cheeks. It was a girl's game. Scotty and her cronies played hardy ball, but a puddle in the path of the ball splashed them as Scotty gave the final kick. The recess bell halted them then. Giggling with the spray all over their faces, they rubbed away the mist while dashing back to their seats.

Gary seemed to have forgotten his anger for a moment. He looked almost peacefully at the spelling words on the board: rheumatism and pneumonia. Miss Orne pointed with her yard stick while the children with blank faces followed with their eyes much as a beagle watches uninteresting prey.

Scotty was most attentive to the window where the fire had been or maybe she just wondered. The landscape, with clear yet stark lines, silhouetted the Gothic Hall in the distance. "Rheumatism" and "pneumonia" what a substitute! Because she was a good girl, printing well and following directions, Miss Orne had not noticed Scotty wasn't paying much attention to school. Discipline was the order of the day, very often masking the bright, brilliant, and brooding kid.

It really was silly, thought Scotty, she could spend hours looking at the pond watching for fish to jump at the dry rounds she threw in as a teaser, but the blackboard, how dull. Everything about nature was mysterious and fascinating, and then there was Miss Orne with her pear bosom, Ben Franklin specs, and screeching blackboard.

The milk was warm today, in the carton with its waxy glaze, like liquid medicine. They ate from lunch boxes on their desks, peanut butter and jelly. Two more hours and she would be fishing with Barbara. It would be right then; she wouldn't feel the void of the blackboard. Little did she know, bringing the sea and blackboard together would be her quest in life. And the end of the two hours came. As she looked down at her tattered navy sneakers, she mumbled, "Away with you, Gerry and Gary!" and darted onto the road. The rain had left rainbows of oil in the gutters and curious worms wiggling here and there. As she walked around, an ale can in her path, she recalled Zig and pulled out the crisp bill he had handed her in the morning. George Washington with his stoic smile gave her no inkling as to the giver's generosity. Folding the green bill very neatly into squares, she deposited it again into her pocket. This time she walked on more gingerly; she knew not why.

"Scotty!" the man with the English hat called out as he nodded and tipped his hat. Here was a man who knew her name but she did not know his. They passed each day as he walked home from Bigelow's Potato Chip Factory. A happy man with a bulging nose, perhaps he drank ale, as many of the old-timers did.

She never spoke to him but always waved in some salute fashion and kept walking. She was happy in motion, steady, and constant. Past the Sundry Store at the corner of Pond Street, dreams of Licorice Nips and Jujubes popped into her mind, and then she saw the pond and heard the ducks. They must be fed, those darlings. They too liked the fresh bread molded into bait for the fish.

The house, sad in the afternoon sun, cast a sultry hollow gripping Scotty as she entered the kitchen to neither brother nor mother nor anyone. The void worse than fight longed for Patti Page and that dreaded song for company with Eric at a distance. Strange, the Paine house right next to Old Burial Hill should have been lonely, but for Scotty it did not feel lonely outside in the cemetery. Romantic men who forged the future of the States were in the Hill. There were tatters and tale spinners in those tombs. Scotty thought that there was nothing sad or lonely about the dead. Sadness lies in empty living.

Popping on her old jeans and sneakers, she darted downstairs to the kitchen closet where she kept her fishing hooks and string. No pole just a line, that's all that was needed. Darting out of the house through the lion's lair, the ducks waddled quickly after her, squawking and pleading for their fair share of day-old bread. Like Gretel, she dropped a line of bread behind her. And the mallards, their webbed feet flapping, followed her for a time but stopped just short of her side of the landing. Scotty skipped now to see her friend.

"You're here first, Barb! How did you manage that?"

"Well, we had a shorter day today. The nuns had to go to a funeral. All of my pilgrim penguins lined up like a firing squad and proceeded to the requiem mass for Sister Agnes, now with God. One hundred years old she was and wrinkled like a prune. I never knew her when she taught, but I saw her a lot near the grape trellis in the fall plucking all the grapes and nibbling on some as she went. One day I was close by and caught her grape handed with purple lips. She had pretty young eyes in spite of her apple doll complexion, and I loved her tongue, pink and fresh like a tortoise tongue. I saw it when she looked up at me with a scared bandit look, the time I caught her eating grapes. I liked her looks. I guess that's about the same as liking someone. Funny, sometimes you can like people you don't even know."

"Do you like 'em all, Barb?"

"Some are nice; some are witches."

"Not to change the subject, but did you see Neil?"

"Nope, he's sorta bookish this time of year."

There was a seasonal etiquette for the kids. Nobody went to the island in the spring; that was for the summer. Nobody called it soda; it was tonic. Everybody wore a red hat in hunting season; that's just how it was.

"His parents have already planned on Newton Prep School. Getting ready to carry on the family name, you know. Just think, a kid we knew, President of the Bank of Boston."

"Come on, he's just one of us."

"That time is coming, Scotty."

"I guess," she looked melancholy now. "Well, I don't have to worry about that. My dad works for G.E., and I don't know what he does. He's not here anyway. He's in California looking for a house. We'll be moving soon. Haven't thought about it much, guess I don't wanna. Only thing I'm thinking about is that crusty Zig. Do you know what he did? He put his daily bill in my hand today. I just about jumped out of my skin. He came up behind me, scared my gurry out. Didn't say a thing, just looked at me and moved on like in a daze."

"He's crazy, that one. Left his pretty wife and twins for the streets. It takes all kinds," said Bea.

"Got anything to eat Big B, besides those nasty bacon bits?"

Barbara, a lanky kid, favored Scotty's nickname for her, feeling big and little at the same time. Big for big and B for bee. "Yep, I managed to lasso these chocolate chips on the table."

Bea came from a chocolate chip home, cozy and accepting. Her house, a brownstone, and a brownstone mother tending the hearth. Brownstones were best, then came shingles, then brick. That's just how it was. To Scotty's mind Bea's house was a home with gingham pink rimming the lids of row upon row of pickles and preserves of all kinds. Her mum didn't talk too much, but was there, smiling with chocolate chip cookies on the table.

"Mmm, this is good."

Scotty felt a little starved. She sucked the cookie on her tongue so as to not swallow it too fast. How to keep the cookie feeling without swallowing, a good question.

"Now to fishing—first, biggest, most," said Bea.

"You won last time with three fish, but I caught the first! Why don't we just catch, no contest?"

"These cookies, yummy good, even if my mother did make 'em. I've got one more, wanna split it?"

"What a question," Scotty extended her palm. They sat now shoulder to shoulder, legs dangling over the cobblestone landing, and it was quiet while they mouthed their cookies and watched the rippled waters. No bugs hovered over the water in April. It was cool, downright cold, and they wore sweaters.

"I got 'em," said Bea, while a belly gleaming minnow fought water and air for his freedom. As she pulled her string up in the air and onto the landing he wiggled and flapped, wiggled, and flapped.

"First again, you stinker Bea," but Scotty wasn't upset with her. There was no winning or losing, it was just wonderful *being*.

CHAPTER THREE

The nice thing about the kids—they lived without recall or connection. Time for them was a vivid landscape without smog, a face without pimples, an eye full of grace and good cheer, that was it. Words of love and hate could be strewn together because it was that time to love and that time to hate. The staccato performance connected no web of guilt or scorn.

Kate looked cheerful, perhaps peevish, as she greeted Scotty that Friday, the minimum day Geraldine Jones and Teddy Hutch were in for. For Kate had plotted and planned a grueling orientation for these new club members. Scotty was not surprised to see them lined up and sitting on stools in the chicken coop. Kate had bound them for the "Rush."

"What took you so long?" Kate clenched her fist around a paper suggesting the macabre rules for entry into the club.

"We overslept."

To some, Scotty might have seemed stupid, so quickly did she respond to Kate, but the truth of the matter was, she wasn't involved. Acting in part for approval, Scotty obeyed mostly as a spectator, a part, yet not a part of things. Unlike Kate who reeled with delight over the moans and the teeth clenching of poor Gerry and Teddy while exposed to the club induction, Scotty marveled at their emotion, capturing their spirit.

"Watch out! Don't step in that dog do!" Kate piped, later, on the way to the pond.

Teddy jumped to avoid a smear. Everything was wonderful on the way, the warm sun and sunny spirit of youth, the zest for zest. At Shube's, Kate recanted, "Just one bite, Scotty; you can have one bite."

"That's okay, I was just thinking of a peanut butter and marshmallow sandwich. I'll get one at home."

Kate left them at the door. The girls waited outside, staring at the cloudy square glass panes that surrounded Shube's, just above the door. While they gazed, Scotty thought of Neil. She missed him, but why? What did she care about boys? She could outbox, outrun, but not outcurse them. Neil wasn't like that. She thought of his sad smile, his bright eyes, his manner at quiet moments on the beach.

Kate popped out, pickle in hand. "This is your last chance. No then onward."

So, they passed the flower shop, walked past the cemetery and Story School, then straight away to the pond. The mallard ducks were waiting for them. Barbara was fishing on her landing.

"Somebody's over there fishing," said Gerry.

"That's Big Bea."

"What?" asked Teddy.

"That's Barbara Miles, she lives over in that brownstone. We're fishing buddies. Gee, she looks lonely," Scotty mumbled.

"She doesn't look anything of the kind. You can't even see her from here, not her face, anyway. And if she is lonely, she can stay lonely. This is a Hill Club," Kate fired.

"Want some bread to feed the fish?"

"Sounds good," said Teddy and Gerry.

Kate still thought of her closed club.

"Now, just sit up by the lions and I'll run in and get the bread."

"What lions?" said Teddy.

"See them down there by that yellow house? It's the only house on the pond; see it? Never been to my house, have you?"

"Nope," Gerry said. Teddy's head shook no.

"Well, Big B over there is my pond friend. We are fishers and watchers here. We watch the sea a lot, too. It's just over Burial

Hill and up Fountain Park. We watch a lot from Fountain Park. That pickle got your tongue, Kate?"

"Nope, just thinking about the Hill."

"We're at the Pond, Kate, the egging, remember? We're planning for Easter vacation. It was your idea," Scotty teased.

"I know, I know," said Kate in a huff.

"I'll be right back," said Scotty. "The ducks will be here soon. See them there in the middle of the pond? But they are headed this way. I feed 'em here. They eat out of my hand." She paused. "I'll be back in a flash."

She darted in and grabbed the old bread, not moist enough for fish rounds but okay for the ducks.

"Here, we have it. Now don't throw it. They must take it out of your hand. Worked hard to get them to do that, don't spoil 'em."

"Bite or peck, huh?" said Kate.

"Well, they swallow hard sometimes, but never hurt, it's sort of a sweeping feeling on your hand. Just do it. Can't really describe feeding ducks."

So, they all grabbed some bread and held it out. The ducks moved up in a line like confederate soldiers. Sitting on the mound between the lions, the girls fed the waddlers, assembly line fashion.

Scotty looked across the rippling waters. Her black bobbed friend was leaving the landing, homebound. Hill members were engrossed in duck feeding; Scotty pensively searched the waters.

"Neil, where are you?"

"Did you say something?" asked Kate.

"Just thinking about a friend I haven't seen for a while."

Kate was getting the hang of it. They were all quiet enough for Scotty to think. She didn't care much for boys, but Neil wasn't a boy; Neil was Neil. He was a thinker and wonderer too. Why did she get lonely with others? Even with Barb there was a longing, but with Neil she felt the mysterious sea. He was twelve years old, rich, and going away to prep school. She was ten, a pauper, and a wrangler heading West.

The girls tired of feeding the ducks and yawned toward Kate.

"Enough for today, let's get home before dark or I'll be in trouble with all the mothers." The girls followed without protest.

Scotty felt anxious as she saw the gang head back; she walked through Burial Hill, down the steps of the cemetery and up the steps to Fountain Park, where she slipped under the picket fence, down past the sumac and out onto the rock with its crevice haven. Scotty sat for a minute, arms entwined around her bent knees, searching Brown's Island, with its silhouette Mystery House of the pre-Revolution era. Then she glanced to the side of the cliff where Neil's house stood. One of his bedroom windows faced the rock where Scotty crouched. The other window the sea and Brown's Island.

Neil sat at his desk, surveying the island. Then their eyes met. Frozen in a glance, locked in their vision of each other, Neil gestured to Scotty and Scotty waved. She watched him then, as in a silent movie. He closed a book and made his way through his bedroom and down a short corridor to the back entrance of the house. As he drew closer, she marveled at his radiant look in the sun. A handsome boy, with sable eyes, skin both white and pink. Scotty always noticed his face first, but he had an admirable body, as well. He was just as beautiful to her as the sea, and their mutual childlike passion was for nature. As he joined her, they took a last glance at each other and settled back into the crevice. He, too, embraced his legs in a bent position and rested his chin on his knees.

"Gee, I've missed you, Neil."

"I've been here. I mean really been here, studying for Newton Prep. I take the entrance exam tomorrow."

"Sometimes I don't feel like I'm breathing when I go for days without seeing you."

"What about Big B?"

"She's my buddy, too. But there's something in me, Neil, that's more like you. We're more complicated."

"If you wanted complicated, Scotty, you should read some of these sample test questions for entrance to Newton Prep."

"Gosh, Neil, I'm sorry I haven't asked you about how the studying is going."

"Let's talk about something else besides prep schools."

"What, my idiotic girls club? My cousin Kate is on the warpath with zeal for the Hill Club. Oh, it's all a bunch of bunk. You know, Neil, sometimes I don't feel like a girl."

"What brought that on?"

"Do we need an outline of what we're going to talk about?"

"Go on, Scotty, get on with your dreaming."

"Well, sometimes I feel like a pebble rolling along the beach, just collecting sand and growing big, rolling and collecting. But I can't figure out what you are, if you're a rock collector or another pebble, maybe you're a shell close to me on the beach."

"Scotty," Neil waved his arms in front of her, 'I've had enough aggravation with these algebraic equations. Talk to me."

"My friend," she put her arm on his shoulders, "What am I going to do in California without you?"

"And what about me?" he asked, "You've always been a pebble on my shore or cliff. It seems as though you're always just outside my window. Maybe your dad will change his mind."

"I doubt it. On July first he'll be back to help us pack. He has a tool and die job out there. Mum will probably substitute teach."

"Will you come back for visits?"

"Probably not for years. It's too expensive."

"Will you write?"

"What else can I do?"

"Cheer up, Scotty, we'll have our last fling at the old house this summer."

A big tear rolled down her cheek with somewhat more color than usual. They looked out to the island that so intrigued them.

"Do you feel salubrious?"

"What?" said Neil. "What do you know about salubrious!"

"My Uncle Jeep always says 'salubrious.' It just seems like I should say salubrious, too."

"To your health, my sweetheart," he kissed her cheek.

"Health, is that what it means?"

"Yep."

"Well, I better go."

"Me too."

"Mum does wonder about me sometimes," said Scotty. "Your mum just worries about you, Neil."

They wiggled to their feet.

"See ya."

"Yeah, when?" she said.

"For Pete's sake Scotty, you're always in my back yard," and he descended the rock, blowing her a kiss.

Scotty had mixed emotions about the egging of Gary. After all, he did sit in front of her at school. She was sure to hear obscenities after the Hill skit for many a school day. Well, if it had to be, it had to be. He was a bully, a bully against nature, at that.

She walked the streets during the Holy Week, mostly on her own, alone but not lonely. Their holiday was Easter Week. Easter Sunday, the McFinch Clan would celebrate with rite and ritual. Easter Mass, the lily laden church, with statues exposed again after having been masked in purple for 40 weary days. But now, both earth and dome were barren. Each day after school, Scotty roamed the cobblestone ways of Marblehead from Fort Sewell to Gingerbread Hill, at odds, yet connected with this pre-Easter sadness. In keeping with the bleakness of the season, tumultuous Earth had spun hurricane-like winds on the fasting town. Dead fish lined the sidewalks and streets near the old fort. Passing the Barnacle Restaurant, the smell of chowder placated Scotty's weariness as she searched the hibernating eyes of the town folk. Where was the verve of Zig, her mentor? She wondered, as she climbed Gingerbread Hill, how Zig survived these cold months on onc dollar a day. As she sat on her log in front of Black Bird Pond, on top of the hill she could see in the mallard-rippled waters faces of hoboes warming their hands in small fires in the old train station.

On Good Friday, the town closed down at noon. Paine house ritual was no talking between 12 o'clock and three; also, a visit to Star of the Sea Church was mandatory. Scotty liked to be quiet. A forced quiet in the house was fun because her inner dialogue seemed to tidy up life, make it smooth. It was puzzle-fitting time, and what pieces she couldn't quite fit, she just smoothed in. Like Kate for instance, she really wasn't like her cousin, but there was something in Kate that Scotty needed; she just knew it.

Eric seemed to handle the quiet time with comic books. Thank goodness, there was no broken record. He couldn't tease her because he couldn't talk. Maybe she could handle more than one Good Friday a year. At one o'clock, they went to the church; a plaintive few kneeled or walked to the stations of the cross. It seemed sadness was languorous and their sorrow without tears this day. Scotty touched the dry holy water fount and made her way behind her mother to the step-in front of the altar where a metal crucifix lay on a violet pillow. Her mother kissed the wounds of the represented Lord and carefully wiped the crucifix with a soft cloth for the next mourner. Scotty and Eric followed her procedure and then all three quietly sat in a pew and gazed for a time at the open doors of the tabernacle. The ciborium that held the consecrated hosts was gone. The golden walls intrigued Scotty. She gazed pensively at the home of a mysterious King who gave His life for His people.

They stayed only a half hour and then went home. Lois quietly made fried egg sandwiches, Lenten lunch, as Eric browsed through Mad Magazine and Scotty watched the mallards sleeping on the grass by the pond. Scotty, not unhappy, felt that sorrow, like hunger, was temporary but necessary for people.

After lunch, they went their own ways. It was 3 o'clock.

"I'm going to Bea's, Mum."

"Back by six, Scotty."

"Yep."

Eric took off, too, for parts unknown. Scotty sauntered down the green mound, not disturbing the ducks. Eyes cast down; head slightly bent in the same direction; her straight brown hair blew to the wind. The cement path that skirted the pond was cracked.

"Step on a crack and you'll break your mother's back," she recited. Following the web of cracks, careful to walk over the cement etchings, she quickly reached Barb's house. Peering into the crystal-clear kitchen pane, careful not to nose the window, Scotty smiled as she watched Barb putting together a large crossword puzzle on a side table while her mother rolled out pie crust on the kitchen table. Tapping gently, she opened the door. Friends always walked in after a rap.

"Can you play, Barb?"

Mrs. Miles looked up from her pie.

"Hi, Scotty, haven't seen you in a while. Romping around I guess."

"Yep, romping is my hobby, I guess," said Scotty. "But I also like to fish with your daughter. How about it, Barb?" Barb continued to put together the border of her puzzle.

"Let me just finish this one side, Scot."

"Okay."

"Have a cookie, Scotty," Mrs. Miles pointed to the cookie jar atop the refrigerator. Her hands were covered with pie dough, so she could not serve her.

"I love your cookies, Mrs. Miles. Thank you."

"Take more, honey, don't be shy."

Taking a hand of oatmeal cookies, Scotty sat next to Barb pointing to colored patterns that might complete the border.

"Border complete!" Barb kissed her mother and grabbed a sweater. "We're off, Mum."

"Go to church today?"

"Yep, we were there at 12:00."

They both looked down at their sneakers as they walked.

"Gingerbread Hill?"

"Yep," said Scotty. "Doing anything for Easter, Bea?"

"Going to Grandma Miles' house. All the cousins will be there. We color our eggs when we get there and eat 'em up before we leave. No wasting at that house. Grampa Miles hits the juice, you know, the whiskey, and the uncles follow him to the den with their cigars and ale. They hibernate in the den till dinner. The aunties surround my Grandma in the kitchen, helping and tasting all the goodies. We cousins are put outside to make our fun, like your cousins."

"Do you like your cousins?"

"Pretty much. Corky Brown, my uncle Bill's son, is a jerk. Has to have his way always. I guess all families have one. Isn't Kate like that?"

"Kate's strong, all right, but we have some fun times together. She's clever, got some great ideas about everything."

They started ascending the hill. A snooty boxer named Snappy Tom, darted out at them. His curt bark and unfriendly manner reflected his owner's, who did not want anyone on the hill, though it was not private. If Gary had been a dog, he would have been Snappy Tom, thought Scotty.

"Hi, Snappy," the girls said in unison.

They knew Snappy by his bark and the owner by her curious eyes.

"Now, Snappy," said Scotty, "You see us all the time, why not be friendly."

She held out her hand and he snapped at it.

"Snappy, Snappy," a choppy staccato call came from the house. "Stop that! Don't mind him, girls," resounded a plump lady with curly red hair and thin, black glasses bridging her nose. As she drew near, the girls were welcomed by her voice, slow and articulate, but were repulsed by currant-like pupils; her eyes looked stern, the brows were knitted in malicious wrinkles. Her nose, too, looked snooty. A crabapple lady like this was everywhere in town, usually one to a block.

It was more fun when the lady did not come out, thought Scotty. Fun to creep by Snappy while he snoozed in his doghouse. On top of the hill, they nestled on a mound of grass, just short of the open bank that overlooked Black Bird Pond. They sat for a few moments hugging their knees. It was strange, neither Scotty nor Barb were big talkers, but they loved to be together.

"I'll miss you, Big Bea."

"Ditto."

"Will you write?"

"I don't like writing, but I'll do it for you. I'll really try."

"I'm not much of a letter writer either," said Scotty, "but then I've never had to be, my friends were here."

"Does Eric want to go?"

"Nope, his friends are here. My mum wants to stay, too, and well, I've got you, Neil, and the sea. Kate doesn't count, she's family. My dad is the pioneer in the clan. It's in his blood. He had to go. Leave this town, people are too small here. The big mysterious West called to him."

"How are you going?" asked Barb.

"We're getting a trailer."

"Wow, my uncle has one in Beverly, they're neat," said Barb. "Does it have a bathroom and all?"

"Yep, and the sink kinda folds out. I saw the one we're getting in Salem."

"Fun, gee, what fun," Bea spoke slowly, as if she were visualizing the trip west.

"Well, it'll be seven days, eight hours a day, riding, no running around. We'll probably be real tired. Let's not talk about it anymore, Bea. I want to think of the island and our summer fun, about Timmy and his frankfurter stand at Devereaux Beach, those roasted dogs in toasted buns. They were sorta like a mummy, those buns, remember, Barb? And the grape tonic."

"I like the orange," Barb was getting excited.

"Just two more months," said Scotty. "It will be swell to see the Dogwood in Old Burial Hill and the ducklings, the new grass, gosh, I can hardly wait. But I guess we better get back and stop our dreaming, it's almost six."

So, they went down the other side of the hill, passed Grace Oliver's Beach and the fudge store with its heavenly chocolate smell. There were things to feel in those dreamy winter months, intuitions for life.

CHAPTER FOUR

Scotty thought she might see Neil before Easter Sunday, but Saturday was hectic and Lois was supposed to bring a relish dish and stuffed dates to the McFinch Feed. House cleaning was a part of Saturday ritual and there were holiday services to attend. But Scotty thought of Neil and his gathering of the Blue Bloods. She liked to think about the polished rich, but she liked to be part of the McFinch Clan, too; Grampy McFinch hollering at the kids for stealing his Squirt and Grammy McFinch stuffing the kids with goodies. Red roaming, Penny and Candy underfoot, Uncle Jeep into the juice, talking up a storm, and Aunt Marge hanging the laundry—this was home.

Easter Sunday came. Marjorie O'Leary always did the laundry, holidays and weekdays alike, so it was not uncommon to see her in her Sunday best, out hanging clothes when Lois, Eric, and Scotty arrived for their Easter Sunday repast. Aunt Marge still had the chapel veil on her head from Easter Mass while a wooden clothespin dangled from her mouth.

The Paines slipped in quietly to the house, realizing that Aunt Marge would soon be scurrying up the back steps. There was a wonderful smell in the house of ham, greens, pineapple, and doves. Grammy McFinch sat on her rocker in the kitchen, ale in hand. After all, the noon hour had passed and it was perfectly respectable to drink ale after the noon hour, and on a holiday, at that.

Grampy McFinch and Uncle Jeep were watching their black and white television while Red sat to the side swiveling his head to follow the moving figures on the screen. Eric joined the men,

Lois sat with Grammy, and Scotty quickly joined her cousins in the attic where they rummaged through forgotten trunks of jewelry and old gowns from Miss Addie, the original builder of the Hill Street house.

"Hey Scotty," said Kate, a peevish sparkle in her eye, "come on up."

Penny and Candy were looking at themselves in a long mirror. They wore old chemises.

"Cute, I'm so cute," said Candy as she tilted her head and smiled at the girls through the mirror. Penny was shy. She looked at Candy, unmindful of her delicate beauty in the glass.

"Anything for me to wear?" asked Scotty. "That purple taffeta is pretty." She picked the taffeta up and after a quick hug threw it at Kate in playful jest. This might have precipitated a pillow fight but there were no pillows, no more chemises, just jewelry, and they wouldn't start to fling jewelry. In the meantime, the fragrance of ham and pineapple with cloves overwhelmed them. The aroma was rising to every crevice of the attic. Nodding to each other they unfastened chemises quickly and carefully placed them back in the trunk, the taffeta on top, the metal lock thumped closed. Cousins scrambled downstairs but when Scotty pounced on the last step, they took the wrong turn and wound up in the den full of cigar smoke. Choking, they quickly held their noses and tiptoed into the kitchen as in a chorus line. The swinging door finished their entry and just for a time they stood spellbound, looking at the wonderful ham, pies and wondrous other edibles. For Scotty this was one of those rare moments frozen in time, a still life that would always be part of her childhood memories. There was something enchanting about those innocent girls. Delight was in their every vein, giving them an untouchable sensuality.

"Well, don't just stand there, Muffins," said Grammy, we need help setting the table. We'll have to take turns. Lois, Eric,

Scotty, Kate, Candy, and Penny, you'll eat first then Marge, Jeep, and Grampy. Our dining room wasn't made for that many folks."

Of course, Grammy never sat down to a meal; seasoning her food and tasting it filled her. It was wonderful, too wonderful; the kids ate to obesity. They ate ham, yams, mincemeat pie and ginger candy. And the ale played on in the merry voices of a family delighted with life and thankful for their being. Grampy McFinch retired to the den with Uncle Jeep, Eric and Red. Soon, rich Havana vapors encircled their heads like halos of sainted life. "Sagacious, salubrious spirits" piped Uncle Jeep. And in the kitchen, nostrils quivered to pungent smells of Colombian coffee and dandelion wine, which Grammy had made for the aunties. As for the kids, after a prayerful exit, they leaped for the door, sweaters half on and half off, to hunt eggs in the tall patches of grass left ungroomed for the Easter egg hunt. Red, after a time, overwhelmed by the smoke, charged into the yard after them. After all, he was a hunter; his strong teeth held high the wicker basket, while the cousins pilfered verdant blades. On the handle, a violet satin bow trailed the party of adventurers, something like the whipping and thrashing of a kite's tail. Merriment was everywhere, half laughs, half breaths, half barks.

Scotty slipped on some slick grass. Taking respite on her back, eyes to the sky, she saw a glimpse, a dream of Barb, Neil, and Zig as one, like some strange Oriental statue of Buddha with many hands.

"Red, stop, stop, Red!" Red was lapping Scotty's face, the suction of his tongue brushing her cheek like sandpaper while the satin sash flapped in the air. "Stop Red, I'm okay, stop licking me!" She sat up feeling slightly awkward, eye to eye with the beagle. Then she jumped to her feet, ready to resume pursuit of the Easter gems.

"That's it," said Kate, "I counted the eggs, They're all here."

"Divvy up," said Penny.

"We each get one boiled and three jellies," cried Candy.

"Okay," said Kate. They all sat back-to-back in a circle, a bonfire of backs, jellies popping high into the air, then into their mouths. Red's eyes followed, his nose bobbing, his ears flapping. How long could that grand feeling last?

"Grammy's got some marshmallow eggs still," said Kate, "you know the ones, hard on the outside, but with mushy centers."

"Yuck," Penny snarled.

"Well, does anyone like them?"

They all shook their heads.

"No, that's what I thought. Let's hide them for fun in the railroad tracks."

"Can I hide them this time?" asked Penny.

"I guess," Kate paused, "I want to find some too." So, she went into the house to get the marshmallow eggs and to get permission for the gang to go to the railroad tracks. Since it was a holiday, there would be no trains that day, but supper was at six, she reported. The cousins eyed one another and said in unison, "Supper?"

"Well, you know, cold ham and potato salad, only if you want it. It will be on the table to pick at. Now let's get going. You better stay here Red, Grampy's looking for you. Go to the house, Red. Good boy," she said as he followed her directions.

The Abbot Hall clock struck ten times. It was pitch dark as Scotty rang the doorbell at Pete Reed's house. Eric had gone there after the Hill banquet. Now Lois and Scotty were calling for him, homeward bound. Perfunctorily, Scotty marched to the door of 2 Rowland Drive to retrieve her brother, thinking of meeting Neil next day and sharing their gluttonous tales. He would talk of "gateau" or "fromage" and "de la glace." How she loved to hear that French. Scotty had an ear and eye for beauty, and not thinking Neil in the least snobbish for reciting their family meal in French, she savored his reports.

As red sails wakened sailors to a promising storm next morning, Scotty felt anxious that a rain would prevent her appointment. She hastily donned a turtleneck, and hurrying to beat the storm, she darted out to the meeting place. "Neil," she gasped, slightly out of breath, as she looked around the sumac which veiled the rock, "that's my spot."

"I knew you'd be here," he said, "we think alike. Scotty, look at this weather."

Scotty glanced at the landscape, free from her tunnel vision of the trail and gripping her knees, sat in her groove in the rock.

"Isn't it exciting?"

"What?" she asked.

"You know, that peace before the storm."

"Yep, I know, I feel the stillness. It is sort of a feeling I have with you sometimes. But I also feel the rage, the fearful energy of the storm is within me sometimes, too, like a seizure, it rocks me. I could do something about it, that feeling, but I haven't figured just what yet."

"What do you know about seizures, Scotty?"

"Oh, didn't you know Barb gets them? I saw her at home once, her face became fearful and angry like some malicious character took hold of her, then her head slumped, and she fell to the floor. Thank gosh she was at home. Her mother grabbed a tablecloth to make a cushion for her head. It looked like Barb was trying to swallow her tongue. Her mum held it down with her fingers."

"We better be careful with her. Do you know what to do if it happens when we're around?"

"Yep, Mrs. Miles showed me. Mostly make her comfortable, watch that she doesn't hit her head or swallow her tongue. It's just a matter of seconds and she's normal. She's like a storm."

"We're all like the storm, barreling breakers, torrential winds, canvas flapping and slapping the deck, and buoys spinning like tops." His eyes flashed as they scanned from seascape to Scotty. "I would love to capture that thrilling and fearful nature," he spoke passionately as he gazed deeply into

Scotty's opal eyes reflecting his face. "The spirit of creation haunts me."

She kissed his cheek. Her lips soothed him like warm cider. "I don't know what you are saying sometimes, Neil. Maybe I'm too young and you're too old and wise for a kid. But I feel you. I've got the feeling I'll say the same things someday." She encased his arm with hers and they remained joined in an embrace. For a time, they sat without words as part of the landscape.

"Come back, Scotty."

"I'm back," she softened her eyes, "we'll be eating colored eggs for days. Did you do anything exciting at your grandmother's?"

"Same Easter rites went to the Neck after the twelve o'clock services. You knew my grandparents lived on the Neck, didn't you, Scotty?"

"Well, you mentioned, ta, ta, your royalty," she winked teasingly.

"Bea, Frankie, and Tom, my cousins, and then well, my Aunt Winifred and Uncle Alex, my father's brother and family, they were all there, at the Montague Residence. Ta ta," he winked back at her. "Beatrice is my age, but as cousins go, she's nothing like Kate. Bea has a club; about four snips of girls, working on needlepoint and embroidery for hope chests. I like her, of course, a pleasant kid, but so staid. I could easily exchange families with you, Scotty, just for a time, I mean. I would like to escape our congenial Blue Bloods for the hunts with Red and the frightful walks on the upper landing of the water tower. Our family, so planned and methodical could make not hide nor hair of Kate, that desultory character."

"How do you come up with those words, Neil?"

"I read a lot and what I read, becomes me."

"So, what is desultory?"

"Somebody who does what they please whenever it pops into their mind without order."

"Am I desultory?"

"When it comes to me, you are." He tugged their chain. "It seems when you are thinking of me, I'm thinking of you, and we meet."

A teardrop from the sky rolled down her cheek, gathering salt and saving the memory on her tongue. Gotta go, she thought, maybe I can make it back to the house before the downpour, but she stopped deliberately to look him in the eye, an eye of such wonder, and she said, "I love you Neil," then, pulling her hand loose, she darted off. Just before she ducked under the fence to climb the hill, she peered back, to see Neil watching her through the sumac. A tear then matched the raindrop on her cheek. She had never said "I love you" to her mother or father.

Swallow it, Scotty, she thought, I'm only ten and talking to myself. Her heart pounding, she made her way to the house before the storm. The ducks scurried to the bushes, ready to bury their heads into their feathers again.

"April, May, and June," she talked to herself eyes downcast on the cement, watching for cracks. How odd, she seemed to look down or up most of the time.

On Monday, she returned to Gerry School to face Gary again. All good things must come to an end, she thought, trite but true. Gary was reality. His foul mouth, the gurry of life. Perhaps she wouldn't love Neil or Barb as much without the test of Gary.

"Hey, knuckle brain, do any egg smashing this Easter?"

"I colored eggs; we took turns hiding them at my Grammy's and then we ate 'em. I didn't smash 'em."

"Well, I thought you were going to egg me, you pisshead."

"Quiet, Gary. Miss Orne won't be hard of hearing when I bellow what you said into her ear."

"Okay, knuckle brain, I'll shut up for now."

Math led the litany of academics for these fifth graders. Fractions, how droll, but Scotty, feeling playful, wrote "Scotty over Neil equals love."

At recess, the girls played kick ball. Scotty, the captain, kicked the ball to victory. "Get 'em Scotty!" It was the last kick before the end of recess and the Voit went spinning out, under the fence, to the street. Scotty ran outside the school yard to catch the ball, but the gutter snatched the round rubber ball, slapping it onto the rubble of yesterday's storm. Scotty made a triangle at the end of the gutter, just short of Eddie's Sundries. A diagonal step had saved ball and face. Tardiness, like a failing grade, would have made victory into loss. The bell of resumption pulled faceless children to the looming school as a magnet. Scotty flicked particles of rocks and debris off the wet, repulsive ball. With one eye to the backs of her classmates, like sun's rays being absorbed into the brick, she skipped, then ran to catch up.

After school she walked, eyes to the road, searching the pavement for wiggling worms entering the pond boundaries; she noted fish—one, two, three of them, strewn on the sidewalk nearest her house. The ducks greeted her, their waddling "heinies" in natural cadence. Scotty fumbled with her cobalt parka, with fish bread for her friends in her jacket pocket. Usually, she squawked back at them.

"Here you are, my darlings. Didn't get much yesterday, with that storm. It's hard to tell when you fellows need food, for it seems you're always the same size," she said to the ducks. "Perhaps you're squawking a little more today. That's it, you talk when you're hungry. I guess that's true for all of us. We talk more when we're in need."

And after she fed them, she sat on the wet mound between the ceramic lions, the ducks at her feet, quiet now, and they all stared at the pond together. She didn't want the cliff today. She might see Neil, and the memory of her love confession still smarted in her mind. But she wanted to see Barb; she had a craving for Big B. So, spanking her bottom dry, Scotty snuck away from her friends, into the house to drop her book bag. The kitchen was as silent as a tomb. A smidgen of grape jelly dotted the counter where Eric had eaten his English muffin that morning. She hurried out, no reason to stay. Head down again in scrutiny of thc pathway skirting the pond to Barb's. She stopped at Barb's landing to watch a crayfish clutch a dead fly which had floated to the wall of the landing. Then she flung her last morsel of bread from her parka pocket into the pond. Rims of fish surfaced like dolphins to punch the bread into the air then they tugged and pulled at them until the white rounds disappeared and Scotty disappeared into her friend's yard. Her rock garden still waited for narcissus and daffodil to surprise the first days of May.

After two raps she always popped in. "Hi, Mrs. Miles. Is that cookie dough I smell?"

"Why Scotty, it's you! No, that's gingerbread. Want some?"

"Love some," she rubbed her stomach.

"Barb is just changing into play clothes; she'll be right down."

Scotty partook of the Dromedary delight, cupping all crumbs and tossing them greedily into her mouth.

"By golly, where did it go?"

"Wow, that was good. It might not have tasted that great if it didn't smell so good. Don't think me a piggy, Mrs. Miles, I'm really slow. I just eat fast."

They both laughed. This kitchen was better than a dead jam kitchen; Scotty thought of the sticky drop of grape jelly on the lonely counter in her home.

"Hey, Scotty," Barb was pulling through a warm cotton turtleneck as her feet scurried down the runner that looked remarkably royal because of its crimson projection, "What's up?"

"I can't stay away too long you know; I'm addicted to your mum's cookie dough."

"You don't say." Barb gave her mum a peck on the cheek. "You can't have her, she's all mine," and then she paused, "Wonder why I'm so skinny, the aroma alone must be fattening."

"Wanna fish?" asked Scotty.

"Yep, but I'm out of bread. Maybe we should use gingerbread today." The three laughed. Mrs. Miles gave Barb half a bread loaf. Then, quickly she covered the gingerbread with foil, and nudged the girls out the door. They returned by the barren rock garden to the pond.

"So, what about Neil?" Barb asked as she slid onto the edge of the landing, letting her legs hang down over the edge. Scotty joined her.

"Neil?"

"Neil."

"Oh, I saw him yesterday before the storm."

"Did he have a good Easter?"

"Royal, I would say, or Blue Blood; maybe that's the word. We didn't get into food. Can you imagine being in Neil's family?" Scotty said with dreamy eyes.

"Nope, I like my mum's cookie dough just fine." Big B put a morsel of spongy bread onto her fishhook. Strings and fishhooks, that's all they had, and they plopped them into the water.

"But Neil's fine, he's not a big shot. He says what he thinks, and he thinks the Mystery House, Timmy and the frankfurter stand are fun."

"Yep, not cat hurling like Gary," Scotty spouted. "What a way to come back from Easter vacation to that foul-mouthed birdbrain."

Dead silence followed. Barb gazed deeply into the pond at no particular spot with an uncanny stare. She soon elevated her gaze to Scotty's eyes with a cold, menacing, deliberately grotesque look. Never had Scotty seen her friend looking like such a terror.

"It's your fault Scotty, you created Gary."

Scotty winced with pain. Was this a nightmare? Her girlfriend's contorted face and eyes cut her to the quick.

"Me? What did I do?"

"You treat Gary like slime, with your holier than thou attitude. You expect him to be foul, and he is."

"That's unfair B. What's bringing this on?"

Barb continued to talk deliberately slow, unaware of Scotty's retort.

"His father's out of work so he hits the bottle, and his mum's dying of cancer."

"I didn't know that."

But Barb was not listening. She stared into the pond now and began to shake.

Scotty grabbed Barb's arm for fear she would fall into the water, and then Barb, with a jolt, violently slumped into her lap. Paralyzed with fear, Scotty clutched Barb's arm. Bewildered, Scotty realized that this was a seizure.

A few seconds later, Big B sat up. "What happened?"

"Don't you know?"

"I felt angry and helpless and then everything went dark. Did I have a seizure?"

"Yup," Scotty loosened her hold. "Are you okay?"

"Oh yeah, they don't usually last long, but it's embarrassing, especially the foam."

"No foam this time," Scotty patted her friend on the shoulder. "Maybe, we better go home."

"No, really, I'm okay."

"Do you remember anything about the seizure?"

"No, what happened?"

"Well, we were talking about Neil," Scotty hesitated, "and then I brought up Gary. Don't know why exactly, but Neil always makes me feel good and Gary, I dread. I loathe everything about him. Don't you remember?"

"No-o-o," Big B elongated her negative.

"You really don't remember?" Scotty pouted while searching Barb's face.

"No, I get sorta goofy with those seizures. I'm told Grampa Miles had 'em too. Hope I didn't scare you."

"Well, you did scare me a little. Thought you'd fall in the pond. You . . . you . . ." Scotty stuttered, "got kinda angry before you fell."

"My mum says the same thing. I get cantankerous."

"Oh, you and Neil, your words! Just what does cantankerous mean?"

"Grumpy."

"Well, cantankerous, yup, that is how I'd describe you."

Then a sharp tug on her line told Scotty she might have a catch. A small mackerel jetted out of the water and flapped like a griddle cake on the surface. Back into the water, the mackerel pulled Scotty's line like a tug of war under a blanket, then it went limp and Scotty pulled it in.

"Bingo." The two girls giggled together.

On the landing, the tiny fish flapped some more, its scales, like a reflector, made kaleidoscope images of the sun.

"Too small," sighed Scotty, actually relieved to return the fish to the water. The fun for her was in the catching, but not in the keeping.

"Yup," Barb agreed.

Scotty at first struggled to unfasten the hook from the mouth of the mackerel, then nimbly, she released her friend into the rippling water.

"Gotta go, B," Scotty said. "Gotta do some chores at home for Mum before dinner."

"Maybe I'll do the same. I like to clean up after gingerbread dough," Barb winked.

The two then pulled one dangling leg to the landing, then the other; in a bent position they pushed with both hands and launched their bodies to stand.

"So long then, B."

"See ya, Scotty."

Big B watched for a couple of minutes while Scotty, head down, studied the rocks and crevices in the cement, homeward bound. Scotty didn't look back.

"Cantankerous," she whispered. "Was that all she meant? How ridiculous to think that I had a part of Gary. I hate that kid," she grumbled. "He makes me feel miserable," she blurted out. She thought some more about how she endured him like a little martyr. And he knew it. So, she ran hard to stop thinking, to stop the questions, the inner questions.

Lois, home from school, had wiped away the jam spot. Scotty hugged her mother, peaceful again.

CHAPTER FIVE

The days that followed after Easter, the Tuesdays, the Wednesdays, repetitive and familiar, filled Scotty with the natural rhythm that orders serenity in life.

In the back of her mind, as she met the man with the English cap or saw Zig in the distance lingering on some hill, she dared to think of Gary and her judgement of him. His incorrigible character seemed so bizarre, it scared and intrigued her. In limbo with him for a while, she decided on a plan of placid silence. After all, a pleasant countenance endeared her to Zig, so it might work with Gary. Her new mission became smiling at him silently and occasionally picking up papers that he had dropped. Baffled at her conduct, he stopped calling her names, since she had not responded to them. Their relationship took on a new face of resignation. He continued to peck at everyone, but he left her alone. On one occasion he actually accosted Tommy Field who had tripped Scotty for fun.

The Hill Club hadn't met for quite a while. The chicken coop, piled with snow in February, left no hope for comfortable pranks. But on Sundays, after church, when the Paines went to the Hill for family dinner, Kate would outline Spring activities, using Scotty as a sounding board. Finding new things to do was a problem, so Kate focused on new membership, devising more grueling initiations.

Kate reveled in the power of vulpine leadership. By the end of April, only puddles stood between her plans and reality. Scotty, however, wished only to be back to a dry rock or Fountain Park with Neil and Barb to plan island adventures. She had grown bored with the Hill Club. At ten, she could choose adventure and mystery instead of power, a personality treasure that would be buried in California days.

May arrived, pulling crocuses and daffodils from the hills of Old Burial Cemetery. Mother ducks with their new broods began walks around the pond. Cobalt skies and cotton candy clouds were mirrored in the pond while the ceramic lions, stark and alone, became cushioned with the velvet of new grass.

Scotty excitedly picked narcissus to surprise Mr. Graves, the retired lawyer who lived next to them in a secluded area behind a smaller pond that the kids used for ice skating because Redd's Pond didn't always freeze as fast. In retirement, Grampy Graves, as Scotty called him, loved to leave oranges and Licorice Nips in front of Scotty's door, labeled for her. Having no children of his own, Grampy Graves mystified his adopted granddaughter with the kindest of surprises. Scotty favored him with small gifts too, a miniature reindeer candle, Rudolph, was the most notorious present that reigned on his mantel winter and summer alike.

"Oh, Grampy, you caught me!" Scotty exclaimed, bent with her small bouquet at his doormat. She had meant to dart away after a rap on the door, but now she was stuck holding a lone narcissus while the rest of her bouquet of yellow daffodils made the welcome festive.

"Why, Scotty, my little dear." The venerable attorney had the demeanor of a retired Renoir, white and bearded. His pink cheeks now formed apples in a smile for his favorite sweetheart. "I'm looking for my newspaper. Have you seen it? Now here, what have we here?" He bent to hold a daffodil. "This is lots better than my newspaper and I know that Grammy Graves will like this posy, too."

Scotty beamed. She had wanted to surprise him. "I'm glad you like them." She rubbed his cheek with her peach skin and kissed the air, English style.

"Where've you been, my girl? The winter's been lonesome without you, but here you are with the spring."

Scotty smiled, her eyes clear and moist like marbles.

"I missed you as much as you missed me, but gosh, it's just great to be outside again. Drawing cartoons and listening to my brother's stale records can be horrible. I can't believe it. It's really May!" She shivered with delight and smacked her lips as though to taste spring.

"So, what's up, my friend, certainly you've got more to tell me."

"School, mostly, the Hill Club. Well, Barb and I fish sometimes, but it's been too wet for fishing and too wet to sit on the rock at Fountain Park with Neil to plan the treasure hunt at Brown's Island."

Scotty crossed her fingers when she thought of Neil at the rock before the storm. Grampy didn't have to know everything. After all, he knew about the plan to find the treasure. Wasn't that enough? Even Lois didn't know about that.

"Haven't seen you, my dear Gramps, for so long, I can't quite remember what I did tell ya. Did I tell you about meeting Zig in the fall?"

"Nope, don't reckon you did."

"Well, that was some story."

Mrs. Graves, in the kitchen, caught Scotty's attention by waving her rolling pin in the air, in the middle of making an apple pie, as her floured fingers threw Scotty a kiss.

"Well, where was I? Oh yes, Zig. Zig the banker, the banker turned beggar. You know the one."

"Don't hear much these days. We're mostly by ourselves, me and the Mrs., and he's not in the paper. Nope, can't rightly say I know him."

"Well, it's so strange, I mean, I don't know him either, but he gave me his dollar, his last and only dollar that day, and I took it. I don't know him, but I took it. Actually, he pushed it into my hands!"

"Slow down, Scotty."

"Sorry, I'm so excited today." She tried to slow her speech. "Well," Scotty's eyes bee-black pools of intensity, "Zig, a middle-class man, banker, teller actually, gave up his twin girls and wife to walk the streets. Being a bank teller and a man of conscience, he left money for his family in a trust. But for himself he lives on one dollar a day which he gets at the bank daily. Nobody knows where he sleeps, but he's been seen eating with some beggars by the old railroad station. He roams all day and does not speak to anybody.

"One day, I was gazing at the pond just before leaving for school, and he crept up behind me and pressed his dollar in my hand. Not a word, mind ya, but as I looked at him, I realized, we were not strangers. Hard to explain, I had the feeling I knew him as much as I know myself."

"And the dollar?" Graves asked.

"I hid it for a while but then decided to give it to the Church. Put it in the poor box, I did. After all, it didn't belong to me, did it? But I will always remember it."

She blew out air, just a sigh to change the subject, "It seems funny to be here on Sunday. I mean, at home and not on the Hill. Mum's packing is almost done, she is going to California for a visit with my Dad. He found us a house. Wants Mum to be the final judge."

"What about you and Eric?"

"Eric will stay with a friend near school, and I'll go to Aunt Lucretia's. You know, the eldest aunt. She never had children. Grammy and Aunt Marge would take me in a minute, but Aunt Lucretia has first choice; makes me feel important, though I'm a bit too simple and shy for Aunt Lucretia. She married a Frenchman, you know, snooty and mannerly. I'm never quite sure what to do. Maybe that why Mum's putting me there, to submerge me in etiquette, the poised cock-a-button. Funny, huh?" Scotty laughed and Grampy joined her.

The pie was beginning to titillate their nostrils. Grampy Graves made faces now. He licked his lips in anticipation of a sweet feast.

"The pie is still hot but I've some wonderful oatmeal cookies," Grammy said loudly from the kitchen, "How about it, tea and cookies?" So Grampy and Scotty adjourned to the kitchen for their repast of sumptuous sweets and savory tales.

Sunday evening at home, Scotty's anxiety mounted as she thought of her stay with Lucretia. Lois would bring her there soon. They would make their farewells at Lucretia's house. Aunt Marge would drive Lois to the airport at 6:30 Monday morning; no time for goodbyes then.

Aunt Lucretia, the eldest aunt, was handsome and bold, and by far the most theatrical of the family. Her use of slow diction and erudite talk could be mixed with spontaneous nonsense in muffled tones, all of which set her apart as a dramatic personality. Accountable to none, Aunt ruled the Hill with her shocking maneuvers and manipulative ways.

In their younger days, Lois tagged along with Lue; in this case it was the younger girl who was the chaperone.

"That red haired brat, I won't have her around me!"

Scotty heard that story many times from her mother. She had used her aunt's very words. Lois had not wanted to be with her sister on her escapades, her bright red long curls were enough embarrassment, though Grammy McFinch had thought them a radiant family treasure.

"Bite your tongue and watch your feisty temper and you won't have your sister with you," Lois repeated Grammy's part too.

It had all been told to her, through her mother's eyes, how Kitty McFinch would shudder at Lucretia's antics. Lue always had the right word or memory of an incident that could trigger shock from a family member. Oddly enough, in their game of Parcheesi, home, the victory, never reflected home, that secure, warm self. Sadness with supremacy, Lue had no place left to go, such is the case with winning loss.

"I think one day she will be free with nobody to control or impress, but right now she enjoys the power of controlling family feelings like a doctor. She pecks here and there, making sister or cousin alike kick and squirm, because she touches nerves. She says I drink and that your dad had other women. Well, I drink, a little; I miss your dad, but I'm not a drunk and your dad, well, he talks to other women, but he doesn't have other women. I love my sister. I just don't like the way she acts. Maybe I should say 'I want to like my sister.'"

"Mum, are you sure you want me to stay with Auntie Lue? I've never heard you talk so."

"She loves you, Scotty, and you need a little of her, you're too much of a church mouse, maybe I'm the same. Lue knows refinement. She can polish you a bit better than I can. Just look at her regal bridal pictures at Grammy's; oh, and there are so many photos tucked away in her album of visits with mayors, teas with councilmen; she even ate with the Ambassador to France. I'm not jealous, mind you, but I do wonder where she came from, Marge and I are so simple."

Scotty's eyebrows were up and down in amazement as her mother talked. Was this really Lois Paine, her meatloaf and smiles mother, kindergarten teacher? She was completely off the cuff and totally out of character. Or maybe not, maybe there was more to her mum; a crazy, bone feeling told her so.

They reached Aunt Lue's house.

"Come in Marguerite, come in, have you had dinner?" Aunt Lue had suggested to Lois that she not come in with Scotty. Lois had spoken to Lue on the phone with school instruction and other routine matters, and now she said that she wished to check on Eric and turn in early and left.

"Yes, Aunt Lucretia, I did eat, thank you."

"Oh, let's not be so formal, you call me Lue."

Scotty smiled while she nodded, still a bit shy with her new knowledge of her aunt.

"I've been looking forward to this visit with you, Marguerite, it's a bit lonely here without Martin."

Scotty smiled and nodded again, she wanted to tell her aunt to call her Scotty, but she couldn't say it just yet. Lue's dreamy eyes were remembering Uncle Martin now in some French marketplace, where he was on a buying trip. Martin owned a French deli in Salem and Boston. She remembered that Neil had lunch with his father in the Boston deli and told her all about it. Scotty had only visited the Salem bistro, but the smells and ambiance made her long for exotic Parisian places.

What a fanciful living room they sat in now as they chatted, a stuffy paisley chintz sofa and a royal plum velvet upholstered rocker. Fans with pictures of French chateaux lined the walls and over the mantel, a portrait of Lucretia and Martin. There were Swiss chocolates and English toffees in a sweet dish of Rosenthal china.

"Would you like a chocolate?" Lue offered as she saw Scotty's eyes watering at the tasty scene.

"Thank you," Scotty felt awkward with such opulence as she bit halfway through the sweet laden with liqueur. Aunt Lue had a natural grace with this kind of refinement. Somehow Scotty, so natural, became clumsy with this Swiss delicacy under Aunt Lue's scrutiny. It was all so unnerving to her.

That night as she lay in the Eastlake guest bed, she was charmed by the floral wallpaper. She contemplated her family and the strange contrast of its members. Where did Aunt Lue come from, and hadn't her mother asked the same thing? Grampy McFinch, a painter, and Grammy, a cook; Aunt Marge, more the nanny type; and Lois, a little bit of everybody plus some rare quality, she just knew it, sleeping in her. And Lue, what about Aunt Lue?

Aunt Lue began life in ballet slippers, the ballet an avarice for a glimpse of life.

"Listen to me, I'm beginning to talk like Neil," Scotty whispered to the flowers on the wall.

And in her mahogany bed with spiraling bedposts, Aunt Lucretia had her thoughts, too. In her youth she had not been as timid as Scotty; she had been bold, but neither of them had been too timid or too bold to dream and wonder.

At school the next day, Scotty felt flushed as her Aunt dropped her off at Gerry School in her vermilion Buick. The kids, all goggles and giggles, saluted her as might the fans and voters of Elbridge Gerry, one time governor of Massachusetts and Vice President of the United States. The long-ago patriot, for whom the school was named, would have welcomed the greeting perhaps more than this shy schoolgirl of quiet manner. Lovingly, Scotty kissed her aunt goodbye, forgetful that demonstrative partings was a Lois trait, not aunt Lue's. Her niece's wet lips only made her cheeks smart. Lue was used to Victorian distance.

"Goodbye, dear," Lue said, "I'll come for you at three."

"Thank you, Aunt Lue," Scotty couldn't say only "Lue," just as Lue didn't know what to do with kisses.

Sheepishly, Scotty confronted her friends.

"Say now, Scotty, was that your fairy godmother?" said Tommy Field, the tripper.

"My aunt," Scotty snapped, as she tried to kick a can on the school grounds to change the subject. Soon the kids were running after the Coke can until the bell rang.

During the week, the kids adjusted to Aunt Lue's vermilion Buick, much as they adjusted to the gong of Abbot Hall, and Mrs. Orne's lacy hanky that centered her low-cut bodice, buoying up and down as she skirted the room helping boys and girls alike.

After school, aunt and niece had tea with shortbread cookies. High tea was always served on Aunt Lucretia's Royal Daulton or Wedgewood. Supper at seven was not as portentous as tea; it was boiled beef with vegetables and tapioca, a Grammy McFinch supper. After dinner, they took their walk to the end of Bay Street to see the Salem harbor, to check for red sails, predictors of good weather for the morrow. This was their almanac of life.

"Did you ever want children, Aunt Lue?" Scotty asked.

"Martin and I couldn't have children. Shall we sit on this rock for a moment?" Aunt Lue answered, wearier from thought than their walk. "Before we were married, your uncle and I would picnic here. We'd tie our wine bottle on the end of a string and dangle it from these rocks in the cool waters until we ate. We planned for a family; we planned for a house, so many nights, from these rocks. But now," she hesitated, then she sighed. "Can I confide in you, Marguerite?"

Scotty answered with eyes questioning and head nodding affirmatively. Only kids made those requirements, she thought. Only kids made secret promises.

"I have only told this to your grandmother," Aunt Lue said, looking at the water. "Your Uncle Martin is dying of a rare liver disease. He'll not last long. I've wanted to keep the news from Kit and Roy as long as possible, hoping there'd be a miraculous remedy." Aunt Lue didn't look near tears, she was composed as always, even when angry. Her few "damns" were measured, without emotion.

"Well, I'm preparing to take over the stores. It would be impossible now to have a child; no time, you see."

Scotty's eyes spoke of benign resignation. She understood everything, the best she could as a child.

"It's getting a bit chilly, shall we go back?" Aunt Lue took Scotty's hand to pull her up. They walked pensively back to the house. Scotty could not conceive of Uncle Martin dead. She knew nothing of dying.

Lue, seemingly immune to future pain, questioned Scotty with her eyes for new ideas to entertain their evening.

"Would you like to play rummy, Scotty?" She had stopped calling her Marguerite.

"I don't know how."

"Well, it's easy, I'll show you. Shall we give it a try?"

"I tried to play chess with Eric," Scotty sputtered on, "but he was furious when I couldn't understand how to move the 'pond'. 'It's the easiest move, you dummy,' he said. Of course, I know Old Maid; Barb and I play that."

Aunt Lue instructed, and they spent an hour playing the game.

"Now, you've school tomorrow. Let's turn in and I'll catch the news on my radio."

"I'm ready," Scotty yawned. "Shall I do anything in the morning for you, Aunt Lue? I'm used to getting Eric's English muffin and eggnog, mother's coffee, too."

"No dear, I'm a tea drinker, and I'll make it, thank you. I'm the hostess in this family. Maybe I can get you something?"

"I like muffins, too."

"Good, we'll have tea and muffins. Now, good night."

Scotty wanted to peck her aunt on the check, and she looked for permission.

"Kiss me if you must," Lue winked at Scotty, warming up to her innocent affection.

That night, Scotty dreamed of Neil, "I love you, I love you," she mumbled in her subconscious, and she woke up with a start. "Desultory, so that's what I am!" she mumbled, and went back to sleep.

On Friday, Scotty thought about her stay with Aunt Lue. "I like being an only child," she thought, "with pretty floral wallpaper in my bedroom and no holes in the wall, a vanity with a lacy border, and milk glass bedside lamps." But there was something lonely about Lue. Things looked too perfect; it was a no-spill house. Scotty always had a milk mustache or a cock-a-button in her hair, naturally out of order. And even though they talked about meatloaf and laundry, hugging Lois was home. She even missed Eric and his obnoxious "Cross Over the Bridge." After all, wasn't he a teenager, splitting from the clan? He had his rights too. Secretly, she missed the trauma of her family life. And she missed Zig. There was something cozy about the lowly man, a homeliness in the dumps, a friendliness in the slums, a kindliness in Zig, the person.

Now without them, she appreciated them. She had never been without them before; but she also appreciated the rare, unique experience of being an only child with Aunt Lue.

Scotty, packed and ready, waited for Lois.

Lois was on time from the airport; Aunt Marge waited in the car while mother went to fetch the daughter.

"Hello, darling, were you good to Aunt Lue?"

"Your daughter was most pleasant," Lucretia answered for Scotty. Scotty just listened and wondered why the Aunt Lue who now spoke was not the Aunt Lue of her stay.

"She's a rummy player now, Lois, and a tea drinker."

"You'll still get my coffee in the morning, won't you, Scotty?" Lois winked.

Scotty said nothing; she was supposed to listen, but she flashed a slight grin.

"Things okay in California? Ed doing all right?"

"He seems to be ready for us, has a house, a ranch type, seems nice, newest house I'll ever live in! I'm just not ready for the move, but I'm sure it will grow on me."

They had their squabbles, but none of the three sisters wanted to be separated. Marge stayed in the car because she had had some tiff with Lue. They probably wouldn't talk for a week or two. They were all so different, so affected and complicated, but at least Scotty had seen Lue's furtive eye for fun. Maybe duty made Lue think of Martin and his withering life. Lois's return was her return. But Scotty soon drowned out the adults and their pompous talk. She wanted to know about her pioneer father, about California palms and oranges. He sent her a candy crate of miniature oranges, a souvenir. But her mother and aunts talked about duties.

Her imagination now sauntered to Marblehead, to the Barnegat, old pirate haunt of the pre-Revolutionary days. Oakum Harbor was Neil's backyard; she saw him now beckoning her. She heard the shrieks of a woman coming from the island of buried treasures.

"Scotty, you about ready?"

"Yes, Mum, I've been ready. Goodbye, Aunt Lue, thank you for everything. Maybe Eric will play rummy with me now and forget about the chess."

"Goodbye, dear, and you are always very welcome."

"Goodbye Lue, thanks from me, too."

As they left, the elder sister shut the door abruptly, as if dismissing servants. Was there such a thing as brief love?

CHAPTER SIX

As Scotty expected, being back home with its fishhooks, holes in the wall and Eric's records, took on new meaning.

"Hey, Moose," Eric called to Scotty. "Have a good time at Aunt Lue's?" Eric's ruddy skin glowed from neck to cheek as he panted from his run home.

"Yep. You too, Eric?"

"Yes and no. I thought Mum was strict! Peter Reed's mum takes the cake. I ran home to play my record; I haven't heard it in a week."

"Well, I missed Hopalong Cassidy and Zorro, now that you mention it, but I had a more sophisticated time," she batted her eyelashes at him.

Eric loved and hated her, the little angel of the family. "And now, on to my record," he repeated.

Scotty said nothing. Foiled, he retreated to his room. Scotty walked around the kitchen.

"Tea time!" Lois looked cheerful, not merely contained. A week away had relaxed her. It's so strange, Scotty thought, her mum was so comfy and her aunt so imaginative. Two sisters, yet so different.

"Some tea, Scotty?"

"With lots of lemon and sugar."

"Child, sometimes I think I should serve you lemonade." Lois took her sweater off quickly and hung it over Scotty's head the way Ed did when he was home, treating Scotty like a hall tree. Quickly, the tea kettle made hissing sounds and the vapors warmed Scotty's imagination to talk of her father's adventures.

"What's it like, Mum? What's it really like, California?"

Lois steeped the tea bags, "It's warm, the palm trees are tall and the geraniums made bright lawns of red in those Hollywood homes I saw. I remember Fred Astaire's prints in the cement star. The Spanish stucco houses with their tile roofs. Everything seemed new and undergrown, not like here with these old houses and big, old maple trees. Your dad was proud of it all and proud to take me around as if he found the West. As a matter of fact, he has grown a small mustache and looks like Errol Flynn. We toured Universal Studios, feeling somewhat like celebrities. It's so different there." She paused. "I'll let you put in the sugar and I'll close my eyes, this time." They each took a big sip.

"Scotty, how you slurp! It's hard to believe a kid could be so loud and demure at the same time." Scotty grinned.

"The house is nice," Lois continued. "You'll have a bigger room, and no holes in the walls," she blinked with excitement. "Eric will have his very own unit behind the house, as a matter of fact, right off the patio and garden with scads of irises. There are oh, so many irises!"

"Any beach, Mum?"

"Well, we have a drive to the beach, but we can go on Sundays. It's funny to see the ponies," Lois sputtered on.

"My own pony, did you say, Mum?"

"Yes, your own pony, silly! The ponies are oil derricks, pumps that look like ponies on the beach. The beaches have lots of buried oil and when you walk on the sand, your feet look like Sugar Babies, like sugary licorice," she stopped. "I'm scared to leave Marblehead, I know, but I'm beginning to feel your Dad's adventure."

Eric lit a fire that night, a colored log, and they worked by candlelight, he on a sketch of a headless horseman, for art, and Scotty copied cartoons from the paper. Lois, being both mother and father now for another month, sat in the Windsor rocker and read the Sunday news.

Eric was sick the next day. He usually had many colds. After serving her mother coffee, Scotty brought Eric his eggnog and English muffin. Kleenex was strewn by the bedsides and nightstands. Eric continued to sneeze and blow. "He must be sick," she whispered, as his Gothic Church radio played only mumbled, low key sounds of the news.

She liked to be with her brother; she just didn't like to talk to him. When he was sick, he didn't talk much, and Scotty would lie on the floor in his room making card houses while they listened to "Amos and Andy." He didn't have enough strength to tease. She liked to slip in at such times and look at his Nordic countenance and compare their resemblance. But it all passed when he grew strong and played man again. Now she and Lois must go to school. Eric would stay at home with his ginger ale and Campbell's soup.

The ducks came running when Scotty passed through the lions' path and down to the cement skirting the pond. "Did you miss me, my dears?" She tore into her brown lunch bag for a crust of white bread from her peanut butter and jelly sandwich. "Peanut butter and jelly sandwiches, food fit for a king," she spoke to the ducks as she shared her crusts. "Avaricious, aren't we? Gee, Neil would be proud of me and my duck lingo. That's all you get now." Wrapping up her sandwich again, she walked along. It was good to walk to school again. The limo service didn't sit well with her; she never would have made a proper queen. Oh, it was all right to cheer her on in kick ball, but to take notice of her alone, why that was Scotty's job. To take stock of to notice; and she noticed Gary looking helplessly at the fraction on the board. Fifth grade math was not his pleasure, and he looked vulnerable and puzzled.

"Gary," Scotty stopped before his desk, "I've missed you."

"What?" Gary looked more puzzled, if that were possible.

"Why, I've been here, and you've been here at Gerry."

"Well, I've been staying at my aunt's, and I felt as if I haven't been here."

"Scotty, are you crazy? What are you talking about?"

"Oh, nothing, I just missed you."

He understood. They understood each other and she sat down. In ten minutes, she had answered the fractions and showed him her page. "Make any sense?"

"Now I understand you."

She did a little pointing with explanation of Miss Orne for him now and returned the page to her desk. It was strange how things between them changed after that. They didn't talk that much but there developed a friendliness and an acceptance apparently indicative to them both. Each morning after that fraction, Scotty made some gesture to talk and on Friday, she asked about his mother. She had never mentioned to Barb that she knew about Gary's mother, the information spat out in hate of sickness. But she did wonder why Barb had never told her of Gary's mother and her cancer when she was okay. Scotty thought they were friends, but then Barb didn't talk a lot, nor did she complain or gossip. She liked that about her friend so that was that.

"Gary, I'm sorry your mother is sick."

"You know about my mother?"

"I've only heard from my friend that she's very ill."

"My mother has cancer, but never much talks about it. I'm not even sure what cancer is. But I hear my dad talk to her about it. He's kinda down in the dumps. No work at Graves Boat Yard and my mum's sick. She's so weak. Sometimes, she can't get out of bed. He doesn't come home much, my dad. Guess he can't take it, my mum sick and all, and no work and all. I feel like I don't belong there 'cause I want to eat and there's no food." He got a mean look in his eye. What else could he do? Gary was a proud kid.

Scotty felt a tear on her cheek. So quickly it rolled over her frozen cheek, numbed by the pain of existence. Rubbing the tear into her skin, she took on a common cocker spaniel stare of animal candor. "My aunt brings us some food, my mum's sister. She doesn't have much, but she brings us chowder sometimes on Friday. Her husband is a painter, he works pretty much. So, she brings us chowder and Boston brown bread and we get cans and bread pretty much. I help at Schube's after school, sweep the floor. They can't pay me, I'm too young, but they give me cans of food and bread. Sometimes I even get Spam. My mum don't eat much. I mostly eat my food and I'm happy to have it."

She bit her cheek. She wanted to cry so much and all along she thought he was a foul-mouthed jerk of a kid. Well, he fooled her with his tough front all right. She was feeling now like she was the foul-minded jerk. She couldn't sit still in her pain so she started to sputter.

"Oh, boy," she said, "We've got troubles."

"Whatcha mean, we?"

"Well, we're friends now. You're just like one of the cats that got thrown into the pond and I gotta help you, I just gotta."

Gary's eyes dimmed in recognition, confirmation of their bond.

"Bet you didn't know, Gary, that most of my friends are bums."

"No, not you."

"Yep, why even the beggar Zig knows me and my friends kiting around at the Barnegat. You know the old pirate hang-out. And we play hopscotch in front of Molly Pitcher's House, the old Brigg House. You know the one?"

"You mean that house on Orne where the wizard lived a way back?"

"Well, not John Diamond but his granddaughter. She was the fortune teller. I can see you're excited just now, but that's not all." She looked both ways then whispered, "Do you know my name?"

"Scotty, are you crazy?"

"My name is Marguerite Scott Paine. And I bet you didn't know that there were only two women accused of witchcraft in our town and put to death. One was Wilmett Redd and the other was Margaret Scott."

"Oh, my gosh," he said.

"My real name is Margaret; they just call me Marguerite 'cause my grandmother was from French-speaking Montreal and I'm her namesake. I am a witch, don't you get it, so don't ever treat me like a drip again." Scotty closed smugly with her arms folded, Captain Hook fashion.

"Gosh, double gosh," he said.

The bell rang and they got busy. Plaguing her mind were thoughts of her father's family. She thought of her namesake, Marguerite Scott, her grandmother, her father's mother. Odd she had not thought much of them lately. When her dad was home, the Paine family went to see the Paine family seniors at least twice a month. Scotty walked home as she thought of Granny and Grandpop, Aunt Winifred and Uncle Richard. Uncle Richard had died of tuberculosis before Scotty was born, but in pictures he looked very much like Edward, lean and muscular, a full head of chestnut hair parted to the side and falling just to the eyebrow, an eyebrow that sadly sloped.

Aunt Winifred never married; she taught grade school and cared for her parents. Lois's only romantic tale of her sister-in-law portrayed a rather plain personality, a young woman with glasses, fairly white, and a motorcycle driver. A ride on that cycle had been the most provocative issue of her life.

It was all so strange; her Granny Marguerite Scott had married Grandpop Paine, a first cousin, in the Montreal circle, a common practice in Canada, but illegal in the States.

In her wedding photo, she looked like Queen Victoria. Handsome, august, a rich bold character, but Scotty had always noticed the tight lace around her throat and the ankles so carefully covered. Regal beauty that dissipated through a marriage realized later as beneath her.

Marguerite Scott came from a more than reputable Montreal family. Her father was a famous architect, her mother a cameo beauty. In the social circle, Marguerite had her coming out party, exposed and admired by the creme de la creme of Montreal's best young men. But she chose Julian, her cousin, on a whim; perhaps the marriage was the most spontaneous gamble of her life.

Scotty would never know because the girl of the picture was never the grandmother she visited, served, and was servant to. When her father was home, the Paines visited their elders in New Hampshire, at their retirement home in Anthram. Subtly, Granny regulated the family, though final decisions were proclaimed by Grandpop Julian.

Scotty knew her grandmother through her care of cottage and garden. They never really talked. Marguerite senior took care of things in a gingerly fashion. Scotty looked on and helped. Granny Marguerite carried the poise of a martyr resigned to the commonness and labor that was below her. Winifred adored her mother, enough to stay an old maid virgin in perpetual sacrifice to her idol. Edward venerated his mother and politely loathed his father, sensing a hidden tenderness and beauty in his mother lost to an insipid father, a staid banking husband who made his mother and their life routine. There were always marguerites in the garden but never in her heart, a heart turned to stone by serving Melba Toast, wide eyed lumpy tapioca, and dusting Van Dyke type portraits of sullen black gowned ancestors. The women in these portraits were mostly tight lipped, hair without fancy, and sat clutching Bibles.

Scotty remained the servant in the family while her brother and cousin, Charlene, celebrated all the tea parties and pigeon feeding in the park. Marguerite doted on the first-born children. Scotty didn't think much of it but came to believe there were some social differences between herself and her brother and cousin because Lois noticed the servant role given her daughter. Scotty sensed only camaraderie with Granny, her whimsical garden, yard hammock, Indian tea pot, and the dinner chimes. She, like Granny, was the stewardess, caretaker of home ritual. Scotty rang the dinner bells. On warm days she brought the elephant tea pot with a small boy on his back to the garden for cups of Orange Pekoe. She carried the oatmeal cookies away. And after tea, she searched for wild strawberries with Granny. Stone by stone, they stepped around sweet william, bachelor's buttons, and alyssum. Perhaps Marguerite saw her own childhood in Scotty. In Scotty, maybe she could control the lovely child she was not or did not allow herself to be. Controlling a free spirit might be her only freedom, now shackled to Julian and his dutiful existence.

"Here we are at Redd's Pond," her daydream had carried her home and she automatically reached into her parka for bread morsels.

"No bread, my dears," she pulled her pocket inside out to prove sincerity. "But I'll get you some inside the house."

The house didn't seem so lonely today. Her thoughts had made visitors for her. She felt a companion of both meaning and life for she understood Gary and her grandmother a hint more. Eric, modeling with balsa wood, sat straight in bed; his butch haircut made him look neat, though the room was a disaster of Kleenex that never made the wastepaper basket.

"Feeling better?" she asked, peeking in at the door.

"Yup."

"I guess you should, after a week in bed," she said, playfully critical. "Can I get you anything?"

"Well, my ginger ale's gone, I could use another bottle."

"Coming right up." Scotty bounced down the cellar steps. It seemed none of the kids ever walked down the steps. A case of tonic, New England's soda pop, lined the cobblestone basement. The distributor delivered one case of tonic per month. All the bottles were labeled with a Marblehead fisherman in rain gear, sailing into the sunrise. Grape, orange, and ginger ale went first. The cream soda and root beer last. The kids always took two steps at a time going up the stairs.

"Sorry, Eric, only root beer. Here you go."

"Thanks, Moose."

"Be nice."

"Why?"

"Because you like me in spite of the fact that I'm an angel."

She blinked at him several times, giving the appearance of a fluttering bird.

"I'm off now."

"Where are you going?"

"To Fountain Park. Back before Mum gets home."

"Okay," he said. He kind of liked having her around, not only when he was sick, but never would say so.

She leaped out onto the lawn. The ducks were at the other end of the pond. "Thank goodness, they can be a bother sometimes." Scotty often talked to herself out loud. She would be thinking inside and then blurt out a word or sentence of her thought. As a matter of fact, she liked to talk to the air. Sometimes she would look around and then begin a wonderful dialogue with herself. "I hope Neil is at the rock. I have so much to tell him." Again, she took two steps at a time, climbing the stairwell at Fountain Park, then down and under the fence, past the sumac, to the rock. A glorious day it was at Oakum Harbor, the old haunt of pirates. Dories gleamed, slapping waves as eagles wailed at the large vessels disturbing their calm waters. Scotty's eyes sparkled as she settled into her rock, arms around her knees, to gaze at the sea. She took in a big gulp of air, and blew it out, a sign of relief. "It's been a whole week." She looked down to Neil's house and turned red. He had been watching her on the rock and was staring at her that very moment. With his feet up on his desk, knees bent, arms around them, in play mockery of her. She waved and he left his desk to meet her on the rock. Not looking, Scotty lingered, waiting for the surprise of his presence.

"Golly, it's good to see you." She waited as his knees touched hers on the rock, and they sat as twins. Then she looked him straight in the eye.

"You still think I'm desultory?"

Neil waited his turn. When they first met, Scotty always sputtered in conversation, like a top, her verve prompting his imagination. She finished abruptly, "You're the only snob I'll ever love."

At fourteen he knew she'd always be a girl and he'd always adore her.

"Did you tell me you went to your aunt's?"

"Yup, there for a week. I was an only child for a week. Aunt Lucretia has no children. It was something like your life, Neil, I guess. Aunt Lue and Uncle Martin are the regal ones in the family, the uppities. For a little fishmonger like me, it was big time being a princess, a lady for a day, week, I should say."

"I don't think I'd like you much if you were an uppity. Stuffy, rich people make me feel sick; they don't flow. They can't say what they think because of etiquette. I'm sick to death of being proper."

"Hey, hey, don't get excited. I'll never be proper; I babble too much, but it's sorta nice to think I could be proper if I wanted, a lady, ta ta," she giggled as she held out her hand for him to kiss it. And then quite instinctively, she talked about Grampy Graves, calming his ego with her loquacious manner.

"I'm able to see Mr. Graves, my dear old attorney, now the weather's better. He lives back of the little pond. You know next to Redd's Pond. He's like a fortune teller for me, something like the people who lived here a way back."

"What's that?" said Neil, still preoccupied with his rage.

"You know, fortune tellers, the people that know more than regular people. My friend, well, we're sitting there very quietly and then he says things, important things I'd never think of, the old lawyer, my friend."

"Like what?"

"Oh, I can't think right offhand, but it's like he knows me and he knows what I'll be like when I'm grown. Like some of those old fortune tellers who used to live back of Old Burial Hill. Molly Pitcher, for one, Old Wizard Diamond's granddaughter."

"He worked with lots of people," Neil said, "Maybe he knew girls like you and how they grew up."

"Well, maybe," Scotty sighed.

"I'm just teasing, I'm sure Mr. Graves has insight and knows you'll grow up to be a beautiful conch shell on the beach and the melody of your waves will be his eternal music."

"How dramatic, Neil, that's so pretty."

"I'm pretty too."

"Neil, you always say these wonderful things and then joke. Sometimes I don't know if I should believe you. Are you serious?"

"I'm playing with you because you're too serious. You always have a sad question in your eyes. You're just a kid; don't think so much."

"I like to think; it's great fun for me. I'm not smart but I have a happy imagination."

"Gee, I wish I could paint you, Scotty. Boy, would I like to capture your spirit!"

"I'll give you a picture of me before I leave."

"Photographs aren't the same."

"Oh Neil, before I forget, I have to tell you about Gary."

"Gary the scum."

"Well, he's not even foam on the sea anymore, he melted; or I did. We're friends now. I found out his mother's dying and he's supporting the family. His dad is out of work and hitting the bottle."

"Wow, that's a mouthful. Well, I'm glad for you anyway. It's hard to be around people who are not kind or real. Sometimes I feel consumed by people like that. I'm always trying to get under the skin of my life. You're so real to me Scotty."

"Yup, squeeze me."

He hugged her.

"Don't fool yourself Neil, you think too much, too. Gotta go."

She kissed his forehead. He watched her disappear. She wouldn't go to Grampy Graves today. It was now late and Scotty needed to be home. She forced a smile then she thought of Neil's words that she thought too much. Granny Paine popped to mind again, and Scotty thought of the wonderful miniature silver tea set that Granny had given her. It was always more fun to imagine Granny's tea parties with her doilies than to be at any other tea parties. Maybe Granny had known Scotty better than Lois imagined. Granny and she shared imagination, while Scotty perhaps shared the hidden passion of her mother, a true Marbleheader. In her criticism of Granny, did Lois want to be joined to both of them?

At home now, she popped in to have a look at Eric.

"It looks like it snowed in here Eric. You've got so much Kleenex on the floor!"

"It's likely to be sand soon, Scotty, not snow. We're in the middle of May; only three more weeks of school. Hope I don't get any summer colds; they're the worst."

"How's your root beer holding out?"

"Okay, no more, thanks. I'm getting tired of it after a week, and I don't like it flat like you do."

Scotty liked to take a glass of tonic and put it by her bed at night so in the morning it would be bubbleless. She liked to drink it like that.

"Mum will be home any minute. I'll set the table. She told me this morning we'll have chicken a la king tonight. Oh, I hate that," said Scotty.

CHAPTER SEVEN

Sunday would be Mother's Day. Scotty had two presents in mind, one for Lois and one for Mrs. Doliber, Gary's mum. Nothing elaborate, geranium baskets would do nicely for the summer. She had saved some money from odd jobs. Besides, Scotty wanted desperately to meet Mrs. Doliber. She had a curiosity to see someone who was dying, "Maybe I am a witch," she thought. I must be a witch named for my Granny. We both must be witches, so curious and imaginative.

Death was not so scary for Scotty. She lived, after all, right next door to a cemetery. Old Burial Hill was her front yard. There were lots of famous personages buried there. General John Glover, the famous patriot who ferried Washington over the Delaware, was buried there, as was the gallant Captain James Mugford Jr., who sailed the schooner "Franklin" with his crew. They were the first American Navy, and they took the British ship "Hope" on May Day 1776.

Cemeteries were part of the town, many times the center of town, in Old New England. Old Burial Hill had been the first meeting place of the town. Life was not long for many of the early settlers; whole families were buried in the cemeteries, dead from epidemics and common illnesses. Many a Sunday, folks would visit the cemetery and read the epitaphs and sometimes ludicrous tales of the dead. One such silly story was about Hannah. Scotty often thought of the inscription that read:

> "Here lies the body of Old Aunt Hannah
> Who found her death from a banana.
> It wasn't the fruit that laid her low
> But the skin of the thing that made her go."

"Scotty, I'm home," she heard her mother announce. But Scotty kept thinking of Marblehead. It was a nice old town with not too much history, just enough not to worry about dates and an incentive to imagine about it. After the War of 1812, Marblehead's naval significance waned. Paint, shoe, and glue factories opened and grew in town. Fishing and sailing became the pastimes. The rich and poor got along something like on a Yankee plantation. The merchant princes and tax collectors became the factory owners and bankers. The naval crews and fishermen now manned the factories, but they were all connected by a net of tales and dreams.

So much of Marblehead history was passed on by story from granny to grandchild. Bits and pieces of events, happy memories related by tykes walking to school, were told to them by fishermen from their nostalgia of old. From beggars to dreamers, the story was written on their faces, how the sea, man, and time meshed. Those who stayed close to the sea were saved by the water table and by the land that distilled their roots. They became the stories they told, growing from history into history. But certain folks, by their sense of ego, grew into the gossips and crabapples of town, untouched by the beauty that surrounded them; the nature that was to be their heaven became their hell. Impossible to ignore, these hotheads wound up as town officers, school principals, and sometimes men of the law. Not all of course, there were a good many successors of the early forefathers, those legendary romantics.

The aroma of dinner revived Scotty and brought her to the present. Lois was used to Scotty's dreamy aloofness and patiently awaited her daughter's presence.

"Mum, why do you like chicken a la king? It looks awful and tastes terrible."

Lois laughed, "I'm afraid I don't cook like your Grammy McFinch. But you know I don't cook for a living. Between teaching and laundry and you two, what else is there but stew, meatloaf and chicken a la king?"

"Subs, Mum, submarine sandwiches."

"You sound like Eric, with your submarine sandwiches."

"Well, let's have them tomorrow instead of beans and hamburgers. We always have beans and hamburgers on Saturday. This family is too predictable."

"You are right, my dear, we'll have subs tomorrow," said Lois and she tugged Scotty's straight brown hair.

"You sure, Mum? I was really just kidding. Just now I was thinking of our American Navy and Old Burial Hill; it made me spirited, I guess, and a tad giddy."

"I'm sure," said Lois, "I love subs as much as you do. I just like some prying and pleading every once and awhile."

"Are we dancing tonight, Mum?"

The kids took ballroom dancing on Friday nights with Miss Bell in the Old Hall across from the Post Office on Front Street. Miss Bell brought to mind the saloon town madam, that flamingo, slinky look in scarlet from head to toe. Her lips reminded Scotty of the Halloween lips of red wax she bought at the penny candy store. Those lips seemed to stand by themselves.

"Well, Eric won't be going, not after a week home from school with a cold, but Kate and you may go."

It only cost one dollar. Scotty loved to look at Miss Bell's nephew. He always came with her to the dances. Every coy miss wanted to dance with Miss Bell's nephew; his name might have been Neil, too. Scotty couldn't quite remember. This new belle was excited just watching, never hoping, nor desiring to dance with the young man, prince-like and charming. She could almost taste the pistachio ice cream at Eaton's Soda Fountain after the lesson. Scotty looked up at the television. After dinner, she was with Zorro, her black masked cavalier of the screen, proud on his stallion, as he bid adieu to a widow saved from destruction by roadside bandits. She watched Zorro until they left for the eight o'clock dance.

Scotty wore a simple green plaid dress that evening, with her shiny patent leather flats. Not a frilly type, she liked some lace but only a touch around the collar. Unobtrusive but sweet, she followed Miss Bell's instruction for the waltz step. She danced with the air and then with a girl partner, for there were not enough boys to go around. When she danced with boys, she got red, the flushed look of blush Scotty had wanted as she did the color on her face with the first snow or the hot sun on the first days at Deveraux Beach in the summer.

As she danced now, she saw Neil. She couldn't figure out if it was more fun being with Neil or just dreaming of him. And then there was the ice cream; she never tired of pistachio ice cream. Kate went to Eaton's Soda Fountain after the dance, too.

"I could eat coffee ice cream forever," Kate slurped.

Lois drove each week to the dance. In abeyance, Lois watched her Scotty and the other young dancers, feeling secretively part of their rhythm. Lois ate her ice cream now too, savoring the French vanilla as she savored the life of those young spirits, content to feel vicariously something she had never enjoyed.

She thought back to her courtship of Ed, the double date, how he had charmed her. He had the good looks and manners of the English sort. She had the fervor of those Channel Island people who were the first settlers to Marblehead: those stubborn fishermen, who behaved according to their inner compass, with independent natures that would lead them to freedom from England.

Lois inherited the central nature of the early founders of Marblehead, and she also shared in some way the importance of proper behavior of Marguerite Paine, her mother-in-law, who carefully hid feelings behind duty. Ed Paine had some sense of the true Lois, some intuition for which he'd gladly cross the country. In California, wouldn't Lois be free to be a Marbleheader again? Wouldn't he be free of his mother's Victorian shackles within him?

"Mum, are you done?" Scotty asked in amazement. Her mother wasn't usually lost in a dream.

"Ah, yes. Are we ready?" said Lois.

"Yup, hope they have pistachio ice cream in heaven."

"Why, Scotty, what makes you think you're going to heaven?"

Scotty blushed, "Well, I'm just hoping for anybody who goes there, that they get their right flavor."

"Now, even if you are my daughter, you're pretty sweet, wouldn't you say, Kate?"

Kate patted Scotty on the shoulder, nudging her to the car. Two years older, she was thinking of the boys at Miss Bell's, not of Scotty. It had been a wallflower night for her and she wanted to get home and be ruler of her turf.

They dropped Kate off at the Hill. Lois and Scotty were quiet as they savored different memories. Lois thought of her week in California. The unknown pleased her, mystified her, that boiling blood of adventure she shared with her husband. Those sunsets and palm trees, she still saw them, like the souvenir bracelet she had brought Scotty—blue with orange sky and small palm trees linked like paper doilies around her wrist.

Scotty thought of the geraniums she must buy tomorrow, one for her mum and one for Gary's mum. She shivered when she realized Gary didn't know she would be visiting. What would he say, would he be mad? Did she know him well enough now to come visit unexpectedly?

They buried their thoughts as they entered the house. Eric had made his own fun. The Kleenex sheets were piled knee high again, and balsa wood was everywhere. As they popped in, Scotty threw her hands up in horror.

"Hey, Moose, how were the guys and Miss Bell's knucklebrain nephew?"

Scotty reddened, "Goodnight, Eric."

"Yes, goodnight, Eric," said Lois, "clean-up tomorrow, and school on Monday, for sure."

In her room, Scotty went to bed and a picture of a salmon-colored geranium enveloped her in slumber.

She walked the back roads down Orne Street next day, passed Graves Boat Yard, and she heard echoes of Commodore Nicholson Brighton gathering his men so long ago for the schooner "Hannah," the ship that would leave Marblehead waters, rally in Beverly, then set sail under commission of the Continental Congress and George Washington and capture the British ship "Unity," first prize of the Revolution.

The Old Town House loomed in front of her with its rustic stone edges. The yellow and white building was built in 1727. Later, the famous Marblehead Regiment was recruited there. Languorously, Scotty continued, almost forgetting her purpose. Climbing the hill to Abbot Hall, she listened while the Victorian clock struck ten times. The grounds around the tower, called Washington Square, were once a common gathering place. John Glover practiced with his men, the very men who ferried Washington on the Delaware. Down the hill, she naturally picked up her gait and entered Peach's Florist just at the bottom. Panting awhile, she reclaimed her breath while India bells chimed for Mr. Peach who busied himself in the greenhouse. On Mother's Day, Mr. Peach returned to the shop laden with pots of magenta, salmon and crimson geraniums.

"Well, Scotty, what do you have to say for yourself?" Mr. Peach was huffing, mostly out of breath with anxiety in anticipation of crowds. On Mother's Day, flowers were purchased for mothers, of course, and grandmothers or aunts who had been like mothers, or for wives that would soon be mothers.

Scotty's wide eyes, with their natural glance, calmed him.

"Easy does it, I must tell myself. I always feel about to have a heart attack each Mother's Day, with all those frantic buyers."

"I guess I beat the rush," Scotty beamed.

"My first customer." His brow smooth now, he beamed back.

"Your grandmother is in here all the time. Those fussy boys she cooks for at the Manor want fresh flowers on their table. Can't say I mind, flowers are my business, and Mrs. McFinch is such a trooper, sucking her cloves, all in black, what a Marbleheader. A sight for sore eyes, she is, such a decency about her. Now my friend, I know why you're here; what's the budget this year?"

"Well, Mr. Peach," Scotty put her finger to her lips pretending to think of something she already knew, "Do you have any two-for-one sales?"

"You have two mothers this year, Scotty?"

"Nope, just want to give one to a friend, I mean my friend's mother."

"Well, Scotty," Mr. Peach thought or pretended to think, "Can't be giving free flowers away. Wouldn't make no money that way at all."

Scotty looked at the polished black and white checkerboard floor.

"Such a formal look, you look like a billboard for the Humane Society or a homeless shelter."

"I understand Mr. Peach. I've got five dollars for my mother."

"Oh no, you don't."

"What?"

"Where's your fighting spirit?"

Scotty looked around.

"Inside you, girl! What a kid!" Exasperated, he shuffled back to the greenhouse, dragging a withered leg, uneven from birth.

"Mind the shop a minute, will ya, while I get your flowers."

Scotty nodded. Behind the counter, she looked into the brightness of a May morning silhouetted by the velvet interior of the shop full of violets and begonias. Scotty touched a violet leaf; it tingled softly between her thumb and forefinger. How would she deliver the flowers to Gary's mum?

"Mrs. Doliber, I was in the neighborhood," she prepared her speech. "Well, Gary and I have been school friends. I didn't like him at first, but then I didn't know he had a sick mother. Bunk, bunk, I'm no good at speeches! I always wind up blurting out some silly truth."

"What's that?" Mr. Peach was back, pots in hand. "Did I hear you talking to somebody?"

"No, I was just planning what I'm going to say when I give the flowers."

"That's the nice thing about something beautiful, Scotty. You don't have to do much talking. The flowers being lovely and all, nope, I don't like to say much, the flowers do my talking."

"Well, that's okay for Mum, but for my friend's mum, I mean, I don't know her."

"Take it easy Scotty. Just give her the flowers and smile, she'll make the connection." Scotty beamed.

"Now here's your pots, not fancy mind you, but it's the flowers that count."

"Geranium red is sort of like barnyard red, isn't it, Mr. Peach?"

He blinked his eyes in affirmation.

"Oh, they'll love these."

"Okay, my little love, now off with ya. I have a busy day ahead."

The five dollars lay on the counter; its green could not compare to the value of this sale. Mr. Peach put one pot under each of her arms.

"Under the yoke, you are."

He opened the door and Scotty was off into the bright day. When she arrived at 12 Orne Street, she noted the shaky cottage with unkempt hedge in front. She tiptoed to the door, the color of bleached gray, and put her mother's pot behind a Canterbury bush at the side of the door. She would pick it up on the way home. There was no bell, but a brass door rap, the figurehead of a ship. As she grasped for the golden woman to announce her presence, Scotty was surprised when the door opened, pulling the brass rap from her hand. Startled but not frightened, she watched the door open slowly to expose a tired, hollow-eyed woman ghostly white. Her hair a gray-blond, hung shoulder length, finely combed but uneven on the ends, and clumps of hair were missing, exposing the scalp. She was in her nightgown of frayed, dotted flannel, worn thin in spots. Her bare feet without slippers showed with long toes that turned out, and ragged nails, neglected, Scotty suspected, from lack of strength.

"Yes, what is it?"

Scotty stammered, "Hello."

"Hello to you."

For a time, all Scotty could do is stare at the serene familiar lips that addressed her, feeling a sense of belabored peace. There was a strange smell of decay coming from the room, a dullness that screened death, but foreshadowed an ominous end. But the lips that addressed her fought for time. "Life, life, life!" they seemed to say.

Scotty regained her nerve, "Mrs. Doliber, you don't know me. I'm a friend of Gary's at school. Actually, we have just become friends lately and he told me about you and your illness. Well, I'm sorry and I wanted to give you these flowers. Maybe they'll cheer you up."

CHAPTER EIGHT

Scotty spoke quickly and ended with a question because she really didn't know what to say or when to stop. The vivid flowers and the girl's sincerity brought a broad smile to Mrs. Doliber's lips, dispelling the morose atmosphere of the house. Scotty responded to the smile with relief.

"So, you like them?"

"They're lovely. Please come in and we'll find a place to put them."

Scotty still held the geraniums as she passed the golden figurehead on the door.

"Sit down," Mrs. Doliber pushed some newspapers off a faded wing back chair to make room for Scotty. The living room had a coziness about it; a red, white, and blue Afghan covered the sofa and across from it stood a black Windsor rocker with a matching footstool.

"Don't be afraid, dear, I won't bite you."

Scotty smiled, with a meek countenance. They both knew Scotty felt shy but the knowledge of death also permeated the room with timidity.

"Here, let me take a look at you," she paused, "What a fine girl. You say you are a school friend of Gary's?"

"Yes, Gary sits in front of me."

"That's strange, he never mentioned such a darling of a girl, but then," she stopped and spoke more quietly, "we don't talk too much anymore. He looks like a lonely puppy around me," Mrs. Doliber stared into the air trying to remember something. "My only son," she spoke with resignation. "God help him now, soon without a mother. My sister will take him. And his father, well his father can go to the devil." The dying woman spoke not with malice but with prophesy.

"We never had much. I go as I came. Gary should have more in his life because he wants it. He grunts, dreams, and sweats for it. His father drinks for it. One can never get ahead like that. Oh, I know I'm not a pretty picture. Can't do much for my family now, but Harry, well, he would have drunk anyway, even if I was in good shape. It's in him. Nobody could believe in him 'cause he never believed in himself. I wanted to believe in him. He drank when I met him but not all the time. Worked hard at the boat yard. Our life was simple. Our entertainment was the tavern, not for the juice, but for the spirited people there, the salt of the earth, they were. But he wasn't like them, those fishermen and boat menders, so manly and brave. They could weather the pain for the pleasure. His pleasure always came first."

The sick woman paused, tired with speech. Scotty felt uncomfortable with the stillness and could feel this woman's reflection, her deep resignation to the end of life as she had known it.

"Can I make you some tea?" Scotty hadn't planned to say that. Service was her energy early in life.

"No dear. How shameful of me not to offer you tea. Would you like tea?"

"Oh, I must go, Mrs. Doliber. I have chores on Saturday." She looked at the geranium on the coffee table.

"Looks like a good place for it," said Scotty, "Now I must get home and hide my Mother's pot."

"Well, it certainly was nice of you to come, dear. I do love flowers, though I don't get in the garden much these days. Gary will be sorry he missed you. Now give me a peck."

Scotty stood awkwardly, she tried to hug Mrs. Doliber over the coffee table, then she walked around the table. It was just one of those out-of-step days for her; sometimes on those days one could learn so much. Her gift had been a surprise even to herself given out of both curiosity and compassion.

"Goodbye, Mrs. Doliber. It was so nice to visit with you."

The broad beam of smile returned to Mrs. Doliber's lips. And Scotty felt a rich glow from the lady figurehead as she passed through the door. The screen door whined as she left, and the giver, still a bit nervous, walked a brisk pace to the end of Orne Street before she remembered she had left her mother's pot back at the Doliber house.

"Oh gosh, going back will be like stealing coffee grounds from Mrs. Boile's." She remembered the Hill Club initiation. "I could almost go back to Mr. Peach's and ask for more flowers. I'd have more nerve to do that. He was so kind, but he has a business to run. I've got to go back to the Doliber's house," she mumbled aloud.

As she backtracked just short of the weathered cottage, Scotty heard an outraged heavy voice. She tiptoed up the stairs and peered through the window. A loutish, swarthy fellow with bloodshot eyes raged at Mrs. Doliber. He cursed her with a nagging voice.

"Buying flowers, and we can't even eat," he cursed. "You galley slut," and he slapped her face. Blood dripped from the corner of Mrs. Doliber's bottom lip. She slumped into the Windsor rocker.

"This is what I think of your flowers!" He held the pot in the air then let it smash on the vinyl floor. Terracotta pieces flew everywhere and Mrs. Doliber buried her face into her knees. She had withdrawn into the seat of the rocker as an embryo in fear of a brutal world. She sobbed in rhythmic heart break.

Scotty was at first paralyzed at the window, then quickly came to life when she saw the village dolt weave to the door in drunken stupor. She jumped off the porch landing and squatted low, out of view until the raucous voice was silent. Peering up above the porch landing, she saw him swerve down the street. A feeling she had never felt before soared in her heart—hatred.

A little numb but not immobile, she climbed onto the porch and without hesitating entered the house to console Mrs. Doliber.

"Oh, Lord," Mrs. Doliber kept repeating, "My son, my son." Even in her pain, she worried for her youngster with such a brute of a father.

Scotty resolutely placed her hands on Mrs. Doliber's throbbing, dwarfed shoulders, "What can I do to help?"

Mrs. Doliber was still for a moment unsure of the soft voice that beckoned to her. Then, she sighed, almost giving up her spirit. "Remember my Gary," she pleaded, her voice as clear as her husband's was scratchy. "He needs something good in his life," she said, and she reached out with her hands without lifting her head.

Scotty took those frail hands, the purple veins prominent as the color of the dying lady's lips. Scotty held those limbs, and then rubbed them, then set them down gently. In the silence that followed, Scotty picked up the geranium, carefully holding the loosened dirt to the roots. She went to the kitchen and out the back door to plant her token of love. It seemed more like a burial than a rite of spring. Back in the house, she found the whisk broom and dustpan in a kitchen closet. Carefully, Scotty removed all traces of the broken clay pot and returned the cleaning tools to the closet. Tiptoeing into the living room, she covered the woman in the rocker who had lifted her legs onto the hassock and appeared now to be resting. As she brought the knitted cover under Mrs. Doliber's chin, Scotty noticed that the blood-stained lips were clean.

"She must have licked them," she thought. She closed the door gently and left. On the porch once more, she took her mother's pot in hand.

The geranium sat until morning at the Lion's Mane. When she entered the house, Eric was in his room without correcting or contributing to the mess already there. Lois, in the kitchen pantry, made a list of food they needed from Shube's. Scotty found the duster and mop on the wall of the cellar steps. Quietly, Saturday chores began. But something had changed for the whimsical girl, some brutal truth had aroused her, as the first slap of the doctor awakens a baby to life. The violence she had witnessed had matured her.

Mother's Day, glorious and warm, tickled the spirit to believe in all things. For a time, even the road slug could be venerated as an act of God and Scotty realized her happiest moments were in simply being, without expectation. Excitement and adventure were there for her, but right now she resided in something like a still life of happiness.

She awoke early and slipped on her faded jeans and Marblehead sweatshirt. Creeping downstairs with navy sneaks in hand, Scotty donned the tennis shoes, weathered by Marblehead roamings. Laconic thought placated her heart as she opened the door; the bright and still day belonged to her. This morning, quiet intimacy followed as she passed the sleeping mallards and yellow daffodils skirting Burial Hill, preaching God's beauty better than any sermon.

"I'll never talk again," she said. But then she had said that about eating, too, at Thanksgiving. No, she was a human being, with despairs like most, forging her personality, trying to understand the contrasts and where she belonged.

Neil's house was still, as she viewed the landscape of Brown's Island and Graves' Boat Yard, so still that only a fleeting seagull's cry could despoil the feeling of eternal serenity.

Scotty wondered at herself sometimes. She wasn't much like other people, who were removed from life, pretending only to belong. She was secretly honest to herself and nature, at home in the world, or the many worlds that connected her. Sauntering back to the house, she recovered her sensibilities as she picked up the geranium and carried it to the house. She put away for a time the maelstrom of yesterday.

Preparing a small breakfast for her mum, a pewter tray helped display the English muffin and coffee, and a single daffodil in a bud vase made the simple meal look elegant. She had snipped the daffodil near the Lion's Mane when she brought in her present.

Eric was still asleep at nine o'clock, but Lois would be getting up soon for Sunday Mass. In fact, the nine o'clock mass usually attended would be the noon mass today. As she entered the room, Lois stretched like a cat. She liked to wake up slowly on weekends.

"Happy Mother's Day, Mum."

"Oh, Scotty, how sweet," Lois said as she rubbed her eyes.

"Remember when I was four and served you cereal with salt on it for Mother's Day? Sugar and salt still look alike to me; there won't be a problem with this English muffin."

Lois could not remember but then she yawned and held her hand to Scotty to pull her up. Mornings were slow for her.

"Gee, I had the best dream." Lois looked at the daffodil as she spoke. "We were in California on the beach, and your father was bringing us Timmy frankfurters and grape tonic. Ed, I said, take off that English cap; it's summer not winter!"

Eric popped his head in the door. Though a teenager of fifteen, he had a look about him of an Alaskan puppy with his golden butch haircut and blue eyes darting out under colorless brows. He wore a terry cloth robe and black open-back slippers that flapped as he entered to present his mum with a card.

"I thought you were asleep," said Scotty.

"I thought you thought I was asleep, Moose."

Eric opened the card for his mum and read his addition to the sentiment, "I owe you a year's supply of free car washes."

"Eric, how thoughtful." Then Lois reached for the card to read the verse quietly.

"My present is in the dining room," Scotty spoke softly, not wishing to compete.

"Let me guess, Stowaway Sweets? I love chocolates."

"Guess again, Mum."

"Then it's got to be from Mr. Peach's shop."

Scotty beamed as her mother took her housecoat and slippers and headed downstairs. But the beam was short lived when a vision of the other flowerpot came to mind. Scotty felt badly for Gary's mum and she didn't feel the full happiness of her gift to her own mother. Strange, it seemed happiness didn't spring from giving, but was earned. She had felt happy with the gift of Zig. "Mmm." There was something of the mysterious and unexpected that would always contribute to her happiness.

Mass at the Gothic church, Star of the Sea, was followed by a trip to the Hill because, of course, Grammy McFinch needed her praises too. Lois had the perfect hat for her, a type of headdress fit for a cardinal, perhaps, with a black veil meshing the front. And for Granny Paine, she had mailed some Stowaway Sweets. Her mother-in-law had a sweet tooth, and would relish the chocolates, she thought.

"Well, this will be our last Mother's Day in Marblehead," Lois said as they pulled up to the homestead.

Red was at the den window barking at Grampy to let him in, so it was Grampy who came to the door to greet Lois, Eric, and Scotty.

"Hello, Pop."

"How we doin'?" said Grampy McFinch with muffled tones, cigar half in, half out of his mouth.

A whirlwind of merriment beset the Paines on entry. Once in the house, Red chased Candy, who in turn chased Penny to the kitchen. Kate stood at the door to stop them, then took fiendish delight in seeing Red overwhelm the little ones with the most unsavory licks of his tongue which felt like flypaper, wet and scratchy.

"Yuck, yuck!" screamed the girls, knocked down by their sudden stop at Kate's broad shoulders. Red wagged his tail triumphantly as he licked first one, then the other of the kids.

Scotty joined as a spectator. For a time, no one noticed her there. In the kitchen, Grammy sat, ale in hand while Marge sat to one side and Lucretia to the other.

"Is it too early, Mum?" Roy McFinch gave an eager eye to Kitty.

"You mean for the juice?"

Grampy winked.

"Well, I guess not, I have my ale here. But please get Red off my little tykes."

"OK, Red, back to the den. Find Eric, back Red!"

Sober after his rummage, Red followed his master's direction and returned to the den, reclining by Grampy's hassock. Grampy followed, anxious to return to his black and white TV. Hopalong Cassidy was on. Television now captivated the hearts of those worn painters and hunters. While Uncle Jeep would retire to the garden one day, for now it was a part-time hobby. He was there now, planting the gifts of the day. Marigolds, from Marge to Grammy, geraniums from Kate to Marge, iris from Lois to Kitty.

"It won't be the same next year. I'll be in California." Lois's voice drooped like a tulip without water.

"We'll come visit when you're settled," said Kitty. "I don't want you to go, but your husband has a wanderlust and so does your daughter. Look at her over there, that cock-a-button, a dream in her eye."

Scotty stood at one end of the kitchen while Kate broke her blockade and the younger cousins recovered their breath from their freakish screams.

"Maybe she's in California now. Hey, there, Miss Scotty."

"Hello, Grammy," Scotty came to her grandmother and hugged her. She was a nurturing queen with those long plaits. Scotty had braided them often. Now they were properly tied behind her head. Those hands, freckled and spotted, had labored to fill many mouths. That sturdy body was the very clout of the earth.

"So, darlin', what do you have to say for yourself?"

"Not much, Grammy."

"Taking care of your mum while your dad's away?"

"Trying. She's so difficult in the morning, getting up, I mean."

"She's better than the rest of them," grinned Grammy as she eyed Lucretia and Marge.

Lucretia had been silent too long. "Scotty certainly made a fine house guest. Though I didn't get coffee in bed. What a charming companion, but she snores a bit."

"I don't," Scotty gasped, turning scarlet.

"Yep, just like young Grammy. Just before bed each night I'd peek in on you. There you were, snoring to beat the band."

Scotty's eyes rolled up and then to the side, trying to avoid obvious embarrassment.

"No harm in snoring, child," said Grammy. "Your Aunt Lue's just trying to get a rise out of you. She's done plenty of that in her life. Just ask your mother."

Lois blinked quietly. Lue fidgeted with the place mats pretending to be putting them in order.

"Good looking, but devious. Maybe an actress is what we want to call her." She was pensive for a moment.

"For you, Grampy, it's the hunt. For you, Uncle Jeep, it's that first burst of green from the chard; for you, Aunt Lue, it's controlling somebody, even for a minute." Kitty McFinch looked at Lucretia with a clear eye then swallowed a gulp of ale.

"Now then, I won't be sending you a knitted poodle with a dollar for your birthday. California's too far for that. How about if I send you two dollars?"

"That would be great, Grammy," and Scotty hugged something she thought was so wonderful, and equally hard to define.

"Now get on with you!"

Her cheeks back to normal, Scotty darted to the front door; its hinges were the squeaks of home. Hopping down the porch steps, the last she leaped like a spirited pony. Grammy sighed at the air of youth; Scotty had more vitality than the human heart could hold.

Lucretia looked up at Kitty McFinch when Scotty left. Lois and Marge pretended to tidy the kitchen.

"I was only kidding with the girl, Kitty."

"Kidding is supposed to make people laugh, not embarrass them. You like to see people squirm too much, Lue. Got better things to do, don't you? Martin's business? Where is Martin? He's home, isn't he?"

"Home from France, you mean, juicing it up. Probably should get home and check on him. We visit his mother tonight. The cancer has him down. Don't know what to say. I'm afraid."

"Maybe 'cause this cancer is something you can't control."

Lue was curt, "Am I the only one singled out here, mother? What about Marge and Lois, they aren't angels. Why me?"

"Cause you're clever. They're learning something from life, you're just spinning your wheels, controlling people."

"Well, I can't control Martin," her eyes spoke with fury. "I'm not so very clever with cancer and death."

Lois and Marge fidgeted with the dishes, learning for the first time about Martin.

Kitty went on, "You can be kind to the man you married and get interested in his business, a business you can carry on for him." Kitty McFinch seemed so dispassionate.

Lucretia rose, "It's all very ironic. Here it is Mother's Day and perhaps I'm wicked, but I'm not a mother, and being clever hasn't helped me there, either," she softened her voice and kissed Kitty on the forehead. "Goodbye, all." She left, not like the free pony, Scotty, but with a stiff gait of disillusionment. The stillness that followed became uncomfortable.

"Well, things are neat here; we better be going," said Lois.

"Have a little ale."

"Not this time, Mum, I'll have my vermouth at home."

Scotty couldn't wait to get home. She wanted to visit her wise Grampy Graves.

CHAPTER NINE

"Grushenka, come in, Grushenka."

"Grampy Graves, this is Scotty."

"Yes, I know, but you remind me so of Grushenka."

"Who is she?" Scotty's eyes caught his in question.

Graves thought Scotty too young to hear of Dostoyevsky's character, who with her dreamlike distance created a sensual attraction for men old and young. He dwelled on Grushenka, almost addicted to the memory of the novel.

"She lost her innocence at eighteen to a Polish soldier who promised to marry her. While terribly hurt and mortified by her loss, in a sense, she gained knowledge, witch-like knowledge." The rest he thought to himself the look of innocence yet the knowledge of lust. It would be like making love to an angel. "I worry about you, Scotty, because you have that dreamlike quality and that witch-like ability. You're marked in some way, you're different. It could be your crowning glory or your demise."

"What's demise?"

"Ruin."

"Grampy, gosh, you're grave," she laughed, "I can play with words too."

"I am sorry. What a gloomy fellow I am. I should be thinking of your charm, but you'll be gone in a month. Perhaps I'll never see you again. Granny Graves and I are too old to travel to California to visit. I worry about your future."

"I am a Marbleheader and I will be back."

"Promise?"

"Promise," she kissed his head. The fine white hairs were soft on her lips. "Here, look what I brought for Granny. Daffodils for Mother's Day."

"Of course, so that's what you are hiding. She's in the kitchen."

The flowers were hidden behind Scotty's back. She pulled them out in the kitchen. Granny couldn't be lonely; she was too busy baking.

"Scotty, you startled me. What do you have there? How beautiful. Daffodils, my favorite!"

"Like them? They're from my garden. Here you are," Scotty kissed Granny's forehead as she held out the flowers.

"Can you wait for these shortbreads?"

"I can always wait for your cookies." She kissed her again. "I don't mean to be mushy, but you're so sweet."

"Think so, do you? You only want me for my cookies."

"Now, you don't think I'm a witch?" she winked at Grampy, who looked up from his easy chair still in fear of his thoughts.

"Of course not, but, like a witch, you'll soon be riding that trailer like a broomstick off into the West. We'll miss you, darlin'."

The green earth took hold of May's last days. The lilacs, the linden trees and the dogwoods bugled the glory of spring. It was easier to study for those final tests and the close of school because, pass or fail, nature would always come back with a new mystery, a new tale of life to coax them on.

A folly for life began in June. At school, Miss Orne no longer chastised Scotty for dreaming at Abbot Hall. It was all over for the year. Gary reconciled himself to the fact that he would only half understand fractions but would completely miss Scotty.

At home, Lois procrastinated with the packing that would change their lives. Eric disappeared with sailing buddies, ready to mutiny as the time drew near to leave.

At the end, Scotty wanted to spend time with Neil and Barb, find the hidden treasure on Brown's Island, and pamper Grampy Graves as best she could. Tenaciously, she clung to that plan but then she'd vacillate with thoughts of flight. She would hide in Marblehead, live in Eric's tree house and fish by night for food. Maybe she'd sneak to Grammy McFinch and steal Red's food at the back door. Maybe Zig would befriend her and show her the life of a vagabond.

The rising sun prompted her to savor every moment of the last days. Sunny days at Deveraux Beach, toasted rectangle buns with frankfurters from Timmy's, grape tonic, Licorice Nips, Sugar Babies; she would never complain if some sand mixed with her sandwich. These were hollyhock days and romps to Crocker Park to swim off the wharf, to spy from Fort Sewell, the bastion for the War of 1812. Scotty could almost touch the spool top fences as she bounced by. She lived with visions of sailboats.

On June fourth, Scotty, Neil, and Barb planned a picnic on the beach at Brown's Island to plan their conquest. School ended June third. While she waited on that meeting day at the beach, Barb unraveled a fishing line, "What a mess," she mumbled.

Neil always waited for his buddies in his bedroom, checking out the window from his desk. He would read until he caught sight of a black bob or a longer brown pageboy. When he spied Barb, he left to greet her while Scotty surfaced into the picture at the same time, and she joined him on the rock staircase descending the cliff.

"Hello, there, how convenient," he said as he took Scotty's hand as she walked down the path. He surprised her and she stumbled.

"Are you okay?"

"Yes," she said, gripping his hand.

"Now go slowly, we don't want Barb to bury us in the old house if we fall down this cliff, deader than Victoria Snow."

When they reached bottom, they were more effusive. "Have you started to pack yet?" Neil asked while they walked toward Barb on the beach.

"Trying to get rid of me?"

"Don't be silly."

"Now I'm silly, am I, for not wanting to pack and leave town?"

"Stop talking, Scotty. I have a present for you, and I want you to pack it and take it to California."

"What is it?"

"I'm not telling you. You can open it on the road."

"Well, Neil Montague, first you call me silly for not being packed and ready to leave town, then you say you have a present for me, but I can't open it. I know I'm not logical, but you don't make sense at all."

"Gosh, you're cantankerous."

"I know it." She pushed him down on the sand and ran toward Barb. Neil's heart raced as he chased his shadow, part of himself. Giddy with high spirit, they both chased each other around Barb.

"Hey, hey, you're getting sand in my face!"

They couldn't stop for a moment, locked in a childish zest for life. Panting and laughing, they stopped to catch their breath on either side of Barb. Barb smiled and methodically wiped the sand off her hair.

"The fun's out there," she pointed to the island, "You dingbats."

Scotty and Neil muffled giggles trying to compose themselves.

"The strategy, the strategy," Barb spoke flamboyantly, covering hurt feelings; nobody chased her in the sand. "When, where, and how? My suggestion is we wait a couple of days until Scotty leaves. If we find the loot, Scotty may have to smuggle it to California. My mum's the kind that will make me turn it in."

"My mum, too," said Scotty.

"Well, my mum will say it belongs to the city and they need it, too," said Neil.

"All right, I leave July first, so let's make it June twenty eighth. What do you say?"

"Sounds good," they both replied.

"Neil, will you check the schedule?"

"Check," said Neil.

"How much time do we have to find the booty?" asked Barb.

"Jake and Johnny are gone about an hour. That June twenty eighth better be a Monday. That's when he goes."

"I checked it out already," said Scotty, "It's on a Monday."

Barb was writing everything with a chewed down yellow pencil on an old grocery bill. "This planning makes me hungry." She pulled out two Pippin apples, offering them to Neil and Scotty.

As Scotty chewed a circle around the apple she asked, "Did you try the water yet, Barb?"

"It's colder than a witch's tit. The Atlantic, you need a tough skin to swim in that water."

"What a nice kid, to pack us a lunch," Neil said as he searched through the basket, finding sandwiches neatly wrapped in waxed paper. "What do we have here, the famous Miles cookies?"

Scotty and Neil rolled their tongues over their upper lips. Barb pouted at them, "This is serious, guys. Finding treasure is big time. When we finish planning, then we can eat."

"Aren't we finished?" Neil smacked his lips in anticipation.

"Let's go back to how," said Barb, "Will we stay together or separate?"

"Please, please, let's stay together," said Scotty. "I'm the type to cover my eyes at spooky movies."

"No!" Neil laughed.

"Neil, you're not even excited," Scotty accused.

"Well, I want to discover the treasure, but if not, give me the gold in your eye."

"Neil Montague, you are the biggest tease. What are you going to give me."

"What are you going to give me?" he asked her the same question, more seriously now.

"The memory of me."

"You peevish devil," he said.

"Witch," she said.

"Hey, hey, what is this, a private conversation? I brought all the plans plus food, and I'm being ignored," Barb sullenly retorted.

"Oh, no, you're not! I'm a flake and he's a clown. We need you to ground us," said Scotty.

They both threw their arms around her and stared at the island.

"So, it's settled; we'll do the search together," Barb said. "Now we can eat."

Barb pulled sandwiches from the bag. "Liverwurst."

"Liverwurst?" Neil snarled.

"Liverwurst, it's good for you."

"Yes, mother, anything for those cookies."

"I love liverwurst," Scotty blurted out.

"You need lots of this stuff because you're too white, Scotty. Must be anemic."

"Yes, mother," she mocked. "I just take after Granny Marguerite. She is sorta white in a pretty way like a porcelain doll. Eric the red is a McFinch, always looks like he's been in the snow."

"Are you scared, Neil?" Scotty squinted her eyes trying to read something inside him.

"About exploring the house or the unknown?"

"The unknown," she said.

"The unknown, no. Only the known fact disturbs me. Not what's coming, just what's there. I read the encyclopedia for fun. I get scared when I lose something valuable, knowledge or somebody. I'm a little scared that you're moving."

Barb coughed.

He took Barb's hand, "Big B and I will romp, but we're all sorta the Three Musketeers. We belong together." Then he took Scotty's hand, too. "Any more liverwurst?" he searched the picnic basket.

"No kidding, you like it?" Barb's eyes sparkled as if she had converted someone. "But it's all gone."

"Oatmeal cookies, oatmeal cookies," he chanted like some petulant kid.

"All right, all right," spoke Barb. "Take them. Take them. You can have mine if you like."

He picked up her hand and kissed it.

She blushed, "Neil Montague, you are such a clown."

They all laughed.

"I'd like one of those cookies," Scotty pleaded.

"My dear," said Barb, "here is a cookie. The cream soda is all we had at home. Would you like one to wash it down?"

"I'll take a sip of yours, Barb."

"I want ginger ale," piped Neil.

"You would. Here, take the cream soda and be glad."

"Well then, it's finished," said Scotty chomping on her cookie. "I know the twenty eighth is a Monday. Let's be here at nine for our conquest of that house."

They each held their food in the air for a toast, one cream soda and two oatmeal cookies raised high.

"To the house," said Neil.

"And everything in it," said Scotty.

For a few minutes they pensively gazed at the 18th century structure faded and tattered by time, but for the imagination of these three, a castle of fortune and treasure.

Then Barb began to put away the waxed paper, folding it neatly and returning it to the picnic basket.

Neil darted to the water, all of a sudden. "Ick, it's cold."

Scotty followed, "What a cream puff! It's just right. Stop your tidying, Big B, and come touch the water," said Scotty.

Barb compulsively hummed. Her Virgo always got the best of her. At the water's edge, she carefully dabbed her foot in and out of the frigid waters.

"It's a good thing we don't have to swim to the island. We'd freeze." As she touched the water with staccato jabs, something seemed to dawn on her. "What about the booty?"

"What about the booty?" they bellowed.

"If we find it, how will we carry it?" she questioned.

"Good point," said Neil, sitting on the sand again, face resting on his knees. "But it'd be great to have such a problem!"

"Let's bring our school satchels," said Scotty.

"Good idea," he said again.

Now in the water, Scotty and Barb looked like rocking horses, ankles in, hands bent to touch the water.

"What about Gary?" asked Barb.

"What about him?" said Scotty.

"You haven't been complaining about him lately, 'cause school's out, is it?"

"No, actually, I see more of him now, I mean his mother."

Neil listened too, now, intent on hearing this conversation.

Barb had not remembered her lecture to Scotty before the seizure, how she had told Scotty of Gary's dying mother. And Neil was quiet now with forgotten omission.

"Well, I learned his mother is dying. He's tough, I mean anybody would be, trying to be strong, I guess."

"Just like that," Barb said. "Why didn't you say something? Have you been to his home?"

"Mother's Day. I gave her a geranium. Wanted to do something nice. Went back later 'cause I forgot my mum's pot and saw the Dolibers fighting. She's such a nice lady, but Mr. Doliber is a thug. Poor Gary, he'll be an orphan soon. Doesn't really have a dad, his dad's drunk all the time."

"Well, now that you mention it," she paused, "My mum did say something about it at the dinner table one night. Didn't think much about it then."

"Well," said Scotty, "we're friends now. Seems strange from hating somebody to liking him. Which reminds me, I should see Mrs. Doliber again."

Neil had been thoughtfully still. But now he spoke quietly.

"Scotty, I read the paper this morning. Mrs. Doliber was in the obituary."

"What? What? But Gary never called me!"

"It's kinda hard to call somebody and tell them that your mum's dead, especially a new friend. Gee, I'm sorry Scotty, I didn't know you cared that much about him."

Gently, he put his arm around her shoulder.

"But why? Why? She was such a kind lady!" Scotty whispered, silent tears sliding down her cheeks.

CHAPTER TEN

She wanted to console Gary but she felt paralyzed as she walked to 12 Orne Street. Like a zombie, she went, but not one word, not one, could she find to express her grief. She remembered a bike accident she had had once, crashing into the school fence. There was a time, just seconds after the fall, before the pain hit, that Scotty had felt this same void. Somehow her walk created a rhythm, like a panting dog. Mrs. Doliber loomed in front of her in an eerie sense of presence. Scotty walked in her bare feet. Her toes, a clear pink, looked like gondolas.

"Gosh," she hit her forehead, "Mrs. Doliber looked like the Wooden Madonna in Church."

Her walk to Gary's house was brisk, but she stood traumatized at the walkway until quite casually the door opened and Gary stepped outside to shake a braided rug. Many such rugs covered the oaken floors of Marblehead homes. His mother had made the rug, no doubt. Gary didn't notice Scotty standing there frozen like a wild rabbit. The door closed again, silencing her fear and she crept up the worn steps to the window, familiar from Mother's Day. Her nose on the windowpane misted the glass; the glare of the sun blocked her vision. Rubbing the glass pane, she peered through the window.

Gary dusted the Windsor chair she had sat in. His face was smooth and calm, without a hint of pain. Scotty had expected him to be crying on that frayed davenport. Her fingernails rapped lightly on the window. He looked up with a glazed eye, his thoughts somewhere in eternity. Dropping the dust cloth, he walked to the door.

"Scotty. So, you heard."

"Why Gary? Why didn't you tell me?"

"I don't know. I just wanted to be by myself for a while. Didn't much want to talk to anybody."

"But Gary, we're friends."

"I know, I know, I just didn't want to cry. I knew I would cry if I told you. My dad's been quiet, too, or out of sight, I should say."

"You know Gary, I never even knew your mother's name."

"Lydia. Pretty, huh? Lydia Doliber. A good name for a good woman. She's buried with her folks at Seaside Cemetery. With all the Redd Clan. They had something to do with that pond a way back."

"Our pond? Redd's Pond?"

He nodded. "But the casket, well, my aunt is making payments on it. Wasn't fancy, but it cost a lot, all that fancy pink metal and roses. She had a wreath of pink roses laid right on top of it. We're Episcopalians; don't go to church much, but pastor Mossom did the service at St. Michael's. He talked about the Good Shepherd, and how a shepherd lays down his life for his sheep. My mum was like a sacrifice too, for God, he said. I don't understand it much, but he was kind. I'm calm now, but don't want to see my pa. He never came to her funeral. Don't want to see him anymore. He was mean to her."

"What will you do?"

"Stay with my aunt. Work at Shube's. But I'll come here to watch her garden, and I'll clean a little, like now."

"I can't cry," said Scotty.

"Why do you want to cry? She's in no more pain. I don't miss her yet, but I know I'll be heart sore after a while. Maybe when the winter pond lays waiting to thaw, and I feel the splashing ducks, or when the angler's line ripples the water, or little master's dinghy is launched for the first time, I'll miss her. Or when I get a headache, I'll feel her strong knitting fingers massaging my head. Or when I smell her chowder, those warm clams will bring me back to life. Maybe after a Northeastern, then I'll lie down and cry. But I'm stuck just now, in the eye of the hurricane."

"I'm not leaving you alone. I'll pester you till I go to California. We'll tend her garden together. I'll plant another geranium, this time a pink one. She'll have the prettiest garden in town, she will."

Scotty kissed his cheek. It was firm and warm.

"You OK?"

"Yeah," he nodded.

"I'll be going then, but I'll be here tomorrow."

"When? I go to Shube's at ten."

"I'll be here at nine."

"Bye."

"Bye."

Scotty wandered home. She usually felt happy or sad, but now she felt a sinister nothing.

That night she dreamed of Zig. Scotty talked to him in her sleep. "How could you do it, Zig? How could you choose nothing; how could you choose poverty?"

Zig was standing in front of the Mystery House while she talked. "Come in," he said. He beckoned with his hands. "It's in there," he whispered, his eyes gleaming. "In there, in there."

"But I must wait for Neil and Barb."

"In there, go now."

Scotty hesitated, but then went inside. She would make excuses later to her friends. The house was filled with light display tables covered with candied jewels. When she walked in and began to look at all the tempting candy, Zig became mesmerized by the wonder and pure delight he felt in this girl. So taken with Scotty's charm, Zig wanted her to have all the candy she wished to eat, for to give her pleasure was a pleasure for him, as well.

Scotty ate and ate. She ate without limits and became very sick. Zig was sad now because he had only wished happiness for the joyous girl.

"I must not allow you to eat candy like that again, my friend; for you know no limits to your pleasure. And I who am older and wiser see that I have hurt you, not helped you, nor satisfied you. As a child, I see you'll never be satisfied. I am older, more mature, and I know my limitations. But I like you, for you have endeared yourself to me with your candor and openness to life. I hope we can be friends and you will visit me here at the Mystery House. I will never give you candy again, though you may look at the candy jewels through the window. Sometimes you will be angry and feel the pain of desire to eat the candies, but you will not be able to get at them. Then think of the pleasure and pain they gave you and use the energy of that pain to do great things, to build castles or climb great mountains. For pleasure is for the moment, but your soulful enthusiasm is the essence of life."

The next morning Scotty rose, her dream like a treasure of the Mystery House buried inside. Though it was summer, Lois insisted on getting up early to pack for California. However, when Scotty brought in the six o'clock instant coffee, Lois greeted her with muffled tones. She then promptly went back to sleep. So, Scotty busied herself around the house dusting and sweeping. In her bedroom, she looked at the eaves for the last time. In the closet size room, the narrow bunk bed, all glossy with pink enamel, the noisy metal spring, and the ominous hole that launched a million nightmares—they would all soon be just a memory. She had little to take with her. She might be taking a satchel of gems from the Mystery House and there was the doll chest, Little Lulu, Sister Sue, the crocheted poodle of Grammy's, and the wonderful miniature silver tea set of doll house size, already packed. She could be packing dishes in the kitchen or curios from the coffee table. But there were no directions from Mum.

Eric shared Lois's efforts to pack. Sleeping until ten in the morning, he ate some Campbell's tomato soup for breakfast and then he was off for the day. Crocker Park, The Corinthian, or Kings Rook, who knew where he would go? What did he do for money, she wondered as she disdainfully picked up a soiled paper tissue, remnant of his springtime cold. Gosh, she thought, he hasn't packed nor even cleaned up the balsa wood from his last project.

At 8:45, Scotty left for Gary's, both mother and brother buried in their rooms as if in a winter blitz. Her dad would be proud of her. They were early birds. A sweet thought then dawned on her, a memory of a forlorn worker home from the Electric Company, metal lunch box in hand, and sleeves rolled up. She saw his gray heavy broadcloth pants and his nails, grimy from mold dies. Sandy strands of hair fell over one eye, a soft blue eye. Home from work, he hung his worn khaki jacket on her head.

"Hall tree, hall tree!"

"What?" said Gary.

"Oh, I'm here already. Gary, you wouldn't believe how old I am, and still always talking to myself."

Gary sat in the black Windsor rocker.

"You OK?" she asked.

"Sure," he said, just to respond, "I don't think it's hit me yet."

She felt his head to see if he had a temperature. "You're OK," she pronounced. Somehow with her strange logic, Scotty thought one must have a fever if one had a heartache . . .

"We better get right to the garden."

"What's it like at your aunt's?"

They pulled tools out as they talked.

"She's got a closet, a big one with a window, for my room. It's kinda homey, with a youth bed; even got room enough for my Shube's sign."

"See your dad?"

"Nope, but I can tell he's been around the house, usually leaves an ale can or two somewhere around."

"I'm so happy with my hands in the dirt," she talked to the worms. "Aren't you afraid the robins will get you?"

Gary dug his fingers into the dirt and buried one hand near Scotty so she would pull at it like a worm.

"You crazy kid. I thought you'd be a basket case and you're playing with me."

Gary looked into her eyes with a slightly tilted head and dreamy eye.

"My mum's taking care of me now. She's pulling some magic upstairs. I have a weird feeling I'm safe."

Scotty half understood. Softly, she tugged on his fingers and talked to them. "I can see you're not afraid of robins." She pushed his fingers back into the loosened dirt. With a final pat, mechanically she put back the yard tools.

"I'm going to Crocker Park, wanta come?"

"Nope. Gotta get to Shube's."

"Well, I really should go home and push my mum to pack but I'm going swimming at Crocker Park. After all, I won't be able to do that much more soon. See you tomorrow at nine?"

"Yup," he said.

"So long, friend," she pecked at his cheek.

As she walked, Scotty felt strangely free as she tossed her hands back and forth in a zestful cadence. Maybe Mrs. Doliber was taking care of her too.

Happily, she viewed the white picket fences, hollyhocks, tall and green without their summer blooms. Carefully she avoided dog do and searched back alleys for garages covered with trailing morning glories. She passed the Herreshoff Castle.

Climbing the hill, she took a short turn on the canvas chain swing that overlooked the float, then down onto the landing, where she prepared to swim. Scotty flung off the seersucker plaid blouse and Bermuda khakis. Off came the navy blue sneaks without unlacing, and neatly she folded the clothes and set them on her shoes.

Her white skin, never at liberty to tan, quivered as she dipped one leg into the frigid waters. Bobbing up and down in her mint green checkered suit, a brown tie fastened the suit with one button centered in the front to two in the back. As her brown hair flapped, she spoke to the water.

"I don't know how the Brownies do it." The Brownies were a group of elderly men who swam all year round in nearly frozen Atlantic waters.

Scotty managed to sit on the float now and dangle both legs in the cold water. Peering down into the greenish blue, she made eggbeater motions with her legs circling together but not touching. Then she sank into the ocean that was above her head, but she held to the wharf, so she was submerged only to her waist, while her elbows and arms lay flat on the landing supporting her. She kicked furiously to keep warm and soon, adjusting to the cold waters, she dipped deeper until only her head was above the sea; from there the breaststroke and scissor kick helped her scout the near-by vessels anchored down and waiting for their mates. She read their names, "John Brown, Samuel Adams, Gloucester." The last boat she questioned, "Marabot?"

"What's that?" she puzzled, and with questioning eyes she paused only seconds before she kicked furiously while some top pressure pushed at her head, submerging Scotty with coughs and bellows. Under the water for a split second, Scotty thought of death and the times she had been helplessly drawn under water by overwhelming rip tides. The pressure, though only seconds, seemed like hours. When the pressure was released, she surfaced, spitting water. Eric was in the haul of the John Adams, grinning with his buddy, Peter Reed.

"Gosh, Eric, you scared the jeepers out of me!"

"I thought it was pretty funny, Moose. What are you doing here?"

"Well, you don't have to be a genius to see I'm swimming. But not for long if you drown me!"

"Just kidding."

"Whose boat are you in?" she treads water and held to the edge.

"My dad's," said Peter.

"All my friends sail," said Eric polishing an invisible badge. "We're all medal winners at the Corinthian Club."

"Well, to the best of my knowledge, we don't have a sailboat, Eric."

"Won all my medals with the help of my friends, right Pete?"

Scotty had never talked to Pete, but he seemed snotty and empty headed.

"Right, Eric," Pete said after some hesitation.

"Well, I'll be going," said Scotty, "I like to swim at Crocker by myself. So long!"

She felt put upon. This part of the sea belonged to her. She hadn't lived long enough to separate from nature and develop an ego with demands and rights, so she'd just mosey on without a fight; she'd flee to another picturesque spot of her own.

"Gee," she grumbled while she pulled her dripping body, knee first, onto the wharf. "What's wrong with me? I never get tired of the kidless wharf or the empty street; but my brother, my cousin, even Barb at times, seem a bother and a bore."

She buttoned her seersucker blouse over the wet suit then pulled the Bermuda shorts up. They were patched with water spots seeping through, but even so, they warmed her. Scotty's hair, droopy with water, slapped her legs as she bent to push her feet into the navy sneaks, using her thumb as a shoe horn, determined to put them on without unlacing. Finished, Scotty's feet gripped the ladder bridging the park in her climb off the wharf. She wouldn't give Eric and Pete the satisfaction of a farewell recognition. The warm rubber of her sneaks made no sound as she stepped onto the gravel and walked along the curb home. She walked head down until she came to Mary Alley Hospital and raised her head briefly to notice the barnyard red clapboard siding. The building didn't look anything like a hospital.

She didn't want to talk to anybody. She just wanted to walk the streets. Content in her solitude, Scotty reached the steps to Fountain Park all too quickly. Driven to her haunt, but frightened even to see Neil now, for she was a part of a feeling both natural and unnatural to man. Moll Flanders, Margaret Scott—Scotty was them for a moment, history itself and incapable of anything but being. One with her dream, she lingered on the hill, viewing the houses near Graves Boat Yard, the flight of seagulls. Then she saw Neil climbing the hill near his house. He stepped carefully around the sumac, on a stone path. The magic bubble broke for her softly like the tide water that breaks in the swimmer's ear, and she returned to reality.

"Shouldn't you be packing?" he called, and he ducked through the hole of the picket fence just down from her.

"Why are you always trying to get rid of me? I thought you liked me!" she pushed at him. He slid down the gravel to the base of the fence again.

"I'm just teasing."

"Just wanted to offer my help, Dum Dum."

He tried to climb the hill again. This time Neil bent to maintain his balance. "Golly, Scotty, let me up there."

"Why? I've already been run out of Crocker Park by my brother. This is my place."

"Our place," he grinned. He put his hands in prayer position. "Please let me up the hill!"

"OK," she said, holding onto the flagpole with one hand and extending the other down the hill. "Is that better?"

"What a Nerd Nose you are," he said when he reached the top, but he didn't say anything while she pulled. They sat on the covered bench. There was something like an open garage that hooded their slatted wooden back bench. They sat for a moment and he took her hand. The peace came back this time, for both of them. It was very still, and they didn't talk for a long while. A lonesome cat brought them back to life as he brushed their knees, passing them with his tail high.

"You're a friendly devil," said Neil.

"What a beautiful tabby," Scotty rubbed the cat's fur, "He looks like Liver Lips, Kate's cat. Oh, my goodness!" She looked some more. "It is Liver Lips! How did you get here?" Then Scotty looked to the steps. There was Kate, furtively pulling herself up the wrought iron railing while she climbed the cement steps. It seemed strange to see Kate there, so out of place for her. Kate belonged to The Hill.

"Kate, what are you doing here?"

"What do ya mean? It's a city park, not private property. I felt like going for a nice walk today. Teddy and Geraldine are on vacation, so the Hill Club doesn't exist right now, and I thought I'd visit my dear cousin plus show Liver Lips what the thugs do to stray cats. So, I brought him in our picnic basket to visit Redd's Pond. You weren't home. Aunt Lois said you might be here."

"This is like the Hill for me; this is my haunt."

Neil coughed and wiggled his fingers in salute.

"Oh," she coughed back, "How rude of me. This is my buddy, Neil. He lives right over there in that fancy windowed house."

"I feel like I know you, Kate, from Scotty's tales of the Hill Club."

"All bad, I hope," Kate returned a peevish grin.

"Well, I got the impression you have spirit and imagination from the reports of those grueling initiations."

Kate puckered her lips in smug acceptance and folding her arms, she said, "You have a pretty good operation here yourself. That's a nifty looking house to explore."

"Yup, there are three to this club," Scotty interjected. "Barb lives next to the pond. I pointed to her that day we planned the egging. Remember?"

"I remember, I remember." Kate sounded a bit defensive. She remembered only too well. How she hadn't wanted to include Barb the day they went to the pond. Now Kate was excluded from their plans. Only Neil, Scotty, and Barb would explore the mystery house.

"Yup, and we even have a date for our treasure hunt," said Scotty, "June 28th."

"Oh, drat," moaned Kate, "I'll be in Winnipesaukee then with Grammy."

Neil and Scotty looked at the grass, avoiding the issue. They knew Kate wanted to be included in their exploration.

"No way. I guess we could have had another person search with us, but Johnny, the watch dog, would never let four people get by him," said Neil.

He and Scotty knew Johnny would be with Jake, but no point in hurting Kate.

"Oh, by the way, Aunt Lois said for you to come home."

"O.K.," said Scotty.

"Here, wait for me. I'll put Liver Lips back in the picnic basket. You'd make a great club member, Liver Lips; I like the way you follow orders."

The fat tabby wanted to go home. Days of conquest were behind him, he meowed languidly at the picnic basket.

"Goodbye, Neil."

"Goodbye Scotty. Nice to have met you, Kate."

Kate wordlessly grinned, thinking of her foiled attempt to join their club.

"Wonder if Liver Lips could find his way home from here by himself," Scotty stroked his head sticking out of the basket.

"I wonder," said Kate. "I wonder."

CHAPTER ELEVEN

As she walked to Gary's next morning, Scotty chanted, "Two more weeks, two more weeks." She was searching the sounds to make a last jingle. The last two weeks were important, but those words just would not make a song. Quiet, salty tears rolled over her cheeks and into her parted lips.

"I'm brave," she said, her lips puckered, her eyes wincing. She didn't look brave, she looked forlorn, soon to be taken away from her land, and be made an orphan. Scotty had no knowledge of bravery except through history's lessons of patriots and puritans.

Would Lois pack today? Next week would be their family turn at Lake Winnipesaukee with Grammy. They would come home and then leave for California. Preparations had to be made.

Tomorrow was Sunday. Scotty didn't want to think about it. She'd go to church by herself. She made stories of her life on the way to the Star of the Sea, the Gothic church. What would it be like going to church in the West? She supposed it would be a mission church and the priests would have bald heads, and rosaries at their brown robed waists. She pictured cactus and sandaled feet and thought of the barefoot Madonna. Maybe it was more natural, but no snow, no boots, no mittens! How dismal! She would worry about Grampy Graves and Zig because they were old, but then she could send a dollar back to Neil. He would give it to Zig. On the other hand, Neil had enough money, he could just give Zig a dollar. Neil would give Zig a dollar when his cheeks smarted, and his stomach gnawed with emptiness. Scotty would be warm but dull, plain and lost in the grandiose

Pacific Coastline, the broad boulevards, the rapid freeways, the tracts of houses with tall, lonely palm trees. The life she was accustomed to leading placed her on a narrow cobblestone, with maples in the distance, the graveyard, the boat yard, lobster traps, the hassock and tonic with Mum, after hurricanes. The Hill Clan, the ale and the cloves; Grammy thrived on those feasts. The kids running for life, the Hill Club and Kate, Scotty pulling the cock-a-buttons from Red's hair, those memories would soon be all gone. But she wasn't done for yet. She'd have Gary, the monster turned mourner, once villain, now friend. She'd promise to write; she'd send him miniature orange crates from California, like her father did. And there was still June twenty eighth. She must take more than memories.

Stone pillars and stained glass kept the Gothic Roman Catholic prayer house cool. When she was eight years old, Scotty had walked into the awesome church while repairmen with hammers made loud sounds in the belfry. Down below, her mother had disappeared into a confessional. While searching, Scotty stumbled into a burgundy velvet drape that boxed off the father confessor, eyeing his Bible through his spectacles, black cassock over his seat just short of his protruding dark leather shoe. Unnoticed, she quickly left, straightening out the curtain. The ominous noise of repairmen and her stumble into the confessional, two years ago, had left a fearful feeling about visiting the church. That feeling was with her now as she sauntered to her center pillar, her place on the Madonna's left side of the Church. She genuflected and moved to the middle of the pew so that she could see the priest, unobscured by the pillar, when he entered to perform his rite. After her usual stare at the crucifix center and the wooden reredos of finely chiseled oak, a quick glance to the high buttresses and stained-glass backdrop, then her eyes dropped down as she made a prayerful gesture with her hands and closed her eyes in reflection.

In summer, the cold stone interior smelled of decaying fern, but scented candles and incense from the glorified monstrance of a prior service, left a sultry atmosphere. For a few moments, Scotty acclimated herself to the heavy darkness, and then, suddenly, a clammy touch to her knee jolted her eyes open. She blinked in amazement, then turned her head gradually to her left and saw the profile of a man, large in stature, kneeling beside her in a slumped position of penitent manner, his left hand touching his brow and covering his eye, while his right hand reached down to the kneeler and fondled Scotty's leg. As she stared at him, without liberty to move away, the man's hand glided higher up her leg. The pew was filled now on both sides, so Scotty could not stand up and walk away without creating a commotion. She sat in shock. The man's hand now moved again and reached above her knee. Scotty tried to block him by placing her hands between her knee and thigh, and there they stayed stymieing the advances of a faceless man, a blur to her side. Traumatized until communion, when her kneeling neighbor removed his hand as if by magic, she stood with the rest of the people to her right, to walk to the front altar. As she reached the center aisle, she sighed at this less than holy service.

After receiving the host, she walked quickly to the side door. As she escaped down the cobblestone path to the sidewalk, she thought, "Why would a person like that even want to go to church?"

She didn't go to Gary's on Sundays. Scotty walked back by way of Story School. Most of the bricks in town were used for schools. Their house by the pond, cozy with its wooden beams and gabled roof, typified the commoner's home. In sight of her home, the usual glee of the familiar gave her no joy today. A laconic tinge clouded her verve of her last summer days in Marblehead. The incident at church merely gave impetus to her inability to connect and find meaning in life, perhaps a goal not within childhood limits. "My life needs connection. I need my own story, my own song. That nerd in church just hit me while I'm at my rock bottom. I'll keep a log, or better yet, I'll keep a final countdown. A calendar, I'll do it on a calendar."

At home now, a note on the kitchen table told her that Lois and Eric went to the Hill after the 12:00 o'clock mass. She probably just missed them.

For some people at the age of ten, the egotistic forces would be well underway. For most kids, the competition in life filled their space. But for Scotty, Neil and Barb, more philosophic by gene, being was discovering their own space, that magic within them scratched finely in the beaches and soon to be made into their inner castles. And that dubious education needed guiding and constant effort as its only reward. Intuition usually came to the old. The young, being dumbfounded by the process of connecting who they were with what they had learned, struggled with terrible space and loneliness. But youth's energy has a way of starting, recklessly darting out to discover treasure in old mystery houses, dashing to begin anywhere, and there to fill in, make the connections. Scotty's attempt at a calendar helped her break up this space and grab hold of her life.

"June's last days. But I need a calendar, a calendar," and then it dawned on her that on her dad's stack of papers, there was a calendar from the National Trust of Boston, a freebie. Scotty raced to the living room, where the old stone fireplace stood mounted against the wall as in an English castle. Near her father's recliner, adjacent to the hearth, a rather plain wicker basket held the mail. The calendar stuck out from the neat pile at the middle. Carefully, she pulled it out and returned the mail, this time uniform on all sides.

"Why didn't I think of this before? And I have the perfect spot for it, over the hole in the wall by my bed." Looking at it, she said, "It's addressed to resident, anyway, and I'm a resident," she said again as she whisked it upstairs into her bedroom and onto the boomerang bed. She thought a moment. On the front of the date keeper, a Marblehead fisherman in his rain gear headed into the horizon, the logo of the town.

"June 12. Today I begin my diary of last days in Marblehead. I'll describe the house so that I won't ever forget. There's enough room for a small paragraph on each day, but I can't be flowery, just the essentials," she outlined to the air. Clearly trying to focus on the house, she walked down to the bottom floor. The warm stone of the fireplace and the bay window, to the right of the grate, overlooked Redd's Pond and Old Burial Hill, creating the flavor of the room, uniting outside and inside. The corduroy recliner and plaid cotton sofa faced the fireplace, leaving a small television in the last corner. Scotty usually nestled on the floor in the evening, changing only the direction of her body to face her fancy.

On into Eric's room, a slight reproach seared her conscience, but she countered, "I'm only here to memorize, not to search. The ordinary clutter of the balsa wood everywhere from unfinished vessels, the unmade bed, the girlie magazine half out of the closet door on the floor, all things seemed right. The headless horseman and the lighthouse in oils, his works, decorated the wall to the right of his bed, and a watercolor of the Graves Boatyard hung above his headboard, again his work. She followed the oak floor with her eyes, the canvas to his mosaic of clutter and then her eyes froze on a black shiny object protruding from under the bed. Dread filled her with half knowledge of the object. Scotty drew near the bed and stooped to gaze without touching.

"It's broken! 'Cross Over the Bridge' is broken, the loathsome reminder of her lost peace. But why? How? It couldn't have been stepped on; Eric is too careful for that."

Sadness filled her. She felt sorry for him. There could be no relief; after all, they'd make another game of it. He could annoy her with something else. He could buy the same record. But nothing helped. She felt sad seeing the record under the bed in a half covered grave. Eric had treasured that melody; could he have destroyed it? She stood again and backed out of the room.

"Whosssh," she said in relief, "It's a good thing I didn't do it." Walking backward, her foot caught at the edge of the door on the hall rug runner. Play made foul for only seconds, the diarist abruptly sauntered onward into the kitchen. She fidgeted with sadness, but not too long; she would make kind memories.

Jam spots stained the formica counters near the lattice window. Outside, the ceramic lions created atmosphere for the ducks perched in wait for their benefactress. Going back to the jam spots with her eyes, "Grammy made this jam," she thought. The sweet and sour taste of family and emptiness. Morning eggnog and after school loneliness muddled together. Looking over the appliances, her eye caught the shine of the kitchen table, an antique painted gray many times, the dune gray of the counters. A decent staircase, better than the cellar high steps but not spirally presidential, led straight up to the master bedroom, Scotty's room and the bathroom. The banister too high for sliding, smudged now with fingerprints of midday snacks, led Scotty onto higher level memories. She peeked onto the pond and cemetery from the top of the steps. Only the dwarfed bedroom, her room, she left for last.

The bathroom at the end of the hall, useful but undecorated, had the essential toilet, sink, and tub. Not a memory but a stage of development to prompt Uncle Jeep's talk, from the privies of her mother's time to the indoor bathroom, "a major step in the defeat of constipation," she could hear Uncle Jeep bellow, in conversation with Grampy McFinch about the first stages of the bathroom at the Hill. "The bath came last," she repeated his words. Aunt Marge used a whole paycheck for that tub. Back to the master bedroom, "Let's not dally; they'll be home soon, Mum and Eric," she mumbled, then stood to appraise that bedroom of the fifties. Neat twin beds, smooth and even bedspreads made of beige cotton and cotton ball fringes at the bottom; a dresser, a bureau, all maple, all smooth and even, tidy, they stood unobtrusively, the seagull wallpaper quietly integrating them. The two windows duplicated the hall window with gables and lattice alike. The only off-center item in the room, an alarm clock, turned toward Lois's bed. The center of the bedstand awaited morning coffee. Two small reading lights clamped to the bedposts provided beams for bedside reading, while a more conspicuous, dusty glass mushroom funneled a glow toward the ceiling, softly ineffective. And lastly, the neat photos perched on the Queen Anne bureau. She counted six. "One each of the children, one each of the grandparents makes four, one of my Dad when he sang in the Boy's Chorus of St. Paul's Cathedral, before his voice cracked, everybody mentioned that when they described these pictures, and my Mum and Dad, young, just before their wedding. Gee," thought Scotty, "Mum's soft eyes and Mona Lisa lips look like the milkmaid on the maple syrup bottle."

Lois's new perm of tight strawberry-blond curls contrasted a face peaceful, yet full of youthful expectation. Ed Paine, like Errol Flynn, boyishly thin, looked sixteen, his blue eyes intelligent yet luminously pure. How could he be twenty-one? Familiar with all things in that room, Scotty stared for a moment at a new picture placed at the front as a focal point, breaking the even numbers of the setting.

"What's this?" Well, she knew, of course. A picture of Aunt Lucretia and Lois, together, arm in arm. Their faces, of course, looked a good deal alike but for Lucretia's more chiseled nose and thinner face. Her hair truly brunette, yet her eyes, the blue eyes of the family, were contradicting: one was soft and furtive while the other glared a stare.

"I've never seen this picture. Gosh, the paper's faded, and those dresses! And that smooth bobbed hair! Why, Aunt Lucretia's hair is shaved on one side! They look a bit silly but friendly, both tilting their heads together like in some puppy pose. Strange," she squinted her eyes and raised them to the far left, "I've been through the whole album but never seen this picture. I wonder why it's standing here in the front like this."

"Are you here, Scotty?" she heard her mother's voice. "We're home."

Scotty marched out of her parents' room clutching her calendar. She walked with purpose into her bedroom and put the calendar on her wall, still seeing the picture in her mind of her aunt's black lashes and eyes, and her mother's softly undiscovered ones.

CHAPTER TWELVE

It felt friendly to wake up the next morning to the calendar on the hole ridden wall. She had not written the first of her paragraphs, but the night's rest helped solidify a few terse thoughts. She wrote as she spoke, "A quiet house, an imaginative cemetery, a broken bridge, and two sisters parted. I don't know why I wrote about the cemetery. I didn't really look at it, but I guess it's part and parcel of the house. So, I'll leave my thoughts just as they come out."

Scotty, refreshed always by slumber, pounced down the steps to get her mother's coffee. Eric's door stood slightly ajar, and she peeped into the quiet chaos. The record was still there and appeared to be pushed farther under the bed. Now, only a black rim showed; it was not nearly as alarming. Eric snored. Scotty now felt allergic to the word "snore," since her chagrin with Aunt Lue's accusations that she snored. Anything that she, herself would blush at she'd never accuse anyone else of.

"I guess he's just breathing heavily," she whispered. "An Alaskan puppy, that's what he looks like with his crewcut and stubby beard, sorta furry and young. How could he be so different when he's awake! Don't know," she put her finger to her lips trying to quiet herself.

Moving into the kitchen, she felt the smooth, gray formica, not unfriendly to her touch. After all, her family lay in their beds. Wasn't family home?

"What a glorious day to go to Deveraux Beach!" Before she knew it the tea kettle whistled, and the Instant Maxwell House steamed her face as she carried her mother's coffee mug upstairs.

Sunday gave way to a giddy Monday for this child who deeply thought or deeply acted. "Mum," she said, "can we go to Deveraux Beach today? Here's your coffee, Mum. It's seven fifteen and here's your coffee, Mum."

Plopping on her father's clean bed, unoccupied for five months, she waited with the coffee steam, to see a movement. Nothing happened. Her mum was fast asleep.

"Won't have many more times like this, Mum," and she waited.

Two eyes blinked open then shut, and a cat like stretch came next. "Goodness, Scotty, it's summer, let a mum rest."

"I know, I know, but Dad will be here soon, and we'll be heading West and we've got so much packing and so many places to go!"

Languorously, Lois got started. She sat up in bed marveling at Scotty's energy. "Where did you come from anyway?"

"The milkman, Mum, I came from the milkman, Granny Paine said so."

Scotty's morning chatter could be abrasive to any sleepy head.

"Eric and I stayed up late."

"Did you pack?"

"I put some newspaper and a box in the middle of the kitchen floor."

Scotty skirted her mother's bed and looked beseechingly into her half-opened eyes. "I'll do it. I'll pack this minute, if you promise we'll go to Deveraux. Come on, Mum, come on!"

"All right, all right, you're just like your dad, Miss Morning Spark. Oh, stop that bouncing on my bed, Scotty, or I'll change my mind."

Scotty stood gingerly and took off down the stairs. Her serfdom won the day. After two hours of arduous effort, two tidy boxes of Sunday dishes pampered in newspaper, lined the dixie gray, one white one gray pattern of linoleum on the floor, and she had made a stab at Eric's room. His scrap balsa wood made its own collage in a paper bag, making the room much more orderly. The eggnog and English muffins consumed without much notice; Lois took the steering wheel at 11:30 for perhaps the last family outing to Deveraux Beach.

The Atlantic coastline made stingy reclining sands. At two o'clock, the bathers looked like a colorful mosaic of bodies as close as could be without touching. Like hopscotch, newcomers bounced from one foot to the next, trying not to land on the belly or back of a sun worshiper, somewhat the way they dodged the orange jellyfish that coated the mud pie shoreline where waters had receded. Footprints turned white with first pressure outlining the sand until small ripples of water erased them from sight, but not memory. Intimately bound to those Atlantic waters, there was a sense of freedom to recall one's roots; a sense of integrity to be a part of history and individual story and a sense of unity in the happiness of being without measure.

"Oh, Mum, there's a place right near the water. Give me the blanket and I'll run down to save it."

Lois and Eric, feet buried in sand, sanguinely responded, being always ten steps ahead of them in the morning, maybe three in the sand. Pulling the faded cotton patchwork quilt, she tore down the sand. Sands not quite ready to grill soles, Deveraux Beach promised choice spots for the early birds, and no lines at Timmy's Frankfurter Stand. On a slight mound, Scotty draped the blanket so as to have a head rest to the sea. Family secured the ends of Scotty's old blanket with shoes and reclined, once more ready to resume their slumber.

"Mum, I know you just had breakfast, but I've been up so early. Can I get my frankfurter and tonic? I'll go again for you and Eric later."

"Let's see, twenty-five cents for the dog and ten cents for the tonic." Lois spoke to the sky, eyes shut, then reaching her hand into her purse, she pulled out her change purse and sat up to find coins for Scotty.

"Here's an extra ten for some potato sticks or a Sugar Daddy."

Scotty kissed her mum while she bent for the money.

"Good idea Scotty, we won't see much beach sand soon; we'll be in the Mojave. Don't worry about our food. Eric can go for us in a while."

Eric, prone on the blanket, gave a snort of approval.

Something so special about childhood made even the air taste good. An evaporating condiment, a special seasoning tasted only in youth could make for a life sustaining memory.

This was the taste of Timmy's Frankfurter Stand. His sundry place sold penny candies, tonic, and frankfurters in toasted rectangular buns. Placid, rotund Timmy, cigar hanging from his mouth, English cap always on his head, catering to the tots like Gulliver to the Lilliputians.

Scotty stood mesmerized, second in line; the stand opened at 12:00. Timmy ordered the Sugar Babies, Good and Plentys, and Jujubes. Scotty salivated at the grilled frankfurters and wondered how Timmy toasted those buns that looked like Egyptian crypts, buns immortal. She watched him as he flattened the buns on the grill with his spatula, then flipped them and flattened them again.

"Wow, it looks good, Timmy."

"What's that, Love?"

Timmy had the kind of smile that never went away. Maybe it had something to do with the fact that he pleased people and felt good about it.

"I'd like one frankfurter, and one grape tonic, please."

"And what would the Little Miss like on her frank?"

"Just a little relish."

"Saw your grandmother the other day in Shube's, what a swell old girl she is."

"As a matter of fact, Timmy, you're like her. You have the same smile, sorta wide like you just ate a whole apple pie and felt content."

"Lord love a duck," Timmy bellowed, "I scorched the frank! Scotty Paine, you're distracting me."

"No matter, I like burnt franks."

So, Timmy winked and placed the frankfurter burnt side down in the bun.

"Now, here you are, a little relish and one of my fancy paper plates."

"It looks like a coffee filter, all folded at the edges," she observed.

"And here's your tonic." He was doing his best to concentrate now.

"Gosh, that looks good. I think heaven must have your hot dogs, Timmy."

"Well, then maybe the good Lord will let me serve 'em up there. Let's hope so," he said, taking Scotty's coins without counting them. "Give my best to your Grammy, now. Kitty McFinch, a right decent old girl."

"I will Timmy, bye." One hand with tonic one hand with frank, Scotty sat on a vermilion slatted bench, covered with a roof. For onlookers at the shore, for grannies and spectators who couldn't take the sun, the pavilion raised on cement provided a bird's eye view of the human menagerie stalking the sunny sands.

During winter months, when neighbors and friends hibernated from snows and frigid winds, one could only surmise their homebound toils. Humid summer sun brought them together to compare notes on absent behavior.

"Mrs. Jacobs is pregnant again," Scotty murmured with frank sausage half in her mouth, the juice squirting up in the air.

Mrs. Jacobs lay on the sand; tykes like stepping stones ran back and forth to the water carrying pails of wet sand for their castles.

"That makes five, one every winter," she chuckled. Then her eyes meandered to Annie Frost, her scrawny wrinkled body lying still on her back.

"A black velour towel? My gosh, she looks silly with that puffy stomach. Poor thing, bet she hit the bottle this winter, brandied coffee, no doubt."

Since her husband, a conductor for the Northern Pacific, passed away, Annie imbibed the juice to placate sad spirits. Lying on her side now, obdurately she struggled with a pack of Camels. Cigarettes soothed her loneliness. Scotty spied the twins next, while drinking her tonic. Sisters of the 1890's, they wore striped bathing suits that defined the covered-up look of their era. With Gibson hairdos, Millie and Gert faced each other in argument. They always debated on the sands, garrulously in a song like banter, their sharp features and cameo skin reminding one of a vintage Coca Cola sign. Eccentrics, their loquacious attitude characterized the old Marbleheader with ale, brandy or tea in hand. The Gibson girls drank from a stainless-steel thermos in cups of picnic plastic.

All done, Scotty wandered back by way of Timmy's again for the redemption coins on her tonic bottle.

"I'll have a Sugar Daddy; hope I don't get sand on it this time," she rubbed her tongue over her upper teeth feeling the grit of bygone days. "Two cents for the bottle and three for the Daddy, seven cents to save."

Scotty didn't speak to Timmy this time, just put the bottle down. He responded by slapping two cents on the counter. She picked up the Sugar Daddy and laid down a dime. Scooping the dime off the counter, he shuffled two cents her way and slapped a nickel down. The nickel's buffalo shone brightly. Done,

Timmy tipped his hat and Scotty left warmed by his glow, a smile that would see her through many storms in life.

CHAPTER THIRTEEN

June 14

It seemed a habit now not to write on the calendar at the end of each day, but in the morning of the following day. The perspective of the night's slumber gave shine to her varied escapades.

"Come here, calendar, you've become my pet."

She gently pulled at the tack in the wall securing her diary.

"Timmy," she wet the pen on her tongue. "Hero of Deveraux Beach, Lord of Franks and Tonic."

"That says it all, really. Well," she reminded herself "this is Gary's morning. Won't wake Mum and Eric," she whispered putting her diary back on the wall.

Oblivious to what she wore, Scotty sneaked to the kitchen door, to realize some private joy in the sunrise, not new yet evenly bright—the world, the ducks, the smooth water of Redd's Pond—"Mine, all mine!"

What she saw became her. For seconds she experienced the magic of the landscape as part of it. Then, eyes cast down, Scotty followed the cracks of the sidewalk almost in tunnel vision to 12 Orne Street. "Gary won't be here yet, so I'll do a little work in the garden by myself."

But when she arrived, Scotty heard sounds, a voice coming from the house. She drew near the window on the porch and hunched so she could peep in. Gary's dad sat on the sofa and spoke to an empty rocker.

"Oh, golly, he's gone mad. Harry Doliber's gone mad!" she thought.

"I'm sorry, Lydia," he looked beseechingly at the rocker. "I'm sorry I was never fancy enough for you. I couldn't make you proud, but I loved you and the boy. I'm not the master of my ship, never have been, never knew how. You were always just good, natural like. I couldn't be like you. I hated you for that but I loved you too. The boy was more like you, your kind. He used my language, but his heart was kind of like yours. I can't cry, Lydia. All I can do is curse, but I loved you. God help me, I loved you," and he put his head down in his lap, his fists clutching on either side.

Harry sat still for a moment, then he stood up in a start. He knew his son would be there in moments to tend his mother's garden. He couldn't face him. Fingering his hair like a comb, he took off out the back door.

"Thank God," thought Scotty, "I could never have hidden from him crouched on this front porch." She went around to the toolshed. A border of salvia met her. "Oh, how pretty, Mrs. Doliber would have loved that red. Mr. Peach must have given them to Gary."

The whole town knew of Lydia Doliber's passing, her orphaned son and drunken husband. A great sympathy followed Gary, even the stray dogs showed deference by following him for blocks in a trail of sorrow.

The garden took on the manicured look of an English park with salvia neatly marching around the rose bush centerpiece. The Mother's Day geranium garnished the back porch where white lattice backed it as the church reredos. No worm could love the garden more, Scotty thought as she took hoe in hand from the toolshed. Spying some neglected hollyhocks by the alley, she summoned some strength to cultivate the nasty soil, uninviting for most plants but the hollyhocks and maybe some nasturtiums. While cultivating, she envisioned a lace curtain in the toolshed window, an old tablecloth remnant she could bring from home.

Gardens were part of New England genes migrating from the imaginations of ancestors; refinement in the garden the best measure of a cultivated sort. A streak of pink made the flowers look wonderful, shrouded so long in green on the stately stalks. Summer awakened Scotty's spirits.

Gary never came. "It's all right," she thought, "he's more sensible now. Had he seen his father?

Scotty tidied up and swept the walk with a broom from the shed.

On her way home she rerouted her path, remembering this day would be for romping and quiet thoughts. Some days she liked to be still. Some enormous peace made her dumb, but not silent or oblivious to the nature around her. What a contrast, to move and be still at the same time. Tenaciously, she enjoyed these moments that came to her, but not always. Some sort of inner compass directed her up Washington Street to the Victorian clock tower of Abbot Hall. Inside, its wall held the memory of the original spirit, "The Spirit of '76" by Archibald Willard.

"What verve," she said aloud then covering her lips, sat in a chair fronting the painting. "It's almost like a wake," Scotty spoke to herself.

The painting, larger than life, portrayed early citizens with the collective spirit of a nation: ready to die, ready to live, ready to suffer for their ideals. All those nebulous ideas made clear in the faces of the drummer, the prone wounded patriot, and the aged hero who drove them on. She sighed an eternal sigh, her somber face held an ugly vacancy, so totally removed yet so totally connected. It seemed odd that such a young person could be made so old with contemplation. A stage coming most often to the elderly, but not always, as the old slow down to outer movement and with the opportunity of retirement to center on inner themes of forgotten ideals and major questions.

Scotty began with these promptings. A contrast in herself being short of learning skills, her intuitive expertise gave her the clout of the Romantic archetypes who came before her.

In the velour cushion of the chair, she sat bringing her elbows down to her knees; cupping hands to her chin, she poked her cheeks now and then, reminding her of life.

Half an hour passed in minutes for the pensive viewer. Actually, Scotty felt more than she thought about the fervor that distilled the nation. A clerk worked quietly at a desk near the entrance to the room. The lady, with thick glasses, pallid skin, and navy suit did not recognize Scotty when she entered on the left. Paperwork preoccupied her, as guard to Willard's work seemed probably a secondary job.

Leaving the Hall as ghostlike as she came, Scotty passed the linden trees, happy in summer bloom. She thought of the Common of old when soldiers readied themselves for the Revolution. Crossing the street, Scotty stared at the Lee Mansion ahead.

"I've never visited that Georgian Glory, as Grammy McFinch calls it. But Uncle Jeep told me George Washington stayed there once after the Revolution and Mum said Lafayette stayed there, too. I know admission costs a quarter and I don't have a penny but I do have some stale bread." She pulled out the bread; the crumbs fell to the sidewalk, as she continued her dialogue and looked up at the "rusticated" building with its cupola and double chimneys. "Aunt Marge says the furniture's something brought back from the West Indies by Colonel Jeremiah Lee who traded with some old codfish, just salt. "Gee, what a time that must have been! Isn't it funny I don't want to see the inside as much as the Mystery House. Fussy antiques aren't me." She pushed her blazer pocket right side in and walked on. Hands behind her back, Scotty shuffled downtown past the Old Town Hall, the back streets to the pond. Winding the back roads home, she thought little about eating, though noontime scents surrounded her. Unlike winter months at noon with chowders simmering into frigid airs, roses and pungent marigolds paved her way home, leaving her only hungry for life. In sloppy navy sneakers, her big toes popped out now and then. As she concentrated on the polished nails, cement, and gravel, dog droppings and then the fragrant trellis rose would reward her like a meandering puppy with a scent pithy to childhood memory.

At Fountain Park, she chose to climb the hill weaving around a granite mound that boarded Old Burial Hill, having in mind to visit Barb, whose house stood on the street nearest Redd's Pond. Usually, Scotty climbed the back steps through the cemetery and down Burial Hill to her home, the only one on Redd's Pond, if you didn't count the lawn and ducks separating the two.

The Miles house, if any, would have the combined smells of summer and winter. Scotty pulled her confused nose out of Mrs. Miles' basil and rosemary garden where she stooped to smell. Quivering nostrils brought her to her feet as she repeated, "Fried scallops."

Her mouth salivating, she knocked at the wooden screen door that reverberated because it was unlatched. Popping in, she saw Mrs. Miles busy as usual at the stove, breadcrumbs and egg on her fingers.

"Doing my cooking early, Scotty. It'll be too hot later. Wanta try one?"

Scotty's eyes buggy, she nodded in silent gratitude. Coming closer to Mrs. Miles, she opened her mouth and Mrs. Miles placed a wee breaded scallop on her tongue. While she chewed, elongating her mouth so as to make the eating last, she listened to Mrs. Miles.

"Barb ran to the store for more breadcrumbs. I never run out but I did this once. She'll be back soon."

As soon as she said it, Barb returned, slamming the screen door, breadcrumbs in hand.

"Hey, Scotty, what's up?"

"Just trying to get my fill of you before I go, and your mum's keeping me filled, guess that's a double memory."

"When's your dad coming?" asked Mrs. Miles. She had finished and was rinsing her hands.

"Mum said he's coming in on June 27th, right when we get back from Winnipesaukee with my Grams. Hope we get it together by then. We're supposed to leave July 1st. Dad expects us to be all ready. My aunt's keeping our furniture, since we'll be living in a trailer to start."

"I don't envy your mum. Packing is rough."

"Well, I don't think she's been overwhelmed yet." Scotty left it at that. "Eric and Mum work at night. I work in the morning. Mum leaves me a note. I do so much and then I'm off. Gotta see my buddies before I go, gotta make some memories."

Barb put her arm around Scotty's shoulder, a tear came from nowhere exposing her feelings.

"May I have just one more, Mrs. Miles? Don't think they have scallops in California. My Dad writes back about abalone. He sent me a pretty ring, but I'll miss my purple mussels all together at Graves Boat Yard. They look like Neptune's Court, kingly purple. Maybe I'll take a whole suitcase of purple mussels. I don't have much to take, after all."

Mrs. Miles held a plate up to Scotty now, her hands clean and apron spotless. "Help yourself" She just knew how to cook: the art of mixing without mess, adept fingerplay, timely seasoning, what a master of the kitchen!

Scotty took two sucks on the fish then chewed slowly as before.

"Mum, can I go out with Scotty?"

"Did you do your chores, your room?"

Bea smiled and nodded.

"Good thing we don't have to move," said Mrs. Miles and she waved good-bye to them.

They were quiet for only seconds outside the house and then both said in unison "Black Bird Pond. Jinx," they giggled.

"We do think alike, and we both like to be led, but you're worse than me. You'd stay around your mum's cookie dough all day if I didn't get you, and I have no reason to my wandering."

They both looked down at their sneaks. Bea's sneaks, the weathered navy of summer worn with spots at the big toes, but no holes. The sneaks represented her even temper, certainly not Scotty's. Even except for the diseased seizures that altered her personality at times and intrigued Scotty since Barb had found the righteous weakness of Scotty's ego through seizure.

"Are we simpletons, you and I? Barb, let me look at you."

Bea knew enough not to talk now when Scotty got started with this inane conversation. She'd just weather it out like the winds of a hurricane. Complying, Bea resignedly turned toward Scotty. So much unidentified character hid behind the lanky Bea with her black bob to the ear and her tree brown eyes of the constant and the grounded. While Scotty's chestnut hair to the chin was more flamboyant, as were the blue eyes, sometimes like a kaleidoscope with green and yellow. They wore neat khaki Bermuda shorts and faded pastel blouses, buttoned down and worn loosely over their shorts.

The blouses were ironed by young girls who practiced on play clothes and who made wrinkles by accident in ironing unsmoothed patches. They would then try to unwrinkle them by ironing anew with wet rags placed on top of the wrinkle. A diligent time, the fifties, defined with labor; that connected, repetitive life that slowed man to appreciation.

"Are you getting excited about the search?" asked Bea, feeling Scotty had regained her senses.

"Yes and no, because it is the end for me even if we do find the loot. We're moving no matter what. We're moving West no matter what."

They marched past the street side of Redd's Pond and looked at the array of lobster traps.

"It's different out there, you know. There are orange crates instead of lobster traps," Scotty lectured.

The girls walked in cadence. They looked rather uniform except for Scotty's hair being a bit longer and flapping some. As they walked around the corner nearing Gingerbread Hill, they passed the steep and narrow entrance to the Paine house.

"You know, I'll miss trying to get up that hill in the icy snow with Mum. Each time we'd slip down on the ice, the car like a sled on chains, my heart would leap as we'd near the top of the hill again, Mum gunning the motor, just short of the top; we'd slide down again, never knowing for sure if we'd get home with the car."

"Nature gives us questions here, keeps us wondering. My Dad writes back in California, the sun always shines, the palms sway but don't droop. The raging sea excites me more than the speed of the cars on the freeways there."

Barb looked at Scotty, "Isn't it funny; I don't see anything different here. It doesn't impress me. It's just there, like the chestnuts in the fall and the dogwood in the spring. That's just how it is. I think I'm part donkey; don't get excited about things like you. But you're right about the cookie dough, sure have a hankering for that."

They stood looking at the street sign to Gingerbread Hill, a steep hill; they waited a few minutes before their climb.

"Think Snappy Tom's still around?" Barb pointed to his dog house.

"Hard to say, I know the Crabapple's there. Gosh isn't it amazing how they live forever in this town? Those prissy bigots, starched up with gossip and cantankerous spirit. They sure live a long time."

"Where's Neil these days?" Bea said as they started their climb. "Haven't seen him since the picnic."

"Well, his dad takes him to work most days in the summer. Learning the bank business early, I suppose. But I think he'll be home Friday. Said something about going to Maine for the weekend to their cottage. I'm going to try and see him Friday. Tomorrow, I'm seeing Grampy Graves, my old buddy."

"He really dotes on you, doesn't he?" asked Barb.

"Well, I don't know who dotes on whom. Gosh, I like him."

They passed Snappy's house but no Snappy and no Crabapple.

"Maybe, they're on vacation," said Bea.

And then the deep blue-black waters of Black Bird Pond reflected the sky before them while they gazed for a grassy mound to continue their talk. A Gremlin's cottage sat to their left. They pounced on the soft verdant grass.

"That cottage was made for Hansel and Gretel or elves, don't you think, Bea?"

"Well, it looks like a Swiss chalet to me. The little old couple have an accent," mused Barb.

As they sat on the grass, their fawn-colored legs bent to opposite sides, they both held themselves up by one hand, palm to the grass. With her free hand, each girl pulled grass and threw it into the pond.

"Ever fished here, Bea?"

"No, can't say I have. Only see mosquitoes and flying bugs hover over this water but never see a fish flash."

"Well, I never thought to fish here," returned Scotty. "The pond always seemed like a big bird bath. I like to watch the black birds here. Wonder why they come? And I never saw any pond water so dark like blue-black and the shimmering of those bird feathers. 'Ataraxia', ever heard that word, Bea?"

"Nope, remember, I'm the dumb donkey."

"Well, Neil told me about that word one day. Peace of mind it means, kinda like what we have here with these quiet waters, without fishing. It kinda slows you down, this water, this still fount."

They sat without talking for a long while.

"What does still water runs deep mean?" said Bea.

"Don't know," returned Scotty.

"The ocean can be still, and it has very deep water," whispered Bea.

"Maybe it'll mean something to us later, lots of things I don't get, not as bad as Gary and fractions, but I got a feeling that's why the adults make us memorize all kinds of things. 'Cause if we repeat them often enough and live long enough, they'll mean something sometime. Just a hunch.

"Now what's happening on June 28th, Barb Bea?"

"The search," Bea returned definitively.

"What time do Johnny and Jake leave for their supplies?" Scotty looked to the pond while she spoke.

"Around 9 or 10 depending on low tide," Barb also looked to the pond while she spoke. "Don't forget to remind Neil to check the tide table in the paper. If I don't hear from you, I'll be sitting on the mussels. Those a way back by the Boat Yard."

"On that old driftwood?"

"Yup."

"Should I bring a flashlight?"

"Good idea, Bea; you're a smart cookie."

"Real cute, Scotty. You got cookie on your brain but there won't be any that day and no cream soda. Treasure hunting is work." Bea's brown eyes looked like Red's eyes when he saw Grampy's pheasant, calculating and direct.

Sauntering home, Scotty took last notice of the fairy-like chalet near the pond whose roof with its clouds mirrored a childhood of whimsy yet solid in the memory of heroes, ambassadors to the Revolution and progenitors of that idealism which was characteristically an American hallmark.

Laconic to their leave, Scotty took the steep road home, the one up the snowy hill, she had just recounted to Bea. When she reached the top at the rear of the house, the bodies of the ceramic lions, (not their manes) held a large note to the ground. Scotty tore the message as she removed it. In two pieces, she read: "How did you like the salvia? Mr. Peach gave them to me. Sorry I didn't get there today; my aunt had some work for me. See you Thursday. Gary."

CHAPTER FOURTEEN

The following day, Scotty decided to visit her old friend, Grampy Graves. Limiting her time with Gary to Tuesday, Thursday, and Friday, Scotty hoped to help them adapt to the impending separation.

"He's a regular kid now," she said to herself. "No more cat heaving, a regular kid. Folks like him or feel sorry for him. Well, they feel something about him, not like when he was a street urchin and they paid no attention." She stopped her inner monologue while she knocked softly on the door to the Graves' Residence (that's what it said on the screen door).

"Anybody home?" Scotty chanted, "Anybody home?"

"Well, if it isn't my Scotty!"

"I'm Grammy's too."

"Will you be mine today, since she's playing bridge?"

"Suppose so, after all, you are my number one sweetheart when Pop's gone."

Graves beamed, then stuttered to change the subject, for he became embarrassed with loving attention. He quipped, "Never did like bridge. When I stopped law, I stopped thinking all the time. Feel a lot better, too. Feel, that's the key word, not everybody feels like you and me. I don't mean attitudes; I mean intuitions."

Scotty's eyes blinked; she sat on the hassock near him, elbows resting on bent knees, cradling her cheeks in cupped hands.

"Some feelings come from our genes and some, I suspect we learn."

Like a mime, her lips lowered, the mask of tragedy, while her mentor took his turn. A fruit bowl sat on the butterfly table near him. A knife lay to one side and a number of fruit plates to the other. At the top, a Rome Beauty with whitish dots surprised her.

"Apples, this time of summer, must have cost you something, that one."

"Yes, well I always must have one apple in my fruit bowl. It's a reminder of hidden beauty and nature's mysterious wonders."

"Guess it's a beauty all right, but that nectarine's got more flavor and looks quite rosy for this time of season."

"Right you are, girl, but the apple carries a sort of mystery from Biblical times."

"Well, I know about that, Adam's fall you mean."

"Do you know, Grushenka?"

"Oh, my goodness, I thought we had done with that. I'm not that nasty character from Dostoyevsky's novel."

"She recovered, you know. She found her way around the nasty part of her life."

"I like sitting with you. You're something like Neil, you know, but you tell stories. Go on, go on, I'll miss you and your stories, my sweetheart." Scotty talked a lingo akin to baby talk when using endearments.

Renoir in his recliner, a pouch of a tummy gave him clout but his character emanated from the perennial sunshine in those eyes that rested on forever rosy cheeks. His reading glasses only magnified his soul.

He took up the apple, "Life is a lot like this apple." He held the apple between the stem and sepal with his middle finger and thumb. Then he pushed the apple around with his index finger, while Scotty marveled at the flawless fruit.

"Some people just spin around like this apple. They stay alive with its shine while others at their prime will cut into the fruit, eager for its essence. Shall we begin?"

"Can I eat some?"

"Don't be like the rest of the movers and shakers. Don't you want to know what's inside?"

"Apple fruit."

"But there's something special in the center," his warm eyes taunted.

"Okay, okay, let's see."

Graves took the fruit plate in hand and placed it on his knees, and then holding the apple just over the plate he took up the paring knife with the art of a master chef and began circling the Rome Beauty with the razor-sharp edge, exploring the entire apple as if to choose a beginning. Then, randomly, the knife almost on its own, bore superficially into the apple, beginning to separate the peel in its course to the inner fruit. Cutting at a languid pace, Graves slowed the process to the inevitable magic.

At first, Scotty looked casual about the common process of peeling the apple, but the surgical process of Graves' adept hand maneuvering through the Rome Beauty slowed down her sensual experience of the fruit. He stopped briefly to expose the fruit and lay back the peel which spiraled and coiled like a snake.

"Why, it's bruised," she said, "But it looked so beautiful from the outside."

"Not much of a spot, we'll cut around it," he winked, "And cut it out when we're finished with the peel. Now," he said as he placed the skin to the side of the plate, reminiscent of a science lecture, "Here is the naked fruit and one small bad spot right here. Well now, in life, to my way of thinking, we need the timeliness of the fruit. We need to appreciate the beauty of its exterior but not wait too long before we cut in. If we had waited too long in this case, the small bad spot would have consumed the rest of the apple. My darling Grushenka bit the rotten spot early in life. She was a bit clumsy in the cutting process. She knew to go in but could have ruined the fruit or butchered the spot cutting out the good with the bad. But the bad part, as fate would have it, gave her the experience of refining her cutting skills and so she went on to cut and eat, removing the seeds and ravishing the pulp."

Scotty wanted to stop her mentor when he mentioned Grushenka's name again. But she drooled for the fruit now and his story of life. Graves could see her eager eyes. He began to cut into the fruit. The bad spot dropped into a nearby basket. He cut a piece and gave it to her.

"It's sweet," she smiled, "out of season and sweet."

"I know my apples, don't I?" he winked again.

As Scotty chewed in slow motion, she looked at a second piece of the porous juicy bit, one drop of apple juice lined her left hand. She licked the drop, savoring and relishing the questionable portion.

"That's how I want you to experience life, slowly and with perception."

"You don't have an evil bone in your body, my dear old owl, you're all wisdom and giving."

"That's not so," he dimmed his eyes to the fruit plate and knife. "Though I've never sought ugliness, I became surrounded by it in my divorce practice. For people can become animals when love turns to hate, and there I was right in the middle. It's something like the policeman turned criminal. I've loved and loathed my clients and Ma Graves has tolerated a lot of perniciousness in me.

"Well, getting back to our story, where were we? Oh yes, looking at life. Do it as you would with a magnifying glass, taste its juice as cider of life, feel every dimension, smell every pore. The deeper you cut, the more precision, and eat as you go." He paused, "The knowledge of good and evil."

"What?" she asked, losing his train of thought.

"When Adam and Eve ate the forbidden apple in Paradise, they realized that the knowledge of good and evil was inside of them; the sin clouded their vision and the vision of all generations. To know themselves became their toil."

She had lost him but would mull over his strange words forever.

CHAPTER FIFTEEN

"One of these days I must speak with Aunt Lucretia," Scotty blurted out next morning. She usually had clear thoughts upon awakening, but two thoughts seemed to clash this morning.

"Quiet Glory," the words popped into her head, "Just right for the apple magic." Her hand reached up the wall, fingers like a tarantula, pulled at the tack. Up she sat, swinging one leg over her bed while her left hand bent under the bed in search of her ballpoint pen.

"Quiet Glory," she repeated, "That's how I feel about Grampy's story. I feel some of the magic from the story, but there's something else. What Barb described as 'better than thou' is just a cover up for something darker in me, some eclipse down the road. But for now, dear thought, Quiet Glory will remind me of the apple story and its hidden star, my star." She touched the pen to her lips and wrote, "June 16, Grampy Graves, The Apple Story, My Quiet Glory."

"Now then, what's this popping into my head about Aunt Lue? I must visit her, maybe Monday. I don't want to say to make up for anything. After all, I didn't make her cross; it was Grammy McFinch at Easter telling her that she manipulated people. Auntie Lue is clever. Kids like me can only blush.

"But today I'll be bored, I'll help pack, sort our stuff. I want to be sad and bored today. I need to make some connection. It's something like Barb's seizures, I think, when I get sad. I need my pain until I get some conclusion. I'll make some sense out of my sorrow, about leaving this town I love."

Scotty didn't see much of her brother and mother now. Like elves, they began their work after she had gone to bed. In the morning while they slept, she did her part to ready the move. Today there was a note from Lois: "Scotty, would you pack the cooking pans. We'll need only a couple for next week. On Friday night we leave for Winnipesaukee, our time with Grammy, yippee! And your Dad comes home on the 27th. It seems like we have a lot to do, but we'll get it done. Love, Mum."

So, she did her duty, and grabbing a muffin from the toaster she cupped the crumbs and juggled out the kitchen door. She liked nothing better than to roam, but first came Gary's house, Thursday morning cultivation at 12 Orne.

Scotty's kind of kid slid her sneakers along the sidewalk, kicking at every loose rock or pebble and looking with such diligence at the path that onlookers would parrot her gait and gaze. Today only a dog followed her, but he lost interest for the spool-turned fence that reeked of another canine friend. Before she knew it, she had walked into Gary's hedge, overgrown onto the walk, that circled to the back yard.

"Oh, my gosh," she said, "We'll need to clip this next."

"Talking to yourself again," said Gary, looking rather cheerful as he stooped to make a border around his salvia with purple mussels.

"Golly, you're artistic. I wanted to take a suitcase of those lovelies with me to California, just to look at. Never thought they could make such a pretty decoration. Are you sure you're not working for Mr. Peach now?"

"Nope, but he offered me a job. Can't eat geraniums like Shube's day old subs. I'd work a day for a soggy submarine sandwich. But Mr. Peach, what a swell guy, he spends time with me, helps me understand a lot about growing things. Ain't it funny how some days you hate people and some days, you love them. I mean, I always thought of Mr. Peach as an ornery old goat. He always looked funny at me, like I was weird or bad. And well, when I came around his shop, he'd start to sweep like he didn't want to look at me, like I was dirt. Maybe he knows about my dad."

"He's just the serious type, a real banker with his pots. You know, making money with this business isn't the easiest job in the world. Some folks don't take flowers seriously."

"My Mum's a flower," he stopped his border to stare at one salvia. "She's more than a flower; she's the inspiration behind this garden."

"You know, Gary Doliber, you never fooled with flowers before. How do you suppose you've made such a beautiful garden? She's the flower and the spirit in you now. Hey, hey what's that on your cheek? You're a former cat mugger after all," and she stooped down to put her arm around him.

Gary grimaced to the point of rainfall, but it all turned to a maudlin grin. "Bet I fooled ya."

"Nope, see right through you, Gary Doliber."

He threw his arm around her shoulder, and they might have wound up on the ground but holding firm, they stood together bracing each other from a fall.

"You know, I never paid any attention to that hedge until I just about fell in it. Got some clippers and I'll give it a once over."

Gary's clear watery blue eyes shone with good nature. The cropped head gave recognition to a face softened with tenderness. His compliance took only the few seconds of understanding her command. He would do anything at her command. And Scotty, not mindful of her power, delighted only in her ability to put a smile where, at one time, there had been only bitterness.

"Gary, you know you don't look like a ragamuffin anymore."

"Nope, my auntie takes care of me. I get my older cousins' clothes and that. Not much room there but we're happy as clams smack dab on top of each other."

"Thanks," Scotty took the clippers. She kept talking as she scissored away. "Now I'll be able to see my cement cracks so I won't break my mother's back." She chanted, "Step on a crack and you'll break your mother's back."

"Are you off to Shube's?" Scotty collected her clippings and put them in an aluminum barrel that Gary had brought with the clippers.

"Yup."

"Well then, I'll put the clippers and barrel away."

"Okay, boss," he saluted her.

Scotty's face turned to a feigned pout in response to his respect.

"No, seriously Gary, we're not going on forever like this. On June twenty seventh, my Dad gets back from Cal and we leave for the West, July first."

Gary looked her in the eyes, "I'm tough and not legless like my Pop. I'll be okay," he said definitively.

"I'm not sure when I'll get back, but I'll write. Your Aunt's on Pleasant Street, right?"

"Right."

"All right, then."

They hugged, one of those hearty embraces, complete with patting each other on the back, a clean-cut loyal sign of friendship, then they departed. She watched him swing his arms down the road with firm resignation and she remembered what Gary had said about Mr. Peach, love, and hate.

"And to think I thought he was a dolt."

Scotty would do anything for anybody, but when it came time for fun there was no one as personable as herself. A loner, one might say, but not a recluse nor lonely. Wandering the streets, she became part of the history she had memorized, part of the town she walked.

"My turn," she said leaving Orne Street headed for Union Street. I'd like to see the Lafayette House once more." And then as if paraphrasing from a book she sputtered, "The Lafayette House was cut apart to accommodate Lafayette's carriage in a visit to Marblehead in 1824. They say he visited once every 4 years after the Revolution," she blinked her eyes as she stood facing the house, "Now, wouldn't I make a good tour guide?"

And then, as if instinct took over, she bellowed, "I'm going to Castle Rock!" Anyone watching would have thought her touched, maybe by the spirit of supposed witches, but Scotty felt in her final days a sense of freedom, an exhilaration that comes sometimes before doom.

"But how can I get there? Maybe with Eric's bike and time enough." Reversing her course, she walked back the way she came, passing the Brigg House on Orne. The story of Moll Picher, the 19th century fortune teller, popped into her mind. Then climbing the back way to Old Burial Hill, Scotty realized, "I've never found the stone of General John Glover, whose men help ferry George Washington over the Delaware. And who was that other patriot buried here?" she thought rubbing her chin, "It was James Mugford, Jr. who gave his life in the first battle on sea when he took the ship Hope in Boston Harbor and then was attacked and killed on his ship, the Franklin, in Marblehead waters.

"What an idiot. I'm rattling on like a magpie. Who cares? I'm happy." Frivolously, she swung her head around to look out of the cemetery. There in the distance the lighthouse marked Marblehead Neck, peninsula of mansions and the merchant princes of this day.

Scotty arrived home to a general clutter of newspaper and boxes. A vacuous feeling overwhelmed her as she stepped over strewn bric-a-brac, half- heartedly packed. The house so still yet replete with unwelcome feeling.

"Why does it always seem like this house is more of a mortuary than the cemetery?"

In the abject quiet, Scotty knew no one was home, so she never called out but tiptoed to the front glassed-in porch that overlooked the pond. That's where the bike would be.

Distracted by the view onto Redd's Pond and Old Burial Hill in the background she commented, "Six hundred soldiers are buried there from the Revolution, but it's not sad like this house. The water, the grass, the elms, the ducks—they're so alive with the courage and idealism of those first heroes of our Country. They're not outside; they're inside of me."

Looking inside again, she spied the bike. Scotty pushed open the screen door and directed the bike down the steps. She walked the bike down the hill and with her left foot on the pedal she coasted, then swung her right leg over the seat and slowly rode until she came off the sidewalk of the Pond and onto the street. Pumping fast, her chestnut hair blew off her ears and out of her face. Scotty traversed the street a couple of times until she saw a car. The summer breeze of flight cooled her passions and after the initial speed, she slowed to a rhythmic pace. The brake pads scraped the wheel rims gently, no annoyance, for a great calm settled inside her, a great self-confidence and openness to her fate.

When Scotty crossed the Causeway to the Neck, an opulence impressed her. Large estates loomed on her left, bridged by verdant landscapes as grandiose in green as the blue sea that looked across from them. Back and forth, she looked from sea to land. The Lydia Pinkham Estate sat next to Castle Rock. Scotty wasn't sure which came first, the estate which was in fact a pink castle, or the naming of the rock. The rock itself had been there for eons.

She came close to the granite and lowered Eric's bike to the grass, for it might have fallen if left on the stand in that rocky terrain. The detail of the rocks and the expanse of their formation paralleled the delicacy of the fairylike castle, so intricate yet so vast.

Lydia Pinkham's fortune came from a pink medicine she concocted to cure women's menstrual pains. Scotty remembered her mum telling the story of that house. That story related to Lois, no doubt from Grammy McFinch, was, like all tales, taken as true.

"I better tie my sneaks. Wouldn't want to trip on that mountain." She re-tied both laces in a double knot. After a mammoth step and some pivots, she sat near a tide pool surrounded with barnacles. That view, the best visual access to the estate, disclosed its shoreline and the charming symmetry of the mansion. A swimming pool, a sun umbrella with table and chairs positioned close to the cliff that sharply dropped to the beach. Hugging her legs, she dreamed of living in the chateau which so many girls coveted for their fairy tales.

"I can never remember seeing anyone there. It's not like it's haunted, just hollow. I know that feeling."

There on the rock, time passed elusively; only the sun could register the end of day, for no schedule gave hint of change, no milkman, no mailman, no man with English hat headed home from work. Waves crashed on the lower part of the rock while the deep sea kept its tide constant.

Then something pulled her up. Scotty wanted to stay right there on the rock, but she needed to get back home. It would take an hour to pedal back, and Lois would wonder if Scotty got home late. A quick view to the front of the rock and the open sea would be enough before she left. So, Scotty jumped and tiptoed over ledges and tide pools, carefully looking to the stones for certain safety. Odd, she thought, there were no tourists on the rock today, for it was a favorite site for visitors to the Neck. She took a last breathtaking gaze at the sea.

Looking ahead she gasped, "It's Zig!"

She caught sight of his profile as she stood up, just as he had caught sight of her those months ago when he gave her the dollar. In his innocent stare to the water, Scotty knew, after the time apart, his reason for giving her the dollar: that they were the same sort of folks, searching for something not clear to them yet.

She did not tarry on her way back home. A feeling of satiation moved her now. Eric and Lois were unruffled at her arrival. After all, dusk came late to summer. They ate, then watched television, "The Millionaire", a program about a philanthropist who gave away one million dollars each year to a worthy person. Each episode showed how the newly rich used their money.

"Imagine if Zig gave me a million dollars. Just imagine." Somehow Scotty felt he had already given her a million's worth in that one dollar.

The next morning Scotty popped up to write her one line on the calendar. "June 17. Dolt-turned-friend Gary, wonderful Marblehead: Lafayette house, Castle Rock, 600 heroes in the cemetery and one in a million, my Zig." She didn't remember even leaving the house that day. The daily routine of packing became like consuming cod liver oil, necessary but disgusting. Nullifying the move, in mind, at least.

Sitting on the rock, Scotty waited her chance to catch a glimpse of Neil. It didn't take long. He was busy packing for their cottage in Maine. Randomly, he neared the window to choose books from his desk for the trip. Waving her hands, Neil responded, trying very hard not to lose his train of thought as he walked to their meeting place. His hallmark of containment vanished as he blurted out his first words, "What you feel, I know."

"What are you talking about Neil? Don't confuse me on my last days here."

"It's not confusing, I want to take a part of you to remember. You're not the only one who can have her memories."

She nodded in surprise.

"Well, I've thought and thought. How is it we're such a team, when I'm so detailed and you just seem to stumble into things. You feel it while I know it."

"And where does Barb fit in?" Scotty mused.

"Oh, Barb, she's sensible. Has a smattering of both, fisherman wise we call it. Practical every day, even a trusty soul good for us. Of course, we're not complete, but we're on our way, in our dispositions to life I mean."

"You may be right," she sighed. I like you even though I'm not like you. And I feel a little frustrated that I can't think as hard or figure things out your way. I'm sort of mousy and sheepish, I guess."

Neil returned, "Well, I feel smug. I'd like to feel humble, but there's something inside me that says I need to think this way and there's something inside me that says I'd never like you if you were like me."

"It sounds very complicated. Can we just talk?" said Scotty.

"Of course."

"You don't seem excited to be going to Maine."

"Well, you know me. I don't get excited over places, I get excited over people, like you."

Scotty blushed and talked quickly to fan the heat. "Barb and I talked about the meeting place June 28th."

"Yes, where?"

"On that driftwood, back of the beach, nine o'clock."

"Good," he said, "I'll make sure to be sick that day. I keep banker's hours, remember."

"Oh, that's right," she said, "You go into Boston with your dad."

"That's okay, haven't had any sick leave," he winked, "I'll have a real headache on the 28th."

"So that's that," she said.

"Yup, that's that," he said, taking her hand.

She blushed again. "I wonder if I'm getting sick, I feel hot."

"No, you're just natural," He took her other hand, and looking deeply into her eyes, kissed her.

It took all her sputter and numbed Scotty for what seemed time immeasurable. "Well," she said, regaining her composure at last, "I'm going to Winnipesaukee with my family to Grammy McFinch's cottage on June 25th. So, what do you think of that?" She said it all to avoid the issue. A new emotion had awakened in her. She couldn't explain it; so, she ignored it or buried it in a hope chest she would eventually take to her wedding.

CHAPTER SIXTEEN

June 19   We all work.

L ike any major project, beginning it took some nerve. Thereafter, it could be fun to figure out where you ever found, kept, or misplaced such a menagerie of trivia. How do you box the furry play monkey on a stick from the carnival, the toy from the Crackerjack box, the coffee pot too old to use but in an aesthetic sense ready to become a planter? Then there were the magazines needing to be read, many years of "Life."

Eric busied himself in his room, a room for much business, while Lois packed memories as she wrapped the pictures on her bureau. Scotty intended to go to the basement to check on forgotten items, but first she hurried to her mother's room thinking she might have forgotten to return the picture of the two sisters. She said not a word as she looked in and saw the picture in question, face down but unwrapped for the move. Not wishing to speak to her mother but relieved to see the pictures back on the bureau, Scotty darted down to the basement.

In the basement there was only one bureau, the lonely furniture of the damp tomb-like room. A macabre sense overtook her as she neared the chest.

"Oh, yes, this sideboard was here when we rented. Uncle Jeep helped Eric move our furniture to the Hill House. We'll send for it later. Won't need it in a trailer."

Though the chest seemed strange to her because it didn't belong to the family, she wanted to open the drawers.

Neurotically she darted to the mahogany lowboy and opened the top drawer.

"Oh, my goodness! Sister Sue! I thought I had packed you." Scotty's first doll looked forlornly at her, one eye open, the other half shut as though she had been blinded. She had been half blinded when Scotty bathed the porcelain head and cloth body of Sister Sue many years back.

"Porcelain eyes have no need for submerging; I wasn't baptizing her after all," she said sadly looking at her horrible mistake. "And here's my tea set. I thought I packed my silver miniatures, but here they are."

And then she thought of her Granny again and the mystery behind her gift. The pretend and make-believe gifts always went to her.

"Oh, the tea set is not make-believe but you must use it in a make-believe way. It's not like a real tea party, like my brother and cousin had. I was always the little servant and dreamer, but then my Granny was, too. A great deal of discipline and detail went into her life. My duty gives me my dreams; a mindless routine, after all, is like roaming the streets. Space and time, that's all I've really ever needed. Wow, I can't believe I'm talking to myself again and what nonsense! Get going, Scotty!" she said, kicking herself.

June 20   The Elk's Picnic

A certain amount of boredom characterized the move; the tedium of packing, nonetheless, was not as bad as the boredom of repetitious winter and sultry summer. Nature's monotony gave vent to patriotic parades and civic picnics. Both reward and custom glowed in eager young eyes who knew winter's lugubrious gestures, of leggings on, leggings off and summer's humid drain, of languorous days and sleepless nights.

The Elk's Picnic rewarded both their imaginations and appetites. Scotty dreamed many times in the winter of finding riches in The Coin Dig at the picnic. A sand box filled with pennies, nickels, and dimes allowed rummaging on the mark of "go" for these kids.

"Get on your mark, get set, go!" Like puppies, they dug with alacrity, they dug with greed. They threw sand tumultuously to expose nickels and copper pennies. Barb, Scotty and Neil stormed the sands together.

"Oh, look at these pennies, all of them! They look more expensive when they're new, don't they?" said Scotty.

"Well, I got a handful of nickels," said Barb, "That suits me just fine."

"Let's see it, Neil," Scotty elbowed him. He held his fists tightly, playfully, as each tried to pry them open.

"Dimes!" they screeched.

"It figures," said Barb, "Neil has the only dimes, silver dimes."

"I always thought nickels cost more than dimes," said Scotty, "They're bigger, after all."

"Well, I always thought the biggest price, the best value," said Neil.

"Oh, I don't think that" said Bea raising her voice as they meandered near the three-legged race, where the crowd grew loud with bonhomie. "My mum's cookies are a perfect example, can't put a price on my mum's cookies. They're free to us with heavenly value."

"You mean heavenly good," said Neil.

"Yupper," said Bea.

"Well, I say the more you have, the more wealthy you are, the more the merrier." He threw an arm around each girl's shoulders. "My happy harem."

"I want a snow cone," said Barb.

Neil's attention turned toward the races, "That looks hard."

"You mean the three-legged race?"

He nodded, his arms around them in close camaraderie,

"Eric does it every year with Peter Reed, and wins too, because Pete is light, runs with his hands like a crab," she grinned sardonically.

"I want a snow cone."

"O.K., there they are next to the cotton candy," said Scotty.

"How could anyone eat that angel hair," Neil jeered.

"I don't like cotton candy either, that much, but it's all for a dollar. Crab roll and lobster tail, hot dogs and tonic, snow cones and cake, all for a dollar."

"Are you selling or do you want some?"

"I want a snow cone," she said emphatically.

"All right, then," and dropping his arms gently, he took off toward the snow cones.

When he returned, Bea smiled with contentment as she slurped the refreshing cherry syrup, sucking a gulp of ice then chomping on it.

"You're a dear," she blurted, like a cow chewing cud.

"Now I want something," said Scotty.

"Yesss," said Neil, "As long as I'm being cavalier, what'll it be, my sweet?"

"Root beer," she said.

"Well, then my scholar, I'll get you a frank."

"Relish only," she said, and Neil beamed with hubris and satisfaction.

So, they all smiled at each other, in line, for Bea was in line again, this time for a cake. She hollered, "Want one?"

They both nodded, a synchronized "yes".

Together again, Scotty noticed Neil's dad. "You mean your illustrious dad is actually going to mingle with us?"

"Yup, he's right over there, Mister Interest Rate himself passing out pens with the Boston Bank logo on them."

"What's it like living with a banker, Neil?"

They sat on a haystack watching Bea who had gobbled her cake and was in line again for penny candy.

"Miss Piggy," he glanced at Bea. "It's like living with Poor Richard's Almanac, a penny saved is a penny earned. Frankly, I don't know where I came from, I'm not a bit serious about finance. I understand it but I'm not interested in it. Oh, I guess I'm just fated to it, a banker but never a miser, too much passion for a Scrooge . . . Not bad, this frankfurter."

"I like relish on mine, too," she said as she watched him chew, then take a big sip of grape tonic.

Neil usually drank root beer, and she drank the grape tonic. They were switching today. "Golly, I never think about my future, I just live," said Scotty, "Live and wonder, and bellow out my happiness. In church, I mean, I sing all the Latin hymns with vigor, but, according to my cousin Kate, I sing all the wrong words. Oh, well, I may not be bright, but I've got spirit."

"You certainly are bright," said Neil, sensing a little sadness in Scotty's voice. "Just as bright as your going-away present. Remember, I never gave it to you at our picnic, I wanted to wait. I've been carrying it around waiting for the right moment." Neil pulled out a purple velvet bag held closed by a golden cord.

"It looks like a jacks bag."

"Two more guesses, no feels," he said.

"Fish hooks?"

"Don't know if you'll be fishing out there; one more guess."

"Oh, I give up."

"It's a . . . It's a . . ." she pulled the bag out of his hand in frustration, yet quite gently. "It's a bronze Marblehead coin! With the fisherman on it! Gosh, it's nice, Neil. Looks like a prize for a contest." She puckered her lips in thought and said, "I'll carry it always, it'll be my good luck charm." The pucker turned to a pout as she hugged him warmly. "You're my best buddy, Neil, you and Bea."

Bea returned with root beer barrels; hand open for her friends to choose their candy. The cellophane rustled.

Scotty wasn't paying any attention to the root beer barrel; she couldn't take her moist eyes off the coin. She rubbed it and held it to the light, the golden sunset glistened behind the fisherman.

"Well, I'm not going to give you my gift now," said Bea. "It's like opening your birthday present early. You'll get it the last day, right before you go."

"That's all right," Scotty hugged Bea, "I didn't expect anything."

And then changing the subject, she said, "You smell like root beer, Bea."

"You too, and you, Neil Montague, have a purple tongue."

Neil nodded in donkey submission. And they meandered on aimlessly, absorbing the radiance and good cheer of the crowd.

Scotty rubbed her coin from time to time, a habit she would have for many years. She would rub the coin when anxious or happy, when preparing for tests or when sad. The Marblehead fisherman sailing into the sunrise would sustain her until she entered another state in life when she would forget herself and the coin's source.

June 21   A Day with Aunt Lue

When she awoke next morning, Scotty popped up her usual zesty self. Then she looked at the calendar.

"Holidays, holidays, so many empty spots on my wall diary. Let's see, I've got nothing for the 18th." Her face flushed as she remembered Neil and his kiss. "It wasn't a normal Neil kiss." She thought for a moment and then she spoke as she wrote, "Neil gets passionate." Then quickly she went to the next omission, the 19th. "Oh, yes," she said, "Sister Sue and Tea Set too, I found them again." For the 20th, "Oh, that's easy, the Elk's Picnic. We pig out and Neil gives me a Marblehead coin remembrance."

"Now today, I have written Aunt Lue, but I don't think I told her I was coming," she mumbled while donning her frock. No jeans today.

She did her house jobs mindlessly and somehow found her way on the road to her destination. "Why didn't I tell her I was coming?" she mumbled, clutching the photos protected by an envelope and walking along the route familiar to her from her week's stay.

Aunt Lucretia's Garden distracted her weariness and anxiety over a confrontation that would not be her fault, yet her problem. Scotty couldn't leave for California without a sense of harmony with an Aunt who prodded the sore points of a family's personality.

"Gosh, they're pretty. Red zinnias, purple mums, and what was that other flower? It looked like a carnation but it had another name. Oh, I'll ask Aunt Lue." The green wooden frame to the screen was securely latched, so Scotty knocked. Aunt Lue greeted her in seconds, composed as always.

"Come in."

Scotty thought of the picture as she entered, comparing the slim girl in the photo with the fuller form of her aunt, who stood before her. She gazed intensely for the furtive eye of the picture, unmindful that she had not even said hello. Scotty, never overly subtle, blurted out, "I came to say goodbye, Aunt Lue."

Half alarmed by Scotty's tone, Lue put her finger to her lips and pointed to the bedroom.

"Uncle Martin is resting. Let's go to the den."

They sat in the knotty pine wall den on a burgundy plaid sofa, turning their knees toward each other. Some of the mums of the garden were on the table. Scotty felt embarrassed to see two even half smiling eyes focus on her. She hoped to see the spurious side of Aunt Lue's nature during her unexpected visit.

But she could see no deception in her aunt, nor anxiety. Uncle Martin was dying of cancer and bedridden, and Aunt Lue seemed unruffled. One would wonder if she had ever loved him, so preoccupied was she with deportment and means.

"Excuse me one moment, I'll shut Martin's door." Leaving for a time, Scotty felt relief from her suspicions. Scotty stared for a time at one knot in the pine wall and then her eyes dropped to the coffee table, where Aunt Lucretia had made a grocery list. Scotty casually glanced at the list, and then her gaze became more scrutinized. What caught her attention was a list of misspelled sundries. Scotty grinned. "Nakpins." "Hmm," she said to herself "maybe she was just writing too fast." But she didn't have a chance to read the whole list, for Aunt Lue was quickly back. Scotty fidgeted with her envelope to expose the pictures of the two sisters when Lucretia was again sitting, their knees touching, face to face. "Well Aunt Lue, I did come to say goodbye," Scotty stuttered, "but I also found this picture and I was curious to ask you about it."

Lucretia looked at the picture, her face now like a sheet, hollow with anxiety. A long pause followed and then she spoke with clear, undisturbed diction, not matching the death in her face, "I didn't want her there that night. Oh, she was an albatross and those stupid cow eyes, so content—she taunted me and I loathed her that night. What passion I was feeling for that boy! Funny, I don't even remember his name now. But it all turned to hate that night with a tag-along angel whom my mother always trusted, who was always responsible, predictable, boring, and she was sabotaging my fun, that little martyr. I hated her that day, maybe even wanted to kill her."

Scotty listened quietly but her face registered every possible feeling. Could this be her aunt? Lucretia taken aback by the forgotten picture seemed to be summoning up some understanding of a situation that originally had blinded her with rage. But it was eerie how she controlled her speech as in a trance or hypnosis. Golly, was this Aunt Lucretia? The same aunt who had made Scotty feel like a princess for days?

As she regained her calm, Lue's eyes mellowed with her mother's softness and candidly with the clearest eye pronounced, "Maybe I was jealous of your mother."

CHAPTER SEVENTEEN

June 22 and 23   All Hands on Board

Anyone who has ever packed for a grand move knows, no matter how many hours of laborious crating and wrapping, it's never over until it's over.

The motivator and instigator, Ed Paine, would soon be with them to help with the move and morale. But without his prodding, mutiny seemed the rule, for there was no rally of emotion, no family beckoning for the move, no dream house that could duplicate their perfect present dwelling. They wanted to turn back before even starting on their trip. Only Ed Paine tenaciously clung to his Midas dream of gold and wonder in the West.

"What a relief" said Scotty, making an inspection of the house to see which room most needed organizing. Peering into Eric's room, she squealed, "Gone!" She took a look under Eric's bed for the broken record, but "Cross Over the Bridge" was missing! Popping her head up again, her face flushed, Scotty felt renewed vigor. Taking two steps at a time upstairs, she went into Lois's room for a short visit. Lois sat on her bed propped with pillows, legs crossed at the ankles. The glasses she wore magnified something deep within her, a dream like translucency; something previously forgotten now glowed in her eyes.

"Is that a love letter from Pop?" Scotty asked. "Not to pry." Scotty peeked into Lois's lap playfully to see what was causing her mother's smile. "Gosh, I've never seen that picture before."

Lois held the picture of the two sisters which Scotty had recently kidnapped and then returned. Scotty's face turned sullen, so sensitive was her conscience to this unpremeditated lie.

"Lucretia's boyfriend took the shot," Lois admitted candidly. "They had been a bit too playful, and I felt compromised as a chaperone, not wanting to be there anyway. My mother made me go. She always made me go to watch my sister. But looking at this picture I don't seem ruffled. Yet you can see Lue's furtive stare. She planned to get away with something, probably already did."

"Look at me, I look like a deer stunned by a car's lights, my eyes so calm, but I was paralyzed with fear that my sister did something wrong and I would get in trouble for it."

Scotty looked at the photo, saying, "Strange, isn't it? I think Aunt Lucretia likes your paralysis. To her, you're peaceful."

"But she gets whatever she wants with her antics," said Lois.

"I'm not sure she's getting what she wants now with Uncle Martin."

After a pause, Lois's far-away look faded. "You're right; you're right. How did you get older than me? Of course, you're right. But why don't I feel you're right? Why don't I feel right?"

"Want some tea, Mum?"

"Good idea."

"Enough of this."

Goodbye, Gary

He stood there thinking, leaning on his hoe as she joined him.

"Here, Butch, it's for you, an orange crate my Dad sent from California."

Gary looked at the miniature, "So this is it?"

"This is it. I'm really going to miss you, Gary."

"Oh, yeah?" he said peevishly. "Why?"

"Well, for one thing, you taught me sometimes we love kids that we really think we hate."

"And you taught me somethin'."

"Oh, yeah?" she mocked him, playfully. "What?"

"You taught me that not all prissy girls who look prissy, are prissy."

They hugged.

"No wet ones this time," she said.

"You all done packing?"

"Well, no and yes. It seems we've been busy at it but only Pop will be the judge as to what we've accomplished. We're going away tonight, tomorrow, and coming home Sunday to pick up my father at the train station."

"Where you going now, Winnipesaukee?"

"Yep."

"Gee, must be nice to swim in a real lake. Never saw a lake. What's it like?"

"Something like Black Bird Pond, but bigger. We swim off of a wharf. The water's clear. I get so excited to go to the lake. Funny, we live by water, but it's different at the lake."

"At night when the moon's so bright, my Grams tells stories about how they used to skinny dip as kids, and then we hear all her tales about Halloween with the horse manure in buckets over the doors, how they'd pull it down on the candy seekers as pranks."

"Why, once my Grammy threw a ketchup bottle at my Grampy when he got jealous. He thought he'd been killed 'cause the bottle broke, dripping ketchup all over him. He thought it was blood."

"And we play cards. Gin Rummy mostly, and Parcheesi. We listen to the crickets on the screened porch and we count our mosquito bites for biggest and most. Got one right on my belly button once and one on my ear lobe. And they have a clubhouse where my Grams rents the cottage. We can play ping pong there and throw horse shoes. Oh, there's archery too."

"Can I come?"

"To the lake?"

"Gary, I never heard you ask for anything. Sounds good to hear you want something besides Shube's Market."

"After this time, won't be going to the lake for a long while, nope, not for a long while."

Scotty gave Gary a final hug and briskly walked home. It wouldn't hit her for years how quickly we give up those loving moments that truly mean something to us and become us.

In her room, she decided to write this evening on the calendar since she wouldn't be home tomorrow.

"Two sisters longing to be each other" and on this day she wrote, "Two friends, Gary and Scotty, become each other."

June 25-26   Lake Winnipesaukee

"Eighty bottles of beer on the wall, eighty bottles of beer," Scotty sang.

"Not that one, Moose," Eric sat in the front seat of the car with Lois.

"Maybe you best be quiet for a while, Scotty," said Lois, "so that the dramamine can take hold. Don't want you to get too excited now and be sick. There will be lots of curves on this trip, maybe even a nap might save your equilibrium."

"Okay," Scotty looked around the Buick; at least she had the back seat to herself. It wouldn't be that way when they traveled westbound. Eric would sit next to her then. Oh, they might play cards but what if he lost? She remembered him throwing a deck of cards at her once. He scared her. After all, he was bigger than she and when he had a tantrum he looked twice as big. Scotty didn't like to fight. She just liked being. Guess I'm like Mum, she thought, there's something else also. Something else.

"Something else in me," she whispered as she fell asleep, mesmerized by the treetops that meshed together as they neared the lake.

Their time at the lake could not be calculated nor remembered as vacation, for the anticipated move West shadowed pleasure, and anxiety took joy's place. The excitement of new nature, the lake reflection of clouds in clear waters, log cottage, the evergreens, the crickets, they were fireflies of past memories.

June 27   Ed Paine comes home

He walked a regular beat down Pond Street. An ordinary man of the town on his way somewhere. The hot June afternoon saw him dressed in a plaid cotton shirt, sleeves rolled up, suspenders showing because his jacket was draped from one shoulder onto his brown trousers. A young man, no doubt, because of his slim body and face without wrinkles. The hair around his head cropped short, longer hairs parted down the center, bobbing back and forth from the wind of his stride. Exposing the man's furrowed brow, the hair drawn back this time with the man's hand, thick and discolored around the nails. He was concentrating or angry, it was hard to tell from the serious nature of his facial expressions.

"It's Dad!" Scotty pointed to the man on the street with his back to them as they neared their destination.

"It can't be your dad. He's due in much later."

Eric kept his nose in a sailing manual.

"It looks like Dad," Scotty's enthusiasm waned in doubt. Scotty turned her head to see the face of the man they passed. "Mum, Mum it is Dad! He's waving!"

Lois looked in the rearview mirror and gasped, "Oh my goodness, he must be early. It is Ed!"

Eric put down the book, being convinced something was happening and when the car stopped, the kids hopped out to greet their father.

Scotty grabbed his waistline and hugged him for seconds before she looked up into his face, "Daddy, you're really home!"

Eric grabbed him around the shoulders in a manly fashion.

Lois exclaimed, "Ed darling, I'm so sorry. We were going to get you at the bus station. Did you come in early?"

She kissed him on the side of the cheek as the children made room for her to reach his cheek.

"Not a sailor's welcome home," he chided, "but it'll do." He reached one arm around Eric, the other around Lois, as Scotty clung to his waist and her mother's with alternating hands.

"You're going to love the trip cross country and we'll go through the Grand Canyon. It's wonderful out there. Those sunsets on the water take your breath away." He sounded excited.

"Dad," said Eric, "you'd think you discovered the West."

"Well, I did," he said, "as you will, soon."

The "soon" scared Lois; she wasn't ready for the move.

"Well, we best get home," Lois said in a cold sweat. "Ed must be exhausted from that long ride. I'll drive, Ed. You'll have enough of it crossing the country. I'm not sure I'll be able to cope with those highways and pikes." So, Eric got in the back seat and Ed took the passenger's seat.

"It's a pity sonny here doesn't drive yet," Ed threw his hand in the back seat to clip Eric's head playfully.

"Dad, they let kids drive on farms in parts of Ohio. Maybe, maybe?"

"Maybe not Eric. There'll be time enough for you to drive in California. We'll make it in a week. I use NoDoz, if you'll just keep talking. Last time I drove alone and saw the Eiffel Tower and pink elephants on the road. I'd rather be awake with my dreams. The Mojave Desert is a mirage during the day, like a distant lake of sand, and the nights are scenes with scads of ants bearing flashlights on their backs, tunnel vision, down mountain cliffs."

"My husband, the poet," said Lois soothed in spirit by his Western visions. But anxiety returned to her when they climbed the hill and stopped in front of the ceramic lions.

Ed jumped out and stood facing the pond; comparison now made him doubt the total Western mystique. A stark feeling from the memory of California grandeur hit him as he looked at comparable beauty, perhaps more glorious in scale and intimacy. He registered his feelings quietly for the time. The family knew his feelings. There was no need to elaborate on them.

But a different anxiety hit him walking into the house. He eyed with depression the strewn newspapers and half packed boxes in the kitchen. "Oh, my God," he said, "I thought you'd be ready." He slumped into a chair exhausted from his trip.

The family looked with shame to the floor. It was a crime not easily defined; a sin not easily forgiven. He looked at them reproachfully. "Why?" he said, "Why? We're moving July first."

CHAPTER EIGHTEEN

June 28   The Search of Brown Island

"Winnipesaukee. Muddled feeling, Dad comes home without fanfare. I'm shivering in my boots about the move." The calendar notes for this morning were different from Scotty's previous serendipitous ones. Scotty was torn with emotions as she hastily dressed to meet her friends.

The day of the search of Brown's Island carried an ominous air. A summer rain wet the beach and sent hovering mist to enchant and taunt the island with the mystery of lost treasure and ghostly Victoria Snow, victim maiden, who presided somewhere in the house overlooking the legacy of wealth and wonder. Seagulls' cry and boat bell sounded the background music of macabre quest.

Neil and Bea waited for Scotty on their driftwood, as planned. Johnny and Jake had left for the flatlands, grocery shopping. As Johnny echoed his last bark, the treasure hunters harkened to the sounds of the fading protector of the island and awaited their late accomplice.

"What's keeping her?"

"A bit edgy, aren't we, Bea?" Neil enjoyed the lull between leaps. "I want to remember these royal mussels and my friends, God bless them, before Harvard and the eventual vault."

"My gosh, it's not like Scotty to be late, she's never late." Bea bit her fingernails, usually an unnoticed fault. Back at the Paine house, Scotty fumbled with Eric's bike.

"Why did I borrow this biker Because you're late Scotty, you're really late," she taunted herself. Descending the hill, she felt her towel slipping from her neck. Down her back it slipped, into the bicycle spokes where it lodged, making the bike wheels lock and stop dead in its tracks.

"Oh, now, look what I've done. Why, oh, why didn't I put the towel into the bicycle pouch! Because I was late and now, I'm never going to get there, and they'll leave without me." Then, from her hard seat on the sidewalk, she remembered and exclaimed, "I've forgotten my sneaks. What a dummy I am." The grease stained her legs from her fitful fight with the bike spoke to give up the towel. Her adrenalin pumping, Scotty forcefully picked up the bike and carried it for several steps until she rested and resuming this labor she made her way to the beach with the speed of a tortoise. At last, the lonely treasure seeker reached the opening to the beach and viewed Brown's Island.

"Oh drat! They left without me. Confound you, bike!"

Scotty didn't worry about the bike now as she let it drop on a sandy part of the beach, between the mussels. "They left without me." She tore off onto the choppy rocks that paved the driveway. The rocks cut her feet. Blood and tears smarted her feelings as she jumped from one rock to the next, trying to avoid the sharp edges and land on the smooth stones until she had reached the beach at the island's edge. Once on land, Scotty ran to the house, appeased slightly by the cool soft sand under her tender feet.

"Crap, Scotty, what took you?"

Neil sat on the porch ledge of the old house, one leg dangling over the railing. Bea sat on the steps.

"Please, I can't talk about it now. Did you go in?"

"Without you?" they said in unison, their voices heeding her trauma.

Calmed by her presence now, Neil said, "We have exactly ten minutes."

"How do you figure?" said Bea.

"I've timed those two before. Jake and Johnny take about one hour for their shopping, give or take a little. In which case, they should be here about ten." Neil looked at his watch and then stared into their eyes, first into Bea's and then into Scotty's, as if concentrating, "It's nine thirty. It will take us 20 minutes to cross the rocks again with Scotty's bare feet." He said this without judgment. "We can't be seen on the path. In five minutes, we can be in my back yard. No time for thinking, follow me."

Scotty was the first to comply, feeling so guilty about her tardiness. What a scene, they looked like a bunch of ragamuffins, especially shoeless Scotty, so disheveled from her flight. Bea poked along behind; it seemed she was more interested in the rules of the hunt than in the treasure.

Neil took charge. Like a troop master, he led his following into the house.

The door, oddly enough, was stuck but unlocked. They opened the door and noticed a wooden floor, a wood Scotty had not seen before, imported no doubt, from the West Indies. A staircase dusted with cobwebs loomed before them. Neil tiptoed up the steps as if not to disturb anyone. Scotty looked ahead of her now and Bea looked at Scotty, keeping track of their leader and his ghostly manner.

She had done it a million times in her dreams. Would Zig be there with jeweled candy? Was it still a dream? The floor creaked at the top. The last step for each sounded their entrance to the second floor. At a quick glance, there appeared to be four rooms. Neil seemed to be by himself as he explored, or maybe he just felt confident that the girls were right behind him and there would be no time for talk. Scotty felt like an intruder and carefully handled nothing in a haunting courtesy, while Neil touched old books by tapping and blowing dust aside to view titles.

"Boswell, Bacon, Shakespeare," he whispered with scratchy throat. The dust muffled his voice, already disguised by beginning fright. A canopy bed, covered to the floor with decrepit sheets laced at the top with mouse droppings stood in the first bedroom.

Bea's brown eyes looked like saucers as she gazed at the canopy and then at a chandelier, whose crystal prisms must have bedazzled the occupant of that feather bed at one time, but now only echoed the cloudy past. They looked at each other in macabre silence, as a pepper grey mouse scurried from under the bed in a room down the hall. Their eyes still gazing at the door, Scotty's white feet and frock added to the atmosphere and nostalgia of the ancient maiden, Victoria Snow. Neil took the lead again after their brief pause. He walked with determination into the hall, or perhaps recall led him on. He eyed his watch—four minutes had passed.

"We have six minutes left," he cautioned as they crept into the next bedroom. They noticed the walls lined with bookcases, an unpretentious double bed centered the room, with a candle laden side table.

"My kind of room," whispered Neil facing them as they circled the bed. The adventurers were warming up to this mysterious, yet fearful exploration.

"No turds," Bea pointed to the bed, not covered with the sheets that lined the other beds and furniture of the estate.

Scotty looked around. "It's not as dusty, either. You don't suppose someone is living here, do you?"

Neil wanted to stay and read all the book titles, but he beckoned them on with his finger, realizing his role as guide. Perhaps this first perfunctory meandering in the manor would help orient the treasure seekers to another more detailed search of the house.

Leaving the room for the hall once more, they trekked along, this time only looking into the other two rooms, for Neil realized the explorers had seen nothing of the downstairs. The two remaining bedrooms, plain in comparison, had no books nor canopy, but one held a cherry wood loveseat, the other a mahogany cradle.

Going downstairs, they stepped, then dusted their footprints behind them, obliterating their trail. The bottom step squeaked.

"Odd, it didn't squeak going up," said Neil in a low voice. A kitchen, living room, dining room, and parlor completed the bottom floor. Neil, Scotty, and Bea kept a steady pace now to see the whole house. A wall size hearth welcomed them into an austere kitchen, where one lonely pot hung centered in the fireplace and a lone row of black brick circled the enclosure, calling to mind the arduous labor of past days in preparing meals. A plain pine table with Shaker chairs portrayed a setting of servitude and travail.

"I think I could have made up some pretty fancy witch tales too, had I worked in this kitchen. It's so sad," said Scotty. "I always dream a lot to get away from sad work." They talked with soft voices but did not whisper. Neil beckoned to them with a petulant brow, realizing they had but two more minutes left for their exploration. The cozy parlor warmed with an Oriental rug on a planked floor. There was a small fireplace and the winged back chair to its side partially exposed, from under its sheet, a rose brocade seat on mahogany legs.

"This seems comfy," said Bea. "Definitely not the servants' quarters."

Their last stop and grand finale took seconds, but it was a magnificent glance, that grand hall with its floor to ceiling paneling, candelabra from the walls and a marble-topped Queen Anne mixing table with two love seats, also Queen Anne.

"Wow," said Neil for the first time truly animated as he pulled his two fellow explorers, hands bonded in a threesome, out the door and down the steps. Scotty cringed in pain as the sharp rocks needled her feet, but the pain this time lacked definition, some sort of adrenalin carried her over the path in semi-sweet delirium. On the slimy shore of seaweed, it seemed odd they had returned but the final sigh of relief hit when the three slumped into Neil's yard on the hammock that overlooked the island. Panting, they watched as Johnny and Jake, in their truck, crossed the rock trail that they had just hobbled over.

"Great timing, Neil, you're a genius," Scotty spoke without notice of her battered feet. And then for several seconds they sat in the silence of their escapade, panting and viewing their unmeasured mystery as though through a window. A warm feeling nurtured their hearts, a collective feeling that they had known the house, felt its beauty, yet the hope of treasure still lay at hand.

Everything blurred in Scotty's mind after that. The goodbye hugs, the walk home without the bike. Neil promised to bring it later; he'd pry the towel loose.

Everything went as planned, for the next two days. Scotty registered, as if in a trance, the hollers of Ed hooking up the trailer to the Buick, Lois throwing the old coffee pot and Victrola inside the car trunk, Eric sweeping up the last remnants of balsa wood, and Scotty leaving her fish hooks by the lion's mane with a farewell scribble to Bea. And then, the car door shut and they backed down the hill for the last time. For the last time they rolled through the narrow town, all eyes on the foreign trailer, and then to the Hill, Village Street, and as in a silent movie, the McFinch Clan lined the hill and waved goodbye to their family, the renegades, the independents.

It seemed so strange that the 1949 trailer-towing Buick was westward bound but not as in "Gone with the Wind," nor as in "The Grapes of Wrath," one for land, one for famine. The Paines moved toward the West toward a new truth redefined in the beauty of each mountain where man was unencumbered by society and narrow Puritanical ways. Whisper of desert wind replaced the gossipy sounds of a small town. Their sacrifice was not in giving up a home but in accepting a new world, uniting in a discriminate way, reaffirming the spirit of the Channel Island people, spiritual yet sensual entrepreneurs of their roots.

CHAPTER NINETEEN

I t was 1973. News of the Vietnam War still shadowed the nation. A vacuous feeling subconsciously affected all.

Marguerite (the name Scotty preferred in her adulthood) had returned to Marblehead for a reunion with her roots and was now standing in front of a historical sign at Fountain Lane near Orne Street.

Marblehead's most celebrated romance began in the old Fountain Inn on Orne Street, whose wooden well still remains in place. Sir Harry Frankland, young and dashing Collector for the Port of Boston, visited the Inn in 1742 and was struck by the beauty of a barefooted fisherman's daughter who was scrubbing the stairs. Her name was Agnes Surriage. He took an interest in her, brought her to Boston where he educated her, and to Hopkinton, Massachusetts, where she presided over his manor house. Subsequently she accompanied him to England, where she was not cordially received by his noble parents. Later he took Agnes to Lisbon with him, just before the great earthquake. When the earthquake struck, Sir Harry Frankland was imprisoned under the ruins of a fallen building and was rescued by almost superhuman efforts of Agnes Surriage herself, with the result that the grateful baronet decided to legitimize their long alliance. Thereafter she was received everywhere as Lady Agnes Frankland.

It was unusually warm on the beach for the first of June. After reading about Agnes Surriage, Marguerite felt a surge of energy as she always did with fanciful romance. She sauntered toward the beach of massive purple mussels, looking ahead to Brown's Island. She searched along the pathway drawn for low tide, but there was no house! The quest of her childhood was gone. Stunned, she searched the sand for a clearing and sat on a slightly wet mound of sand, an island among the mussels. She could neither think nor feel anything for a time. She felt frozen, like a wild animal in fear of a predator.

Marguerite sat to calm herself. What a jolt to find the Mystery House of her youthful dreams obliterated, even though it was not lost to her memory. On the sand as on the cliff, those many years ago, she wrapped her arms around her knees, as she pensively gazed at the vista once so old and familiar and now so new.

Then, in the background, she could see from the corner of her eye, a shade going up and down. Someone was trying to get her attention. As Scotty looked at the house, she suddenly remembered Neil. Could that be Neil Montague looking at her through the windowpane?

And then, as in the long gone past, like in a slow-motion picture, he stepped out of the house and walked to the flat rock stairs that traversed the cliff. Scotty could not quite believe the man who walked toward her was Neil.

"Hello!" he said, "Have you been here long? Don't see too many people here until the middle of June." He stood in her shadow, and they looked at each other without words. He looked remarkably the same. High color in his cheekbones ran down to his stubby beard. A grown Tyrone Power, elegant at first sight, with teal blue eyes accented by black eyebrows and a beard that highlighted his wonderful, sensual gaze. Unshaven, no doubt, for he expected no one on the beach. Sensual, no doubt, for he had no time to disguise his feelings nor comb the thick wavy hair that completed the portrait of raw masculinity.

"Is that really you, Neil?"

"Marguerite Scott Paine," he said in recognition, "Just where have you been all these years? And my God, what happened to your freckles? You're beautiful!" he blurted out.

"You mean freckles aren't beautiful?" she chided.

"No, really . . ." he stuttered.

"Well, Neil Montague, so what about that prickly stuff around your chin, a beard perhaps? You're pretty grown up, I'd say. Seems to me you promised to be a kid forever."

A bit dumbfounded, Neil swung over and sat next to Scotty on her mound. He wrapped his arms around his knees, looking sideways now and resting his head on his knees, continuing the conversation.

"My strange sea fellow, whatever became of you? For years I searched this cliff and beach for my Scotty. It was never the same after you left."

"But you had the sea, Neil."

"I never felt it the way I felt it with you." He took her hand and squeezed it as a blind man clutches his walking stick.

"This will never do, these cold mussels are no place to reunite. We must go up to my place and really talk. What do you say? And perhaps I am old and stubby faced, but I've acquired some skills with that age. I'm somewhat of a gourmet cook now and I'll melt your heart with my chicken Provencal and Pinot Noir. Perhaps I should say, whet your appetite, not melt your heart."

Marguerite's eyes beamed and then she looked candidly into his staring eyes.

"I'd like that," she said.

He jumped up quickly and extended his arm to her, "Scotty," he said and paused.

"I'm Marguerite now. But here in Marblehead, and with you, I feel like Scotty again."

"Scotty . . . I can't get over," Neil continued, "what a flower you've turned into, an iris with those violet blue eyes."

"Now, let's not, get too excited here," she patted his hand. "But I guess you always did say exactly what was on your mind, I just have to get used to it again, that wonderful kid in you."

When he took her hand again, the strangest magic vibrated through her. Hand in hand, they now tiptoed around the purple mussels to the pathway up the cliff.

"And your parents?" she asked.

Neil lowered his voice, "They died two years ago. Mum went first and then Dad."

"Oh, I'm sorry," said Scotty.

"Well, with heart problems and in their seventies, they died just months apart, peacefully in their sleep, private nurse at hand. Not many can do that."

"But enough of death, let's talk about you, my lost friend."

At the top of the cliff now, they paused to view the empty island, near Scotty's old haunt. "Can we sit on the rock again? I was so fond of this rock as a child."

"Of course, we can." he said and she gently pulled him down.

"It's been so long. We were so innocent, so spiritual and sensual together, the truth of dreams, what happened? How did fear replace wonder going West? It wasn't going, it was being West. Without the sea, can you imagine? Los Angeles, most of it dry and plain except for Santa Monica and Pacific Palisades, but we didn't live in that area, we lived inland. I couldn't seem to navigate, couldn't manipulate like most kids. I was like a cat without whiskers, blurting out the right thing always; what a bore. My life soon drowned in dogma, I became lost to my emotions at St. Rose Academy. You went to parochial school, too, didn't you?"

"Not Prep School, but for eight years, I had the penguins," Neil smiled.

"Well, I took everything so seriously in those poor butterfly days," she pouted. "I coped with goodness. From a seagull's wing I dropped to the Church dome. From the mystery of the sea to the mystery of the sacraments, from Nature to intense study and prayer. Gee, Eric didn't do that."

"Eric," Neil said, "Oh, yes, your brother, how did he fare?"

"An angry teenager losing his friends, he could fight, and seemed to move right into the new picture. My new world flowed with ominous penguins of regimentation. A pathway of trees lined my way home and reminded me of the narrow confinement of my teens. New friends and sports replaced my meandering romps through Marblehead with my old buddies," she squeezed his hand. "Oddly enough, I became somewhat of a model for my new peers. My independence seemed attractive among the habits and uniforms, rosaries, mantras, and conformism; different or something."

Neil looked so intent and handsome, his wonderful eyes bridging eternity. Scotty spoke to the sea as she elaborated on the past, not registering his amazing beauty. But then her eyes blinked, and she led to him, "Your turn."

"May I tell you inside?" he asked, not totally lost to the moment. He rose gently and passed her his hand. The same warmth remained in his vigorous grasp. Hand in hand they walked into the side door of his house.

"It seems so strange to walk into a house that I spied on as a child. It's pretty much how I expected it." Scotty noticed the Queen Anne hutch in the dining room first. They walked from a hallway into the center of the living quarters that spaciously divided the two most prominent rooms of the house. "Do you mind if I slip off my shoes, Neil? They are a bit sandy and . . ." without his permission Scotty took off the sandals and leaving them in the hallway, she walked onto the peacock Persian rug centered in the living room. She nestled into a rose brocade Victorian loveseat that faced the bay window overlooking the Barnegat and Brown's Island.

"My dear," Neil's heart felt warmed by her comfort, "my desultory girl, make yourself at home."

"Desultory, that brings back memories. You know, Neil, not one person I've met since you, has called me desultory. I've read the word in books but never heard it used in conversation."

With one leg in a yoga position, Scotty kept to her tradition and fortuitously picked up a needlepoint sitting on the mahogany coffee table. "I love sunflowers, the real ones or Van Gogh's."

"Jessica busies herself with that nonsense. I'd rather paint the sunflowers and be done with it. More fluent, don't you think? You talked of painting way back, but I don't really remember any of your work."

"Let's talk about that later or we'll never eat."

Scotty sat in the loveseat watching him, an artist of efficiency and taste. The Chippendale table set, Neil worked quickly to place Pinot Noir and Chicken Provencal on a pewter tray, garnishing it with mandarin oranges.

"Wedgewood dishware," Scotty gasped as she drew near the table in hopes of helping.

"And why not?" He whisked her into a chair, his body draped at the waist with a dishtowel; then discarding his apron, he lined her lap with a rose-colored linen napkin, and they sat, together, at one end of the luxurious table.

"You're quite the magician! Do you do this often, Neil? Somehow, I don't remember your gourmet nature."

"Scotty, I've learned to be a connoisseur of everything wonderful." He held his crystal wine glass up as he toasted, "To my wonderful, and now beautiful, Scotty."

"And to youth as we knew it," she joined. The sound of a clear, crystal ring gave way to a pregnant silence.

"We have so much to catch up on," Neil gazed deeply into Scotty's eyes, seemingly searching for something forgotten or lost.

"It's really marvelous," Scotty beamed after her first taste of chicken.

He softened his stare with her approval.

"I'm glad," he said. "Now just how long do we have for our nostalgia? Are you here on vacation?"

"I'm visiting Aunt Marge. Do you remember her?"

"I think I do, Kate's mum?"

"Right. Well, Uncle Jeep passed away last year. Cancer took him."

Neil lowered his eyes in pensive appraisal of the loss, remembering the green thumbed uncle.

"All the girls, my cousins, are living out of state. Judging from her letters, Aunt Marge seemed so lonely, so I decided to visit. We are here for the month of June."

"We," he said.

"My daughter, Charlotte, and I. Now shall we go back to prep school?" she patted her lips with her napkin.

"Yes," said Neil. "Prep school and my induction into the material world. Good old Newton Prep, where I learned the difference between wrong and wrong. I became terribly smug in those days. Well, I was in a sea of 'smug.' Snooty rich boys with snooty parents. I developed quite a mordant nature. Society can be like a plague. Everyone played games. The scores were the best grades, the most girls, and the most laughs. Money didn't count, our rich dads covered for us."

"How counterfeit you sounded, Neil, what a rotten kid! But you can't outdo me with your miscreant tales. Dogma can be just as wretched as sin," she gleamed.

His eyes blinked and he listened quite intently.

"Somewhere early in my life of parochial existence, I accepted the premise that the greatest good lay in service to others, and I chased a dream of goodness. I missed the sin of human experience of life. Obedient, even obsequious, to begin with, orphaned to human development, I could have unearthed a monster. I mean, seeing people without an ounce of sensibility might turn someone into a slut, and perhaps I have done as much damage with my good deeds as you with your mischief."

Neil's mouth opened and he sighed, "You mean we're both villains."

Neil controlled his material world. Now off guard, he could only speculate why this lost power felt so peaceful. A serene silence enveloped them and then Scotty casually looked at her watch.

"It's four o'clock! Neil, I must go. Charlie, Charlotte is waiting for me. I promised to take her to the seaside park."

"Well, I'll let you go only if you promise I can see you again."

"It wouldn't be a promise, it would be a wish."

She held her hand out to him. His hand touched hers in warm connection.

"I lost my dream house, but found my friend again, what a day! I'd like to bring Charlie here tomorrow; maybe we can take a walk."

"That would be great," he said.

As she moved to the door, she said, "What did become of our treasure mansion?"

"It burned down years ago."

"What a pity," she said sadly.

CHAPTER TWENTY

"Aunt Marge was forever hanging clothes, and now my daughter is her accomplice."

"Mummy, Mummy," four-year-old Charlie ran to her mother putting the clothespins down on the grass carefully as though she handled china. "Where have you been?"

"I've been to England to visit the Queen."

"No, really Mummy, don't kid; you promised."

"Look at the cock-a-buttons in her hair," said Aunt Marge, "She's just like you, Scotty, and good little helper like her mum, too. Far away she blows, as a ship thrashing in many directions, her wind propels her in search of the unknown."

"Seaside Park? Aunt Marge." Scotty kissed her old nanny. "You seem too serious for hanging clothes, and my goodness, what fancy words. You never talked to Liver Lips like that." She avoided talking of Uncle Jeep just now.

"Well, you told Charlie about Seaside Park and she's expecting to explore it today. Maybe I did get carried away, been practicing my poetry since your uncle's gone, now, so you best be off. You'll have a couple of hours before dinner."

Scotty felt a twinge of guilt. "Maybe we should talk about Jeep."

"No darlin', I'm beyond that point; I'm back to the living part, and you and Charlie bridge me that way. You take me along with your spirits."

"You won't mind, then, if I take Charlie tomorrow to romp around Marblehead?"

"No, indeed not, if you get tired, I'll give you a ride home. Can't take all the little one's time, now, can I? She's made me want to play in the garden again and eat his vegetables, that's what he would have liked."

The next day, they all kissed tenderly before departing. Scotty brought the stroller, should Charlie tire.

"You want to push your stroller for a while, Charlie?"

"Okay, Mummy."

"You're a big girl now, you won't need the stroller all the way."

"Right, Mummy. Right you are, Mummy."

"See that house over there? The one that looks like a cottage with gingerbread around the roof?"

"Yup."

"They used to raise rabbits there, lots of milky white rabbits. And that house next to it was supposed to be haunted. My cousin Kate and I always used to get goose bumps going by that one."

"There are so many windows in the house, Mummy, but the green shades are all pulled down."

"I've never seen them up, Charlie, nor did I ever see anyone go in or come out of that house. Now look there across the street. That nice gray house, that neat colonial with the pretty, even hedge in front. Well, we all wanted to live in that house when we were kids. A banker lived there; I think. Here we are at the bottom now. Will you push for a while? Or we can fold it." The stroller folded so that it could be carried like luggage.

"I like to push the stroller. Too bad I didn't bring Mary Jane."

"We'll take your baby doll next time. Now, on your left," Scotty felt like a tour guide, "see this Seaside Realty sign? Well, it used to be a doughnut shop and they had five cent doughnuts there. Our neighbor on Roland Street, right up there on the next hill," Scotty pointed across the street, "used to send me to buy doughnuts each morning and I got to keep one for myself for going. The jellies were ten cents, but I always got the holey ones, puffed with sugar or glazed. Then there was the Great Dane that lived in that dark red house over there. Poor dog, he was so big, like a horse, and the kids used to ride him. Wore down all his fur so later he'd growl if anybody even touched the spot." Scotty stopped, pulling Charlie by the hand, in front of an unkempt house that looked abandoned. "Now that house over there, the big white one with the green shutters, see across the street? That's the Trucker's house. His son had a crush on me when we were little. Jimmy was my first sweetheart. He was six and had cerebral palsy."

"What's that?"

"Well, when he walked, he had those jerky movements. He wore a steel brace sometimes, and he slurred his words. They had a sing song sound to them, and he stretched them out something like what happens when the record is playing at the wrong speed, a slower speed. We were friends, anyway. It just took Jimmy a little longer to go places and do things. No matter, we romped through the streets of Marblehead, found our gold mines in the chestnut tree by the Dole School. When the men came to spray the trees for us, we hurled ourselves onto the porch hammock, wiggling and giggling together, hands over our faces to block out the poison vapors. We'd go with the town folk after Christmas to burn the Christmas trees at the beach. The bonfires of dry pine needles would send bomb-like flames into the sky as we breathlessly held each other in the excitement and warmth of the flames. When the bullies would ride the Great Dane, Jimmy and I would throw pine cones at them. It was a wonderful world, and then one day somebody told me that Jimmy was different, and different was not okay. All of a sudden, I felt naked and when I covered up, it meant not playing with Jimmy anymore. When I got bigger, I realized that different was what made us special, and Jimmy would always be special for me.

"Up we go!" Scotty pulled Charlie gently to her feet. They plodded on downtown, quiet for a time, the only sound being the squeaks of the wheels on the stroller. "Now, here we are at Hutchy's Potato Chip Factory. It's a nice little store, isn't it, Charlie?" Charlie peered through the window of the vacant shop now. "Teddy Hutch's dad used to own this shop. Sounds funny, but I always bought pickles here. Mr. Hutch had a big pickle jar right on top of his main counter. The best dill besides Shube's, that's where Kate got hers. Want a pickle? Oh, maybe not. It's too early, and they are closed, anyway. Maybe on the way back we can stop at Shube's."

So, they shuffled on to the Warwick Theater. "We watched so many Saturday matinees here. The cartoons were more fun for me than the double features. I used to think heaven was like the Warwick, because they had all those cupids on the ceiling and red velvet curtains, something like the purple velvet that was used to cover all the statues in the old Gothic church, the Star of the Sea, during Lent."

They wandered on into the newer part of the town to the railroad station and five and dime store. "Oh, Charlie, I used to buy all my gifts here, in this five and ten cent store. I got a tiny reindeer here for Grampy Graves one Christmas. He kept it on his mantle all year around."

"Our Grampy's name is McFinch. Who is Grampy Graves?"

"Charlie, you have lots of Grampies. Sometimes people are not related to you but they love you just like they were, and they know you better than your own, real family. Grampy McFinch was always busy painting or hunting. But Grampy Graves knew me, talked to me, gave me little gifts and gifts of his wisdom."

"What's wisdom?" asked Charlie.

"That's what you feel and learn about life, Charlie."

They were at Peach's Florist Shop now, and ready to start the climb to the old part of town. Scotty peered into the shop window. It was hard to see anything, peeking into the dark room. The floors were the same polished black and white linoleum squares that she had remembered as a kid. Somebody darted off into the greenhouse, but she couldn't get a glimpse of him. "I bought many Mother's Day gifts here, Charlie. Geranium was my middle name. Charlie, are you tired?"

"A little."

"Can we climb the hill? Then we can sit on the lawn at the Post Office. It's a fancy building, and across the street from it, there is a fancy ballroom where I used to go for dancing lessons. Think you can make it, Charlie? Golly," Scotty squeezed Charlie's hand, "just like old times! And here I am with you, my daughter." She gave Charlie a hug. "Charlie, if you can get up this hill to the Post Office, then I'll push you down the hill in the stroller and we'll go to the Old Town. We'll window shop, what do you say?"

"What's window shop?"

"We'll look into the windows of those old quaint houses with things for sale, and we'll dream about all that we'd like to buy and what fun we'd have with so many things. But we won't buy anything, we'll just look."

Charlie responded by stiffly walking up the hill, holding on to the stroller. The grand houses and giant oaks that shaded the walk gave respite from the hot summer sun, but they could not prevent humid drops of sweat from dotting their brows. Mother and daughter sighed when they reached the top, and then rear ends landed simultaneously on their grassy destination.

"We should have bought a postcard to send to Grammy and Grampy in California."

"Wait till we see the whole town, Mummy, then we can choose."

"You're right, Charlie. See that house across from us? That used to be the great ballroom of Miss Ruby Bell. She always reminded me of a flamenco dancer, with her jet-black hair pulled back into a tight bun, and rouge on her cheeks to match the color of her bright dress, a tight dress that flared at the ankles for elaborate dances, swoons and kicks. Don't ask me,

Charlie, what any of that means. Just take it for granted, you'll understand the dance lingo one day."

"What's lingo?"

Scott laughed. Charlie's little head bobbed, not at all frustrated by her mother's babbling. They rose together and, as agreed, Charlie got back into the stroller for the downhill navigation.

"Golly, you're getting heavy, Charlie."

"Want me to walk, Mummy?"

"Nope, that wasn't the deal." Scotty panted to the bottom and then blew through her lips a sigh of relief. "Now let me get my bearings. Now, oh yes, there it is, the Miniature Shop that I wanted to surprise you with."

Charlie knew what miniatures were. Almost every toy given to her by her mother was a miniature.

"Maybe I'm the collector and you, Charlie, are my excuse for buying these tiny collectibles," and then looking around Scotty said, "it is so much like I remember it, the Old Town I mean, and the Miniature Shop."

"Look, Mummy, at that big yellow house. I'm not the only one I know who makes my houses yellow."

"You know, they used to paint a lot of these old houses yellow. Not anymore, though."

Charlie shook her head vigorously, exaggerating it in a silly way so common to giddy tots.

"Well, little one, that yellow house is the Police Station and it used to be a meeting hallway back when. The old bank across the street, see how that building is smaller than our buildings now and how it sits almost on the street? Well, folks were smaller a long time ago and they needed only tiny houses. The Miniature Shop has tiny houses, too, let's go and see."

Scotty steered the stroller over the curb and then directed it up again onto the sidewalk in front of the shop window where an assortment of tiny items made regular teddies and porcelain dolls look like giants. Her mother's sudden silence alerted Charlie to her mother's uneasiness. "Mummy, Mummy, say something!" Charlie turned her head back and up toward her mother and saw a stunned look on her face. "What is it? Mummy, what is it?"

"It's my tea set! My miniature silver service Granny Paine gave me!" Scotty's pale and contorted face was reflected in the glass, a mirror to Charlie and a vision to Scotty who pictured her Victorian grandmother with a Gibson hairdo, no bangs, and a lace choker.

"Too many tea parties," Scotty blurted out, not making sense.

"Mummy, there is no such thing as too many tea parties."

"You are a child, Charlie. My grandmother gave me a wonderful silver set of dishes with a magnificent little tea set just like those in the window, exactly. I guess as I look at them now, I can see her stoic restraint, because that was all she could do, Charlie. Granny dutifully cared for family and had lovely tea parties. She never told me that; she never had to. It was our secret. She shared her silver service with me. Service, service, service," Scotty repeated in a rote-like fashion. "But Granny also shared her imagination. In our imagination, we are always free to love and create. It took us girls some time to figure that out, that from duty and Cotton Mather parameters we can make wonder."

"Cotton what? Oh, Mummy," Charlie looked forlorn, "I don't know what you're talking about."

Scotty giggled and said, "Sorry, Charlie. I don't know if I can explain. Cotton Mather was a Congregational minister, a religious man and very strict. Strict meant that there were lots of things he said you couldn't do. It seemed like everything you did or wanted to do was bad. He believed in witches, people who were against God and for the devil. They had the power to do evil, a secret power. Anyway, that's how it all got started. Some little girls made up bad stories about people a long time ago. Well, if you think you are bad, then you will be bad, and these little girls, one of them was the minister's daughter, used to call some folks witches.

"Marguerite Scott was the only person called a witch in Marblehead and she was killed for it. Marguerite was my granny. Granny came from Montreal, Canada, and she lived among the French, although she was English. Her last name was Scott before she married Grandpop. Marguerite is Margaret in English. I think it's kind of interesting, Charlie, that a woman with a witch's name could have such magic. A magic that could make me wonder about the good. Granny helped me imagine the bright and polished inside of the service of life.

"The silver service inspired my creations at home with fanciful parties. The tiniest of sets brought me with Alice in Wonderland through a minute lock into a fairy tale world of my own making. And in real life, Granny showed me the magic of service by walking to the creek and creating baskets of moss and rocks so beautiful in their arrangement, to be sold at church bazaars.

"She let me ring the Indian dinner bells that hung from the kitchen ceiling to announce the time for our repast. Meal preparation took such a long time in my Granny's day. But what a table she laid: starched, white linen tablecloth and starched napkins with silver napkin rings, initialed for each member of the family. I still see the golden tea holder, a sieve to catch the tea leaves, and there were the silver dove wings that held the serving knife above the table so as not to soil it. Eating celebrated life. Manners and etiquette helped us savor every morsel that was carefully and lovingly prepared by Marguerite Scott.

"And then there was the incredible garden. We had the best of everything in my grandmother's garden. Whimsical bachelor's buttons, sweet william, alyssum. We had Victorian lace for our tea table, an Indian elephant teapot. We sat on striped canvas patio chairs with sunken seats and watched goldfinch and Anna's Hummingbird. We ate oatmeal cookies and drank lemonade in glasses skirted in wicker dresses. We had purple lips, fat bellies. Orange Pekoe for the grownups and naps in the hammocks for the kids; hours of nothing, idle peace, slapping mosquitoes. Blueberry picking at the neighbors' farm. We had thc best of everything and nothing."

"Mummy, how could you say all that in one breath, without stopping?"

Scotty smiled. "I was named for my Granny, Marguerite Scott."

"I'm thirsty, are you?" Charlie clapped her hands.

"All right, this way, my dear, to the King's Rock." In no time at all they stood before a shop with a prominent window and many panes. Scotty and Charlie, from her stroller, tried to peer into one of the window panes. Small brown tables and chairs were placed close to one another, and a bar stood against the wall with demitasse cups and mugs. The brightest part of the room was the enormous bronze coffee maker.

"Oh, Mummy, look at that gold statue! It looks like it belongs in the church!"

"Charlie, that's not a monstrance, that's a coffee machine."

"It seems so dark and gloomy in there, Mum."

"Not at all, dark places are good places to ponder undistracted, as we are, with so much of the natural beauty of this town."

When they entered, a waiter, seemingly from a shadow, came to greet them, his white apron appearing almost ghostly in front of them.

"May we sit by the window?" asked Scotty. He nodded. Not many people came to the coffee house in the summer. The desolate room sat like a somber, darkened closet.

No sooner had they sat down, than a beggar outside crossed their path in the window, reminding Scotty of Zig of long ago.

The lone man, disheveled, with a stubby beard and long unkempt hair clutched a wrinkled brown paper bag containing a bottle. The neck, Scotty recognized, was a pint of Bitters.

"I once knew a man like that," Scotty told Charlie.

"Like what, Mummy?"

"Like that man that just walked by outside. He gave me a dollar, and that was all the money he had."

"Why did he give you the dollar, Mum?"

"He liked the way I looked, I guess. Well, now, this is some day," Scotty said as she propped Charlie in her window seat with a pillow from the stroller.

The lanky waiter came to their table. "One hot cider and one black coffee," Scotty ordered. The waiter nodded. As they waited for the drinks, another man walked by outside, a hunchbacked man with a top hat and glasses. He seemed to be memorizing the sidewalk as he walked with a cane toward the ocean.

"How odd," said Scotty. "That man looks like Grampy Graves, the wise old man in my childhood. I knew him better, I mean. He told me stories and his wife gave me cookies. Like my own grandfather, he was."

Scotty signaled to the waiter. "May I order an apple? Just a whole apple." The waiter nodded and went to get the order. Scotty snapped her fingers. "I forgot something," she said to Charlie. She stepped to the next table and took a knife from the place setting. "I guess I'll just share with you one of those magical stories. But you will have to do some guessing. And I have to wait for the apple." Charlie looked like an alert puppy, after the waiter brought the apple. As Scotty held the apple in her hand and extended it to the air, she asked, "What do you suppose is in the apple?"

"Don't be silly, Mummy, there's an apple inside."

"Yes, of course, but there is also something else."

"Seeds."

"Yes, go on."

"Juice."

"Good. Go on. It's how seeds are formed in the apple that makes this story so special. Well, Charlie, you did your guessing, so I guess I can show you." Their hot drinks were there by then and Scotty took the saucer from her coffee cup to cut the apple on. She started slowly cutting the apple, and then went quickly as if chopping it in half. She opened the apple exposing both halves to Charlie.

"Oh, Mummy! It's a star!"

Scotty set the apple halves down, their design turned up as a decoration for the table.

"How is your cider, Charlie?"

"It's hot, but I like hot drinks, even in the summer."

"Well, your Mum would be doomed without her coffee."

Scotty held her hands on both sides of the cup and brought it slowly to her lips, as if delighted yet repulsed by a sudden thought. "I learned to drink coffee in Europe the year I met your Daddy."

"You don't talk much about it, Mum."

"Well, Charlie, your Daddy was not allowed to leave his country, Russia, where I met him, and I wanted to go home to the United States. He wanted to come with me, but his government would not allow it. You may understand it later, but this I'm sure you understand. It's fun to travel and to hear about places and see other people. I always wanted to do that, I was always curious about life and wanted to see everything, just like what's inside the apple, and I did. Then I came home a happier person from my experience. Your Daddy gave me you to take home. I feel he is here in you so when I talk to you, I talk to you both.

"I think I know what you mean."

"Are we finished?"

"Let's go." Scotty left the money on the table. The waiter stood back in the darkness, but his apron showed and his head broke the shadow with a final nod. They left into the bright sun. Charlie clutched the apple stars to hold in her lap in the stroller.

"Where's your friend's house, Mummy?"

"It won't be long, Charlie."

Silently they plodded on, the stroller squeaking on the grating gravel.

And then for the second time, Scotty recognized the historical sign that told of Harry Frankland and Agnes Surriage. Charlie couldn't read the sign yet. All in due time. Strolling down the pathway to the mussels and driftwood, they left the stroller, as Scotty had left the bike so many years ago. Hand in hand they climbed the path to Neil's house.

CHAPTER TWENTY-ONE

"So this is Charlie! She looks so much like you, Scotty."

"Yes, Neil, this is my baby cake."

"Mummy, don't talk like that, I'm a big girl."

"I know, my darling, my sweetheart. I love to call you by fond names. I'm a Mummy, you're my baby."

Charlie felt comfortable with Neil. She liked his handsome eyes. Children love beauty. "You wouldn't call Neil baby cake, Mum." Charlie was a precocious child.

"I beg your pardon, Miss Charlie, I want you to know that your mother once called me a magic conch."

"What's a conch?"

"I'll show it to you, but first, let's have a chat. Neil, this is my daughter, Charlotte Paine."

"Charlotte Paine Kent pretty soon," said Charlie.

"Miss Kent, is it?" Neil blinked questioningly and looked at Scotty.

Scotty winked, "We'll get to that."

"Of course, Miss Charlie, in good time. Now would you like some lemonade or what about some ice cream from Abby May's?"

"I love ice cream. Do you have peanut butter?"

"Well, last time I looked we had chocolate swirl."

"That will be fine," said Charlie.

"Decisive, good, I like that quality,"

"Neil, I know what you mean but I don't know what you're talking about," Charlie floored him.

"Quite a kid, you have here. Reminds me of somebody I once knew."

Neil held up the ice cream in front of Scotty.

"No, no thanks, maybe later."

"Take my hand then," he said to Charlie, "little lady, and we'll sit you at the table."

Scotty smiled as she watched them move toward the table.

"And when you're done, I want to show you that wonderful conch."

Charlie's sparkling smile impressed him.

"Say, where did you get that cute face?"

"My Mummy gave it to me."

"Gosh, you're a sweetheart."

"You may kiss me," Charlie turned her cheek to Neil.

"You know, Charlie, your mother gave me some memories."

"What's a memory?" she tilted her head in question.

"A memory, my dear, is a wonderful feeling someone gives you whenever you think of them."

"Oh, I know, like my cat, Tinkerbell, I can almost feel her furry hide when I think of her."

"Something like that."

"Now, Charlie, your mother and I have many memories to catch up on, so I'll show you that wonderful conch and you may examine it with the many other shells near it. I am sure that the little boy that owns the collection would love to share them with you. I know you'll be careful."

Charlie beamed, a trait of her mother's, seemingly hypnotized by Neil's speech. And then she slurped her ice cream, as before.

At the bay window, Scotty and Neil held hands, settling into the past on the love seat.

"Where were we? Your college days."

"My college days," he began. "I think I finished with Newton Prep. Well, smugness and lechery did not seem becoming to me, so I arduously took on the role of scholar. What else could I do? At Harvard, the undisciplined life became a challenge for me.

The freedom to choose classes and professors exhilarated my normal quest for learning. There appeared to be flexibility between my planned marriage to a business and accounting career. My future, of course, was to be bank president, like Dad. I lost myself in my minors, history and literature. Literature, my hobby of old, became my escape now from grueling math classes and the accounting business at hand.

Hesse, Hegel, Thoreau, Lawrence, Maugham, Tolstoy, they all intrigued me. My mind became a great joy to me. And my old preoccupation with vice turned to hibernation with wonder. In my head I was planning grand cocktail parties, asking the masters about the themes of mankind. My affluent family allowed for vacations in Europe to bridge my knowledge with those places memorized for tests. What lay ahead of me now was the business of life. I began my banking career. I was yet to find my true and lasting nature, but I did find love for a time with Jessica."

"Mummy, mummy, I dropped the conch," Charlie came running to Scotty who gulped, her yearning for Neil's words foiled for a time with Charlie's dilemma.

"Let me see," said Neil.

"I broke it," she cried with heart-rending sobs.

"Wait just a minute now," Neil said gently, "give me the shell." As she gave it to him, the jagged edge rubbed his palm.

He held the gastropod minus a spiral in one hand and, patting Charlie gently on the shoulder, he left the room.

When Neil returned, he held in his hand what appeared to be the same conch with its spiral back again.

"Voila! I keep spares for such occasions," he whispered to Scotty, "Jeffrey's on the clumsy side."

Charlie clapped her hands. "How did you do that, Neil?"

"Magic, I guess."

"Well, I think we've visited long enough for today," Scotty pronounced, feeling reassured yet stymied for she wanted to hear more from Neil.

"May I come back, Neil? I promise not to break anything again," asked Charlie.

"I'd be devastated if you didn't come back."

"What's devastated?"

Neil searched her cobalt blue eyes, "Something like how you feel when those beautiful shells disappear, and you never see them again."

"Aunt M is taking Charlie for a tea party to Salem tomorrow."

"We're going to Bailey's for ice cream, too."

"Hurrah!" Neil cheered.

"A shopping spree, preschool, big stuff, eh, Charlie?"

"Yep."

"Are you going, too, Scotty?"

"No, afraid not, too many letters to catch up on. Besides, Aunt M wants to have Charlie all to herself sometimes."

"Don't be stuffy and work all day. Have lunch with me. I love talking about old times."

"I would like that if I'm not making a nuisance of myself."

"Don't be ridiculous."

"I'm not ridiculous, I just want you to beg and beseech."

"All right then, pretty please."

"What time tomorrow?" she said.

"Eleven o'clock?"

"Bye, Charlie," said Neil. Charlie waved; she was already onto dreams of Salem.

CHAPTER TWENTY-TWO

When they met the next day, Neil anxiously answered the door as if dwelling on something. "Scotty, are you married?" he blurted the words, so out of character with his usually charming and faultless manners.

She entered, closed the door and taking his hand, sat down with him near the bay window, once again.

"No, I'm not married. Let me tell you about Charlie. We're jumping the gun a bit, it all happened after college, but here goes.

Just out of college, I had decided to visit the Soviet Union during the summer of '68. The Russians invaded Czechoslovakia that year, what an exciting summer for a green student set free from study.

"Konstantin Belikov, Konstantin Belikov, Konstantin Belikov, I can see myself writing his name in the sand after I made my Russian connection and returned home after my Russian affair.

"We met on Gorky Street in Moscow. He seemed to pick me out of a crowd of silly college girls, as if he knew me instantly. He edged his way into our line and introduced himself, and then with skeptical eyes he said, 'Do you steal icons?' He appeared so serious but cute. I laughed and he shied and we smiled and then laughed together. 'Well, before I defend myself,' I said, 'do you think I should be talking to a perfect stranger?'"

"Maggie, my friend, looking at Konstantin now, smiled, but we all kept our march, heading back to the Peking Hotel where we stayed.

"'I work for interest,' he said.

"'Go on,' I said.

"'Yes, well, your American accent made me wonder if you're finding your way all right in my city.'

"'Yes, we're quite all right, thanks, and about the icons, well, I don't steal icons, but I would like to steal you. I like cute men.'

"'Cute, what means 'cute'? I have not the word in my dictionary.'

"'Cute means clever and handsome,' I said feeling now so amused as my girlfriends turned green with envy. He looked serious and arrogant to start but I just unhinged him with my quick thoughts. As a matter of fact, generally shy, he pushed some button in me to be recklessly honest and immediate. Whatever happened on that walk bonded us for my three days in Moscow. His name was Konstantin Belikov, or Kostja, for short, as he bid me call him.

"Kostja arrived the following morning at the breakfast table of the Peking Hotel. Serge, his brother, came as chaperon. Interesting, I thought, weren't chaperons supposed to be old ladies? Everything interested me about him, including my disappointment that he did not belong to the K.G.B., which would have made him in my eyes dangerous and mysterious. Since I was the suspected statue stealer, there we were together comparing our lives while we toured the circus, Lenin's Library, some factories, and other Soviet establishments. In the park, I grimaced at a communal cup at a juice stand, a mere kopeck a cup. A drunken man slept on the park bench. The images went by so quickly from the bus we entered from the back where everybody paid their token on the merit system.

"Nimbly, we picked each other's brains, stopping now and then for 'moroznoye,' the Russian word for ice cream. I tried very hard not to stick out. But my smile gave me away and I laughed entirely too much for a Soviet. Oh, I forgot, my shoes were too clean, too.

"Their faces were sad, but sad or not, their complexions shone like begonias, almost translucent and pink. Transportation was mainly by foot, and they all looked healthy, except for their teeth. So many of the old had mouths that were full of gold, while the young had whittled down teeth, maybe from grinding them in frustration. Neil, we had to take showers in the hotel basement. Can you imagine their difficult life?"

He shook his head, engrossed in Scotty's tale.

"Serious, studious, effective, I said, wow, how deeply conscious, those Russians, and the ones that met the Americans seemed to value our high spirit and spontaneity, like me, ha, ha.

"Oh well, I liked Kostja because he knew me. No one I ever met knew my sad face meant serious thought, not unhappiness. And I thought to myself that not everybody that laughs is happy, nor everybody that cries is sad. When we parted at the train station, he held my hands through the open car doors. 'Take off your sunglasses, darling,' he said, 'may I see your eyes one last time?' Then he looked down at his hand which he had made into a fist and opening it he presented to me a sparkling new ruble. 'Keep this ruble for good luck, and remember, the closer you get to your ideals, the closer we will be together.' When we kissed, tears rolled down his serious face. I see him still standing on the platform waving, waving into the distance. Little did I know, I waved with Charlie.

"The night before our parting we had walked alone through the Kremlin. St. Basil's seemed a glowing beacon. The Belikov flat lay adjacent to Red Square. The senior Belikovs were on holiday at the Black Sea, and so they left a quiet flat for their son. At midnight, torrential rain drove us to the foyer of their apartment as unavoidable fate took hold. Relieved, yet powerless for the moment, I became overwhelmed with his caresses."

Scotty became silent for a while, remembering how Kostja's body grew hard against hers. His tongue circled her lips and penetrated her mouth, as a million sparks ignited her womb. He carried her almost paralyzed into the bedroom in expectation of magical bliss.

"Saving my innocence for so long, it was amazing, I gave so freely that night. He walked me back to my hotel in the dawn's early light. Just before I fell asleep, I felt both the sacrifice and the sacrament of my eventful night with Kostja. Yet, a remorse followed my soul for days, a mixture of joy and sorrow, the sorrow no doubt due to the strict upbringing. I didn't know it yet, of course, but Charlotte came to me that night.

"Arriving back in San Francisco with morning sickness, I managed to rent a cottage in the East Bay near San Francisco and found a job as a substitute teacher under the name of Mrs. Charles Paine, widowed wife of Colonel Charles Paine, lost in the Vietnam War. I don't know how I found the gumption to tell Mum and Dad, nor the determination to keep Charlie. But I am so happy I had the strength.

"You poor dear, Neil, I really unloaded on you. You must be bored to death. I also feel a little sheepish telling you this stuff" she lowered her eyes.

"On the contrary, my dear, a former lecher relishes such details of passion."

Relieved, Scotty took on the smuggest of smiles, feeling comfortable in his acceptance, but not resigned. "And now in keeping with my inquisitive nature, perhaps you'll tell me about Jessica and Jeffrey. I've heard of your family. How goes it, Neil? Tell me about Jessica."

He looked at her now, forefinger and thumb in a "v" shape cupping his chin while his elbow rested on a knee bent and raised to support his new stance, shoeless, his heel rested on the edge of the Victorian loveseat.

"Jessica, oh yes, Jessica my beautiful, perfect wife, Jessica. We met at prep school, Andover Academy, at a Junior dance. The greatest good, I thought was Jessica Goode. This was what

I wanted to marry. Jessica, yes, my classical beauty, from the Flemish golden red curls, so whimsical when she pulled her hair back, to her slender goddess white ankles and dimpled feet—I adored her. The litany of her perfection never seemed to stop. In between a supple body, alluring yet motherly, her voice was like an angel with soft, perfect diction. English, from the best London stock, bankers. Good mind, good cook, good bedfellow, never ruffled—always placid, occasionally coy, predictable, dispassionate. I thought she was everything, but I am still missing something."

"Where are she and Jeffrey, now?" asked Scotty, still not satisfied with the information given.

"In England for the month, visiting relatives. Your turn, again," he said, slightly out of breath and wanting to change the subject. He wanted to hear more from Scotty. "Anybody after K?"

"Not until Stuart. I met Stu when Charlie was three. Leave it to me for a comical meeting. I was just leaving my gynecologist's office one rainy, dismal day. In the elevator I had noticed a smart, well dressed conservative type of man, lean and tall with large glasses, my intellectual type. Leaving the elevator, we seemed together in our every motion. We both left the medical building and saluted the turbid sky with our umbrellas, which immediately became entwined. After a tug o' war, we playfully laughed and scurried back into the lobby. Then we sat both umbrellas down and chatted.

"Stuart is a surgeon, fifteen years my senior. He had lost his wife six months prior to our meeting. She had died of breast cancer, and he seemed gloomy, you know, no facial expressions, sad, real sad. But when we talked and laughed, he seemed so animated. After all, it was pretty funny the way we latched onto each other," she winked at Neil, "I knew from the beginning we had a connection."

"How did we get here, Neil?" Suddenly, they were in the bedroom. Scotty was so engrossed in thought that she had been unmindful of Neil's hand gently leading her to his bedroom. "Gee, I'm sorry for monopolizing our talk."

Neil was untying Scotty's summer halter dress.

"Not at all, I'm savoring every word."

"I'm not really hot, Neil; I don't need to take off my dress."

"Oh no?" he said playfully as he pulled off his tee shirt, "All of a sudden I feel quite warm."

"Is this a bedroom scene?" she grinned.

He nodded.

"Well, then, may I say, you have such a dramatic brow."

Half-dressed she kneeled on the bed. Softly she kissed his right brow while she circled the left with her finger. "Are they like seagull wings?" she talked in sultry passion, in the trance of love. "And your nose, I like to be near its chiseled grace." Scotty kissed the nose from the brow to its quivering nostrils. "And your eyes, how they pierce me with a martyr's cause, never have I been shy of those eyes. I was blind without them."

"My angel," he kneeled too, bringing her hands to his lips with eager kisses. How he longed to receive her! They fell on the bed in an embrace. As their faces mirrored each other on the pillows, Neil murmured softly, "Scotty, you make me so happy. I can't imagine life without you. I want you so much. Thank you for coming back to me. There is something in you that is me, waiting to be discovered. I love the me in you."

"That sounds very suggestive, Neil." She kissed his nose and as they lay on the bed, the buds of tender passion ready to bloom, Scotty, on her back, gazed at the ceiling for a moment while Neil stared with the diligence of a lover.

"The ceiling has stars," Scotty said dreamily.

"Rather tacky, wouldn't you say." He didn't blink nor did he change his focus.

"My Mum and Dad had stars like that in their bedroom, golly, I felt secure crawling into bed with my mother when I had nightmares. I just stared at those stars, those cheap, sparkly sandpaper stars; odd how it calmed me."

Neil rolled over to join Scotty with her view. "We never changed the house after their passing." He seemed far away from his whispered reply.

Sensing his regained reality, Scotty spoke, "Stuart and I are to be married in September. It seems almost planned," she said whimsically.

"Oh," he said.

"You look just like Barb with that look, right before her seizure."

"Why, thank you," Neil said mordantly.

"No, no, don't misunderstand, she tried to be serious, almost mad to prevent her seizure."

"Well, I'm certainly not mad, my old sweetheart, but perhaps a tad possessive, the male in me, I guess. Go on, about this Indian marriage."

"What?" Scotty said.

"I just mean, I think of the Indian culture when I think of planned marriages."

"You mean the Indians from India?"

He nodded.

"Well, maybe in part, but really, I felt everything was planned. Somehow, I was on a rail, a train you might say, that would put me in Kostja's path, Stu's path, but don't forget Neil, you were first in my path." Scotty turned and rolled over on top of him. And then holding herself up so she could clearly see his face, she changed right before him from wonder to desire.

CHAPTER TWENTY-THREE

A unt Marge said nothing to Scotty the next morning, but let Charlie do the talking. "Mummy, where were you last night? You didn't tuck me in and I wanted to tell you about our trip to Salem! Did you see Neil?" Charlie ran all her sentences together trying not to forget anything, and not knowing just what she should ask first.

"Yes, dear, I saw Neil and we talked for so long about old times and the things we did when we were children. But I did tuck you in. You were fast asleep and didn't feel my kiss."

Scotty's calmness reassured Charlie and Aunt Marge as well. Everything was okay.

"It was wonderful to be with Charlie in Salem," said Aunt Marge. "I felt like a kid again on my first shopping spree. Never thought I could be happy again," she paused and sniffled, "after Jeep." She stopped and bit her cheek determined not to cry. Then hugging her niece's daughter, Marjorie looked at Scotty and said, "She's got so much of your spirit, we could call her Cock-a-button Two." Aunt M paused again, this time with momentum, "I've got an idea. Let's go to Winnipesaukee for a week, just for old times. The Pine Real Estate agency sends me a notice each year that our cottage has been saved for the same time in the summer that it always was with Kitty. But I don't respond, I don't much think of it anymore. But let's go while you're here."

"Oh Mummy, let's go!" Charlie implored. "You told me so many stories about the lake. Please, let's go."

"Why is it that you always want to go, Charlie, you're just like your grandfather, Ed Paine."

Now both of them were beaming at Scotty, convinced of their plan. Scotty hesitated before she spoke. "Aunt M, I think it's a wonderful plan," she fidgeted with the words, "I do," she hesitated, "but I need to work some things out here."

Marge looked more serene now as she said, "Of course, Scotty, I understand. Maybe it would be best if Charlie and I go and give you some time to sort things out."

Now Scotty beamed, it had never entered her mind that Aunt M and Charlie might go to the lake by themselves.

"Would you mind, Aunt M?"

"I'd adore taking Charlie! Or does that sound too much like Lucretia?"

"Oh my gosh, I've almost forgotten Aunt Lue. What is she up to these days? Mum mentions her every once and awhile. Says she's received a postcard or call."

"Well, your Aunt Lucretia is quite a person in Parisian society now."

Charlie sat on Scotty's lap and they both voraciously listened to Aunt M talk about the famous in their family.

"Yes, ma'am, she really outdid herself, our eldest sister, she did. Everything seemed to happen after Martin passed away. Things were quiet for a couple of months, then she popped up at the Hill and told Kitty she was going back to school. She would be taking over Martin's business all right, the two delis and all, but first she was going back to school to get help with a learning disability she had, dyslexia. Well, we were flabbergasted! Never heard of dyslexia before. Lue told us she was having trouble spelling and nobody told her anything at school about it, just that she was a bad speller. Well, taking over the business would be a big responsibility; she had to write and she just couldn't do it. She was so embarrassed with some of the food companies she dealt with when they didn't understand her orders. You'll remember she was virtually doing everything before Martin went; well, she liked the business and has always been very business-wise and extremely well spoken, so she was determined to carry on and do a good job until she could afford a secretary. Yup, she really did it. She writes perfect English and French now," Aunt M raised her eyebrows and pursed her lips with pride. "We knew she was different; mother always knew she'd be a real winner when she stopped spinning her wheels and really attacked life. Don't you remember that blow up those many Easters ago?"

"How could I forget! I felt like I caused it with my mousy blushes."

Charlie's hands were folded; Scotty's arms were around her and her hands held Charlie's clasped fingers. She listened with rapt attention to the banter of Aunt M, feeling almost like Scotty many years ago, feeling the security of a nurturing nanny and being in the arms of her mother, well, it was double heaven.

"We were happy for her, and she became so successful that she moved to Paris and now corresponds with the Boston and Salem deli shops. We get wonderful presents and cards through the mail, and we have all pretty much accepted the fact that she's a huge cultural and financial giant, though we remain common Marbleheaders. Funny, we're all content now; we are who we are."

"Wow," Scotty let out her breath in surprise. And Marge sat there shaking her head, just slightly reminiscent of a petit mal seizure, smacking her lips as if she were blotting lipstick.

Talk like that took time to digest, but in a timely fashion Scotty returned to their Winnipesaukee trip. "So, it's planned. You and Charlie will go to the lake for a week."

"Shall we, Charlie?" Aunt M winked at Charlie.

"Yes, yes!" she flapped her hands. "Let's go."

It was fun for Scotty to watch them prepare for the trip. Aunt M lugged out Grampy McFinch's old fishing pole from the closet in the den.

"You know, Charlie, your great grandfather used to sit in that tattered wingback chair."

"Mummy, it's got birds on it."

"And the fabric matches the hassock, Charlie. Your great grampy would rest his feet on that puffy stool. And his old beagle, Red, would sleep right alongside of him, his whiskers quivering while he dreamt of pheasants and rabbits. A deer head was mounted on that wall, but it's not there anymore. Well, they would rest there for hours, Grampy puffing on one of his Havanas. Sometimes, my little cousins would come in to try and catch one of his smoke rings. Your great grandfather looked like Popeye, especially when he didn't shave for a week. But your great grandmother was not like Olive Oyl. She was taller, or maybe she just seemed taller than Grampy because she was stout. Oh, she was the best cook, Grammy McFinch, and I loved to braid her hair while she drank ale. They both ate their spinach, though! Your great uncle and grampy had a wonderful garden. It looked just like the one Peter Rabbit got into."

Scotty tugged at Charlie's hand. "Let's go see it!" They ran down the back stairs to see the garden and the old chicken coop of cousin Kate's Hill Club secret meetings.

"Charlie, you'll never believe that your Grammy Lois had a pet hen that laid double-yolk eggs right on this middle step; one a day, or do I mean two a day? Isn't that silly?"

Charlie clapped her hands with spontaneous delight and then they both hopped over that step as if it were sacred. At the base of the stairs there was a little window through which Scotty looked out.

"Oh, Charlie, the garden is not as big as I remembered, but maybe it's because I'm bigger now, so everything else seems smaller. Let's see what you think."

Scotty opened the door. Mother and daughter squinted at the sun, their hands shading the glare. Coming from the stone basement and the cool rock containment, the backyard seemed so vast. They were overtaken by the urge to run toward the sunny field of cock-a-buttons and wild peppermint, so they ran making new footprints where Red once chased Scotty. Now Scotty ran pulling Charlie, pulling her into nostalgia of bygone days.

"What's this, Mummy?"

Scotty pointed to a plant with a big, green, leafy top. "What do you think it is, Charlie?"

"It's a carrot."

"Aunt Margie is doing a pretty good job with this garden, don't you think?"

CHAPTER TWENTY-FOUR

"I feel like the Fuller Brush man," Scotty said as she entered, suitcase in hand, "But I'm not quite sure what it is that I'm selling." Scotty looked almost like Charlie with a childlike pout and a tilt of the head, so common to her childhood stance.

"Well, I'm buying whatever you are selling," Neil said. "Let's take a look at everything." Neil spoke with composure, but his eyes searched hers with a tumultuous spirit. How odd that Scotty had the power to sever and connect him at the same time, a visceral magician of sorts.

"Five glorious days to share," she said, "Aunt M and Charlie will be gone for five days to Lake Winnipesaukee."

Neil couldn't think or plan anything or compose himself. "I want you, Marguerite. I want to make love to you forever."

Neil pulled Scotty down onto the Persian rug in front of the bay window to the sea and as they rode the tides of passion, they calmed their spirits to reclaim memories of a nurturing past now locked in the hearts of each other.

"I've never been so happily exhausted; but if I could compare it to anything it might be the feeling I have after cutting grass or eating two pieces of pie; sort of the feeling of hard work and complete comfort at the same time."

"Oh, Scotty, you'll never change with your strange comparisons and your desultory spark."

As Scotty began to plead her case, Neil covered her lips with his fingers and then removing them as quickly, his mouth drew close to hers as he said with hot whispers, "I adore you, I love you." Then he smiled and said, "But even Shakespeare took a break from the passion of his tragedy; let's sit up and look at what we've missed all these years together."

Tenderly, he pulled her up by her supple hands, undecorated with rings. He lodged a needlepoint pillow behind her neck on the cabriole leg of the Victorian chaise lounge, and then took another pillow for himself.

"Now, isn't this better than the rock, our childhood perch? We are much more comfortable, and we have the same view!"

"It's much more comfortable, but not so suspenseful as those days when the gulls squawked in our ears and the dinghies slapped the water, while those cold winds left us muffling our speech through turtlenecks drawn over our mouths and noses, hands bound in our sleeves like muffs."

"You are right, darling, of course you are right, but could we reminisce in that pain? That was our time to feel."

"And this is the time to talk about our childhood. I think I would agree with you that we have had enough pain aside from nature's ordinary miseries."

"So, childhood, childhood," he said.

"Whatever happened to Zig?"

"Zig?" asked Neil, puzzled.

"Yes," said Scotty, "That desperate character neither fish nor fowl, looking for something outside the duty of his world."

"Correct me if I am wrong," said Neil, "Zig, the banker?"

"Bank teller," she interjected, "Left his family to walk the streets."

"A bum."

"Well, not exactly, I would have called him a magnanimous loafer. After all, he did provide for his family."

"Lived on a dollar a day, is that the guy?" said Neil.

"You didn't know Zig, did you Neil?"

"Just heard of him, really, in fact you may have been the one who told me about him. It's been so long ago. Refresh my memory."

Neil listened while he tried subtly to fondle Scotty's breast.

"Well," said Scotty as she slapped Neil's hand with a quick pat. "He was a wise man. I never really spoke to him but I knew him so well. He has always been a rabbit's foot for me in life, a symbol of good luck."

"Why?" said Neil.

"He gave me his only dollar one day. He only lived on a dollar a day. He just stuck it in my hand as I passed him one day. Very unusual, don't you think? I never even asked him for anything and I was too bashful to return it to him. I didn't want to offend him."

"Oh, I remember now," Neil combed his wavy hair with his fingers while he concentrated. "I think I heard that he's an artist now. No banking for him anymore," said Neil. "Thank goodness it just worked out for me. There's money in banking and leisure to paint. I suppose I'm a painter at heart, too. But I lack his drive. I'm only driven to you, now," he raised his arms and embraced her.

"Uncle, uncle!" cried Scotty.

"You don't get out of it that easily," said Neil.

Kissing her tenderly, he loosened his embrace but didn't let go. He would never completely let go again. For to lose his shell was to lose all memory of his soul.

"Am I boring you, Neil?"

"Nothing you could say or ask would bore me. After all, your story is my story, in part anyway."

"Well, part of that story had Gary Doliber. Gary Doliber, my imagined foe turned friend."

"Are you ready for this, Scotty? He finished high school and then went on to work full time for Mr. Peach. Poor old Peach had a stroke and was pretty much paralyzed, but his brain and writing hand were good so he gave the orders and did the bills and Gary took charge of all the physical work. Since Peach was a widower with no kids, he doted on Gary, feeling, I guess, that they were both loners. When Peach died, wouldn't you know it, he left everything he had to Gary. Gary got married. Married a girl that looked just like Lydia Doliber. Sweet girl, a peasant look about her with rosy cheeks, and they had a little girl, a spitting image of her mum. They live in the old Doliber house at 12 Orne Street. The hedges and the garden are out of this world."

"What about Gary's dad?"

"Noisy Doliber got into a brawl near Barnegat. It was just after you left town. They cut him up pretty badly with broken ale bottles and he bled to death in the gutter before anybody found him. Sad." He sighed then asked, "What about your parents, Scotty, Lois and Ed Paine? Your dad was so fired up about moving West, did his passion last?"

"I'm not so sure my dad's destination was ever really the West. His desire was for the mysterious and the unknown. He could never be satisfied with Los Angeles. Some of his wanderlust was the desire for the unknown. He discovered the ravishing beauty of Yosemite, the peace and clarity of the Mojave, and the almost outer world terrain of Lake Shasta and the Mammoth area. But there was always a loneliness, acerbated by his desire to travel. He needed to move, but he did not realize he ought also to move inside, into his inner self. My mother was more easily contented; she asserted herself in the teaching profession. And as Ed thought, he saw Lois assert herself unencumbered by her sisters, exposing a naturalism and independence so typical of the true Marbleheader. But again, it was a hard tradition to break, that tradition of women to be totally giving. She had the personality and the special verve that kept her going with the evening studies and won her a degree. But she really didn't understand it. Everybody loved Lois, the kindergarten teacher; she just didn't love herself.

"So, they harassed each other with giving and duty, totally ignoring how they could share their uniqueness through personal understanding. I always thought, myself, that marriage was a learning situation, not a state of heavenly bliss. I always sensed that it was another type of working relationship, another job. I mean, I know there is a special attraction between two people but real marriage is work."

"I know," he lowered his eyes. "We all know deep down inside."

Scotty beamed, "Thank you for having me. I appreciate it. Thank you. And I'm having such a good time telling you my stories, I want to say more."

"Continue," he said.

"Can I tell you anything?"

"You can tell me anything."

"Well," she paused, "I think I've lived before. I seem to understand my emotions more quickly than most. My lust for Kostja, then my hate for him when he abandoned me. Some people deal with addictions all of their lives. I think I've learned more quickly. Perhaps this life is my summation. It's all so strange, the dreams and the characters, I mean, they seem to explain my life. I have found great purpose in my myths."

Neil's pupils were so large they seemed like saucers.

"Zig was only the beginning. There was Attorney Graves and the nun, the burning barn, and the lover rejected. Through them all a web of dreams connecting castles with hidden rooms and hidden beaches with white sands.

"When we lived at the pond those many years ago, there was the dearest man, Grampy Graves, I called him."

"Yes, I do remember him vaguely. You called him your mentor."

"He was the sweetest thing, a little stooped fellow, wore a hat. Don't know much about hats but its brim came low, almost to his brow. And what a strange house he lived in. It was green with a low cement fence around it, like a castle. His wife was like Barb's mum, always baking and always sweet. They didn't have any children so they adopted me, couldn't help it I suppose, I was always in their backyard staring at their goldfish. Couldn't figure out how those fish got so big. Grampy Graves used to stare at me from the window. Yep, he stared at me a long time wondering about me, I guess like I wondered about the fish. Well, he started his magic with me by leaving dried apricots and oranges on my porch. He made sure to leave them after school when he knew I was home. My dear old friend would watch from behind a bush to see my glee as I opened the door and found the mysterious, unexpected presents.

"Grampy Graves began my life of surprise and wonder. And Zig was roaming the streets in those days, somewhere between outer dogma and inner awareness. What did it mean that he gave me his only dollar? And my friends, we were all kind of crazy about nature. You, Bea and me, we were all shrouded from life. Childhood recollections were of quiet distance from the world, not from fear but from forgotten spiritual connection. Distracted, I became a perpetual pout and a pain to my family. But as I connected my characters and my dreams, I came to realize those who sought the truth were marked with the same pain. Somewhat like a cat without whiskers, my best defense was no defense. This guileless bravado most common to youth lingered into my adulthood. I stubbornly refused to cope with my ego, discounting it as the lost dream of another life. Where others learned self-defense, my openness set me apart, rightly and wrongly. You can't give what you don't have. The giving came to represent the duty and dogma that replaced nature in my life. By some unknown way, my mind accepted this new parochial way, but my soul slept in the most wonderful hope of the other life. The sacraments, my opiate, protected me from the law of life."

"What do you mean by the law of life," Neil whispered, hardly knowing he had spoken.

"The life of total experience. My parochial existence allotted only one choice, the good, the kind, the most virtuous choice, but I never really knew who I was until I had taken the wrong steps, the less than virtuous decisions, and made some of those wrong choices. I could tell from the mirror, it just wasn't me but some constrained butterfly, body pulsating feverishly because it was unable to fly, unable to be, the way nature meant it to be. So, I tried harder and harder and all in the wrong direction. It happened this way.

"In the sixth grade, in the prime of my idealism, I burned with veneration for one nun whom I meant to please by following her into religious life. Oh, it seems so far away and long ago. I feel so stupid. Are you sure you want to hear this?"

"I want to hear everything; spit it out," said Neil.

"Well, I'll never forget, it happened around two compositions. The first was to be written about someone who the writer considered to be a modern-day saint, and the second was to be a free choice. I blushed when I found out that somebody wrote about me. Imagine—me a saint. I was the inconspicuous type, didn't like it much, but I was really devastated when I got an 'F' for my second composition. Can't remember now who I thought the saint, but my second composition was called 'The Barn.' About the saint, I think it's fair to say in retrospect, the sister who had taken religious vows had hoped for that title. Maybe she hadn't hoped for that but I know she didn't expect anyone to write about me. Nor did I expect a failing mark for my 'Barn.' Though I had written nothing, she could have let me think and write it at home. I had wanted to write about a red barn and all the wonderful animal life inside it. I realized later the barn represented me and I couldn't express my unrealized experiences. I would dream about the barn later as myself while the animals inside would come to represent those who influenced my life. But for the time, my teacher, the nun, hated me for my rather idiotic simplicity and peer admiration, while I idolized her. What a comedy, what 'Ishcabibble?'"

Neil squeezed her, "I know your life hasn't been like my silliness, all charted and planned by your fussy parents."

She puckered her lips, and he kissed them.

Neil continued, "I've controlled my life, yes, but it's been an empty life. I feel sometimes as if I have controlled nothing. Jessica and I are so much alike, and Jeffrey is a carbon copy of us. Our predictability is loathsome for me sometimes. Let's walk."

He had to be in motion. "Let's walk to Brown's Island like in old times. It's low tide and I'll tell you some more about Jessica." Neil was sober to the point of anger, abating a confession of spurious life.

CHAPTER TWENTY-FIVE

In five days, Neil and Scotty had bathed, dressed, and eaten together, but all without intention. Neil had provided a steady menu, quite edible, and then sleep was peaceful. In each other's arms, they awoke mornings to begin new discussions and discoveries. Order prevailed quite naturally as if they were one person.

"I told you about Jessica."

Scotty nodded, her hand clutched his as it once did in those old days of excitement and wonder. They were crossing on the rock pathway now. Scotty's heart thumped, but she knew not why.

"It seemed like a great package, her English father banker, Jessica's admirable beauty, cameo beauty. But a delicate arrogance covered her inexperience. Jaded with the pleasantries of life, her range was fine but narrow, or perhaps limited to society's best. We were cut out for each other, or so our society would have thought. Did she want more from life than simple opulence? I thought so. I always thought she wanted something more; no, I felt it in my bones. Maybe I judged that from her beauty, but it was not forthcoming."

Neil sighed, he let in a big gulp of air and let it out slowly, leaving his lips to go on with his tale of life.

"And as for me, I love the secrecy of the slums. In the gutter, I have seen rainbows. At bank luncheons, many times, I would find myself leaving early to walk the back streets of Boston. Searching faces of want and sloth, lust and suffering, truer to me than the most vapid commonness of my life with Jessica. I'm a great banker; I just hate it. Would rather paint. Never talked about my life like this to anyone, not even to myself."

"You mean you talk to yourself?" she hugged his arm.

"Oh, God, I love you. I've been starved for you."

"Famine makes us appreciate our food, love, the real communication of life," she whispered in his ear.

"How can you be so silly and a poet at the same time. Give me that peevish look."

"Oh, no, you don't. You'll have to take it." Scotty ran dodging the sharp rocks on the low tide path to the island. Out of breath, they sat for a moment on some driftwood edging the shore. They gazed in pregnant silence.

"What happened to our Mystery House, Neil?"

Neil spoke softly as not to scare away a special thought, "It burned down the summer you left. They say it was a prank, some kids playing with fire. Nobody really knows, it was a terrible loss to me, especially after your departure."

"I wonder if my red barn had something to do with the Mystery House. It burned down in my dreams. Gosh, we had so many plans for that house. And what about Barb? What became of Barbara Miles?"

"I met her folks one day," said Neil. "They still have that greystone by the pond. They told me she moved to Springfield, married a plumber, and has four children. Her folks said she is quite happy."

"Any college?"

"Nope."

"Very even, wasn't she," said Scotty, "Very basic, always content."

"More placid than our rip tides, Scotty."

"Yep, that was Barb."

Neil stood up and took Scotty's hand. Shells and rocks crackled underfoot as they trekked away from the wood and onto the grassy grounds that skirted only a dream of their

Mystery House. Gulls hovered, scanning for prey, while fresh salty air refreshed memories of their past.

"And what about Kostja? Did he ever find out about Charlie?"

"We're jumping around here, aren't we? But then, that's how we always were, spitting it out however it came. Well, about dear Kostja, I decided to bury my bitterness with him, because of Charlie. Hopeful at first, I wrote to him, thinking Kostja would find some way of uniting us as a family. Year bled into year as I waited in vain for answers. Answers to questions I would eventually respond to myself. I learned to hate him in those years. He taught me to hate." Scotty's piercing eyes became soft, when she said, "I learned to love better after that, I loved more discriminately. But, let's not be so glum because my first affair went amuck. There have been lots of beautiful love stories, right nearby in fact, did you know about that story of Agnes Surriage and Harry Frankland, their romance at the Fountain Inn in 1742?"

"No, I read about it for the first time just before you came," said Neil.

"Odd isn't it," she said, "The sign has been there for years and I never, never noticed when I lived here. We are very much like them, aren't we Neil?"

"Well, we are minus the earthquake and their eventual union," his eyes captured hers in a stare.

"Maybe our union was the earthquake," she said, her eyes still fixed without a blink at his, "a fire to propel us for life."

They continued to walk with arms around each other's waists. Scotty looked down at the rubble, which was once their dream, "I don't know where you stop and I begin, Neil."

"You know it's the end of the week and we have to get back to real life," Scotty could not raise her eyes to his. She kicked at the clutter of splintered wood.

"Why?" he said.

"Duty." She stopped kicking, but still looked awkwardly to the ground. "It shouldn't be that hard when you think about it. I don't want you; I am you, Neil. And someone can't miss oneself, or can one?"

"Keep talking," he said, eyes now to the ground as well.

"There is some collective will between us. I found myself again in our childhood memories and just like when we were kids, you're still teaching me."

"I know life, but I can only feel it with you."

"Don't be absurd, Neil, how could you teach me what you don't know." Scotty pointed her finger playfully at him. Neil lowered his eyes to concentrate on what she was saying. "You taught me that I don't belong to love, but love belongs to me and I belong to myself. You inspire me by wanting me. I know it isn't just having me, but there is something beyond us, some Truth. Something you want from Jessica is something I want to be. Doesn't every woman? Someone who tempts you but is also your salvation. What can I make of it? Are we addicted? I don't think so. Maybe I should say, committed.

"Darling," she held both his hands and peered into his eyes. "I'll always want you because I'll always want me. Let us keep our dream in the sanctuary of our heart. Let it be a star in our path that will pull us time and again from life's abyss. I've known your passion, yet I've also known your peace. Both are important for they have balanced my life.

"How could I learn so much from you in these few days?" she continued. "Well, Neil Montague, you didn't teach me, you just reminded me. I knew love, like the sea, cannot be captured, but runs freely in the veins of those who would not possess it. I am me again, joyfully, naturally me again!"

Tears rolled from Neil's eyes, bright tears, burning tears.

"I know a man," Scotty went on, "who truly believes in knowledge. He is high among others in reverence of nature and love of God. His identity is my identity, mystic and contemplative. So sensual is our union. But to stay together would be our ruin. The very energy that ignites us would destroy us, because for man, truth is not constant nor pleasure eternal. But I know that bliss, and in time, all pain will be endured because of it. The friction of our parting and loss can help us both make the poetry and painting of our dreams and keep our passion forever."

He sobbed into her breast, and they walked to the house for their last night together.

CHAPTER TWENTY-SIX

One last time, Scotty read the note she would leave on his pillow:

Dearest Neil,

As you sleep, I can talk in peace, without your arguments, though they be true. Did we love more when we feared each other, when passion meant possibility? Could we conjure up eternal lust from a desert of pleasure, or should we be content to ponder the sensual, to tease love? Is responsibility our security? It at least appears to be our lot and we could never sacrifice to love what we sacrifice to duty. I leave you confused and full of doubt. I think the power of love that attracts us has only been a ploy. How foolish to think we could be martyrs in the world of today. But maybe we can sacrifice ourselves for others because we have known ourselves. Perhaps tragedy is reality but not a burden when seen in a temporal world. And maybe our beliefs are stronger than life and every part of us that loves.

Marguerite

ABOUT THE AUTHOR

S. Scott, a native of Marblehead, Massachusetts, shares her Dylan Thomas vision of New England during the fifties. As a child, all she wanted to do was walk the streets, a spectator of life, wanting nothing from anyone, and not enough from herself. Looking for a vocation, she looked for herself, and struggled for a new innocence beyond the machinery of life. Sincerity became her motive, and like a pearl she found herself anew each time she struggled to be herself, to feel the magic—the spirit of all things.

The author, once employed by Disneyland as a magician in Merlin's Magic Shop, has also been a kindergarten and Special Education teacher. She is the founder of the Quaint Corner Children's Museum in Altoona, Pennsylvania, and currently resides in Alameda, California.

"My existence has always been filled with the wonder of nature and the magic of life. Hopefully, I can pique this awareness in my readers."

The author has also published a trilogy of novelettes, *Maggoty*, and five books of poetry, *From Sage to Song*, *Water Table*, *Voyage from a Lady Slipper*, *I Am a Superfluous Woman*, and *Daybreak*, all of which are available on major internet bookseller sites.

www.ingramcontent.com/pod-product-compliance
Lightning Source LLC
Chambersburg PA
CBHW032228050726
47591CB00001B/316